Laurie
Here's to you
and your future. Hope
finding much and a
in this book and the
few laughs along
way. Gives our love
to Margie & Nan

Love W[...] &

Hopefully we can come visit
soon!!.

Suddenly

A Christmas Trilogy

William Michael Cuccia

authorHOUSE®

AuthorHouse™
1663 Liberty Drive
Bloomington, IN 47403
www.authorhouse.com
Phone: 1 (800) 839-8640

Published by AuthorHouse 10/10/2016

ISBN: 978-1-5246-4391-1 (sc)
ISBN: 978-1-5246-4392-8 (hc)
ISBN: 978-1-5246-4390-4 (e)

Library of Congress Control Number: 2016916670

Print information available on the last page.

To the One and Only

Do not forget to show hospitality to strangers, for by so doing some people have shown hospitality to angels without knowing it.

—Hebrews 13:2 NIV

CONTENTS

A CHRISTMAS TALE

CHAPTER 1

And Shiny Is His Name

God was alone. Not a star in the sky; there was only darkness. Suddenly the words "Let there be light" smacked the darkness. Trillions of God particles penetrated the dark void, and there was light, luminous light. God spoke again, and the unseen realm called the heavens became His residence. He continued to speak things into existence, and at some point, He created living creatures He called messengers.

These messengers were like God in many ways, but they were not God. There is only one God. The messengers were powerful, but they were not all-powerful. They would be everlasting but not eternal. Limited in knowledge, they depended on God for direction and guidance.

Only God can freely move about in the invisible places of eternity—past, present, and future. Only God can always be present everywhere. His created messengers were ever dependent on Him for truth and wisdom. When God spoke, with free will these messengers responded and were available to His beckoning call.

Yes, long ago God created angels, carriers of God's life-giving messages, ministering spirits. Angels with long, flowing hair. Muscular beings with excellent singing voices. All angels have wings; some even have six wings. Their beauty and power are reflections of God's glory.

The word angel means "messenger of God."

This is a tale about one of God's messengers, an angel who was very different from the rest. He wasn't strong, he couldn't sing, he didn't have wings, and he didn't have long, flowing hair. God had uniquely designed him to reflect His glory.

One of the ways angels earn their wings is by delivering messages from God on Christmas Eve. Christmas came and went year after year. Thousands of Christmases had come and gone, and this angel hadn't earned his wings. It wasn't that God didn't want him to have wings. This angel always got pushed to the back of the line when Gabriel, one of the archangels, announced Christmas assignments.

The little castaway would cry out to God from the back of the line. "Father, can You see me? I'm the one in the back with my hands waving. Do You see me? I'm the little, bald, wingless one. If You hear me, please let me go and tell earth all about the wonders of who You are."

This angel was created for a unique purpose. God had put in his heart the desire to be special. God made him for the purpose of bringing messages of healing to people on earth who had lost hope. Lost ones who were on the brink of giving up. What this angel didn't realize was that God heard the cry of his heart. God witnessed every teardrop. He had delayed his purposes for a reason. The waiting prepared the little angel for what God planned for humanity. God perceived him as a finished product who could be used to accomplish great things.

The little, bald, wingless one viewed himself the way others perceived him, not the way God had designed him. The other angels made fun of him. He didn't have one angel friend. He shied away from the crowd. The pain of being made fun of isolated him. His only friend was loneliness. The poor little castaway had given up all hope of ever earning his wings.

Oh, and Shiny was his name.

All the angels called him Shiny because he was bald. He was the only bald angel in heaven. God called him Shiny for a very different reason. When God appeared, His glory reflected off the little bald angel's head. It would shine so brightly all of heaven would light up. All the angels would cover their faces with their wings and bow before the glory of God.

Once God's glory lifted, the angels would direct their attention back to the little bald angel and return to making fun of him. Rufus, a magnanimous and boisterous angel, yelled out, "Hey, look! There goes Shiny, lighting it up." All the angels in heaven let out thunderous laughs, causing the earth to quake.

The little bald angel walked away, mumbling, "How will I ever earn my wings so I can fly to earth and help people?"

During his long walks home, he talked to God, asking questions about his seemly hopeless condition. "Father, You know I have lost all hope, but I still believe You are good, and only You can make something good out of me. Only You are good."

God heard Shiny's cry and decided it was time to respond.

One day when the other angels were just hanging out in heaven singing "Holy, Holy, Holy," God showed up. "I have a special assignment this Christmas, and I need an angel who wants to earn his wings."

God had only one angel in mind.

The heavens were silenced after God spoke. There was a hush all over the world. On earth, it was a silent night. All the angels in heaven waited to hear Shiny's name, but God kept silent. God patiently waited for Shiny to respond to His request. He loves when others step forward in faith and respond to His call.

Suddenly an angel had the courage to speak up. "There's only one angel who doesn't have his wings."

Another chimed in, "And he's bald too!"

God affirmed, "And Shiny is his name!"

Shiny hid his head in his hands and hoped no one would see him. He was so used to being made fun of he thought God might be doing the same. Shiny had hit rock bottom.

God had ordained that it was time to call Shiny out. The bald angel would soon learn that God the Father never makes fun of His created ones. He loves all His created ones just the way He designed them. Shiny would learn there's nothing that could separate him from the love of God.

Shiny didn't have the courage to respond, so he continued to hide his little bald head in his hands and hoped everyone would go away and leave him alone.

Again there was silence. Suddenly someone sneezed, and the silence was broken. The sneeze caused rain to fall upon the earth.

"Who sneezed?" asked God.

Herald, the lead singer of the angels, responded, "Hark, it was him Lord, the little, bald, wingless one."

"The little, bald, wingless one?" God repeated.

God saw Shiny differently than everyone else did. God didn't see his flaws; He saw Shiny's potential. God saw the finished work.

God called out to Shiny, "Come here, My little friend, and let Me share a message of hope I have for you."

Shiny inched toward God, and then it happened again. God's glory reflected off Shiny's head, and heaven lit up! Blinded by the light, all the angels ran around, bumping into one another, and a third of the angels in heaven got black eyes from doing so. That's how a black eye got the name "a shiner."

God wrapped his arms around Shiny and consoled him. "I have messages of hope I want you to deliver. The first message is for a blind man who lives on Third Street. Go tell him that I'm going to heal his blind eyes on Christmas Eve. Once you've delivered the message to the blind man, come home, and I'll give you the second message."

Shiny didn't know what to say, so he just sat there. He sat there with his little bald head in his hands, but his heart was fluttering like the wings of a hummingbird.

God broke the silence. "What's wrong, little friend?"

With his heart fluttering even faster, Shiny answered, "I don't know if I can do this. I don't mean to be disrespectful, but I am the least of all the angels. I have no hair, I can't sing, I'm weak, and on top of that, I have no wings."

God made His face shine upon the little bald angel, and tiny wings appeared on his back. When God smiles, wonderful things happen. Shiny would discover that he didn't have to earn anything from God. All he had to do was trust God and know He would be faithful to accomplish everything in him that would bring glory to God.

God explained to Shiny that his wings would develop as he stepped out in faith and trusted God to back up his act. He encouraged Shiny to be strong and courageous and know that God would always be with him.

Shiny soon learned the true purpose of his wings. Wings could be used to get God's attention. They would become a tool for Shiny to commune with God. Who needs wings to fly when God is with you?

Whenever Shiny needed God's help, all he had to do was flap his wings, and God would be faithful to show up. Then God was silent.

Shiny looked, and God was gone.

"Hey, where'd You go? I thought You were going to be with me."

Shiny flapped his wings and began to float gently upward. He was a natural when it came to flying. Shiny would find out that he could do just about anything when he trusted God to provide the strength he needed. He found himself hovering in the air while he thought, *This is easy and fun too.*

Shiny heard, "I'm right here. I will be with you wherever you go. I will never leave you. My Spirit is always with you. By the way, if you lower one wing, you will turn in that direction. Your wings will help you fly on the wind of My Spirit. It's a whole new way to commune with Me."

For the first time, the little bald angel had a smile on his face and a flicker of hope in his heart. He lowered his left wing and took off like a dive-bomber—and abruptly hit the ground.

Well, maybe he wasn't quite the natural at navigating turns, but the little bald angel was determined. He was determined to learn the ways of God and how he could be used most effectively in God's plans.

Shiny thought, *Just maybe I can do this with God's help. Maybe I can fulfill God's purposes for my life. And just maybe the other angels will stop making fun of me.*

Suddenly the other angels were able to see again. They couldn't believe their eyes—the little bald angel had wings!

Rufus blustered from above the crowd, "Oh look, little baldy has rent-a-wings. What do you think you're going to do with those wings—bring peace on earth or something?"

All the angels laughed. Again Shiny was being made fun of by the other angels.

With his shoulders slumped, he turned and walked away, not feeling quite as shiny as he had moments before.

CHAPTER 2

The Earth Tunnel

T he day had arrived for Shiny to go to earth and deliver the message to the blind man on Third Street.

Fear gripped Shiny. He still lacked the confidence to believe God could accomplish everything he planned on doing. He didn't know how he would get to earth. He didn't even know which way earth was.

Discouraging thoughts bombarded him as he was ironing his wings. No one told him you weren't supposed to sleep on your back when you have wings, so his wings got wrinkled in his sleep. Shiny ironed all his wrinkles out, and he was ready to go. He stepped out of his high-rise apartment, and it seemed like the day was different.

Well, maybe not. When Shiny stepped out of his apartment, Rufus was standing there with the other angels. "Where do you think you're going with those wings?"

Shiny answered Rufus. "I-I'm going to visit the blind man on Third Street. God told me he's going to heal the blind man on Christmas Eve. God said to bring him a message, and then the blind man will believe and see again."

The angels laughed. They knew God was more than capable of performing the miracle, but they thought Shiny would surely find a way to mess up God's assignment.

Rufus clamored, "You're headed the wrong way if you think you're going to earth. The earth tunnel is that way."

Hearing more angel laughter, the little bald angel turned and walked the other way. He walked and walked and walked. Shiny could still hear the other angels laughing in the distance. With each step, he could feel his confidence beginning to fade.

Shiny thought, *What was I thinking? I should just turn around and go home. Maybe God will forget about me. Maybe the other angels will forget about me too.* But he didn't quit. He kept moving forward, and with each step, he was reminded of the blind man, a man who had prayed for years, hoping God could still do miracles.

Shiny continued to walk in the direction of the earth tunnel. As the laughter faded off in the distance, he heard a very strange roaring up ahead. It sounded like the roar of a lion echoing in a canyon.

The roaring grew louder with each step Shiny took. The sound seemed to energize Shiny with renewed strength. The little bald angel thought, *That sound is so beautiful and yet powerful. It seems to be coming from the direction of the earth tunnel. I wonder what it is.*

A fly flew up to Shiny. He thought, *I didn't know there were flies in heaven* as he shooed at him with his wings.

God interrupted, "I'm right here. Keep walking; the earth tunnel is straight ahead, and be sure to stay on the right. By the way, that roar is the sound of the saints cheering home their loved ones. You'll be amazed when you see the incredible homecoming reception."

Shiny was confused. *Stay on the right? I wonder why I have to stay on the right. I wonder what our Father means by homecoming reception.* The roar of the cheering saints was now deafening. Well, not deafening, because no one is deaf in heaven. The sound was loud and very energizing.

Freddy the fly called out to Shiny as he buzzed around the little bald angel's head. "Believe me—you'll want to stay on the right, because people are coming to heaven from earth, and they'll be coming up on your left. They'll be coming so fast it will appear to be a beautiful blur of light, but check them out on your way to earth. It's cool."

God read Shiny's thoughts. "Yes, My little angel friend, the fly has a name. Remember I assigned Adam to name them all."

As Shiny approached the earth tunnel, a sign on the right side of the road read Earth Tunnel Straight Ahead. He looked up ahead and was utterly amazed by what he saw. On the left was an enormous stadium filled with people cheering from every nation on earth. Many in the crowd were holding up signs and banners. As Shiny approached the tunnel, its entrance appeared as majestic as the Grand Canyon. The entrance of the earth tunnel was so high you couldn't see the top. The sides stretched to the east and west as far as the eye could see. The light emanating from the tunnel appeared as colors reflecting from a prism. It was like a massive rainbow with every color you could imagine spilling out from the entrance.

Shiny felt even smaller as he approached the mammoth mouth of the tunnel.

Suddenly—yes, when you're in heaven, things always happen suddenly—Shiny was filled with excitement. He could feel his strength returning. God's words were booming loud and clear with each heartbeat. As he inched closer to the tunnel, he felt something he'd never experienced.

Courage surged through Shiny. He had the urge to sing God's praises. He'd never sung in public before, out of fear of being ridiculed. He would only sing in the shower when he was alone.

Overtaken by courage, Shiny sang. You might say this was his debut or the first public appearance of the Shiny that God had intended. He couldn't think of anything other than "Holy, Holy, Holy," but it sounded beautiful. Even the birds along the road joined in with him.

Shiny arrived at the entrance of the tunnel, and before his eyes, a scene was unveiled that would be etched in his mind forever. As he looked to the left of the entrance of the earth tunnel, people were flying out of the tunnel faster than the speed of light. What first appeared to be a rainbow at the mouth of the tunnel was, in reality, people of every color coming home to heaven. As they flew out of the tunnel, they would land softly on a landing pad made of gold dust.

They were caught by family and friends as they landed, being directed into the stadium.

The reception stadium was half-moon shaped with seating that went on for as far as the eye could see. In the stands were family members and friends of people coming home to heaven, cheering with all their might.

As Shiny surveyed the incredible event, he spotted large banners and signs scattered throughout the stadium, welcoming the saints home. In big red letters, one sign read, "It is finished." Another said, "Well done, good and faithful servant." The largest banner of all, held by angels flying overhead, announced, "Welcome to your Father's house."

Standing at the cavernous entrance, Shiny continued to watch the events unfold before him.

At the center of the Stadium, Shiny saw King Jesus sitting on His throne; Jesus, regal in all His glory, positioned to receive His children. Redeemed souls were coming to their eternal home in heaven. The King of kings would welcome the new arrivals with open arms and lavish them with rewards for a job well done.

Shiny's eyes were filled with tears as he drew his attention back to the cavernous entrance, thinking, *What do I do now? Do I just walk in or do I take a leap of faith? What do I do?* The bald angel was overwhelmed with emotion. What he had just witnessed made him feel unworthy.

Then faith rose up, and Shiny declared, "God is with me; God promised He would be with me. Plus God knows all my thoughts, so I will put my trust in God and go forward with His plan."

One of the birds who was flying around the stadium chirped, "Flap your wings, silly."

With renewed confidence, Shiny responded, "Oh yeah, thanks."

Shiny began flapping his wings, and God spoke. "Shiny, it's time. You're ready, and I believe in you! Here's how it works. I will swing you around by your wings three times. The third time, I will fling you into the tunnel. Remember to stay to the right. Before you know it, you'll be on earth."

The little bald angel was puzzled. "Father, I don't mean to be disrespectful, but you're going to swing me around by my wings? You've got to be joking."

A gust of wind picked Shiny up and spun him around. "One, two ..."

Shiny responded, "I guess You were serious."

"Three!"

The wind of God flung Shiny into the tunnel. All Shiny could see was a blur of multicolored light. He glanced to his left, and there was an eternal blur of faces smiling back at him. People of every age and race were speeding by, rejoicing with one harmonious voice. The sound was unbelievable—singing, rejoicing, shouts of joy and triumph, all blending into one marvelous melody. Just for fun, some of the people held hands and formed a V formation like a flock of birds. They would take turns at the point, joy exuding from each of them. Shiny witnessed the triumphant celebration as he raced past them.

Suddenly—yes, in heaven everything happens suddenly, especially in the earth tunnel—someone racing by hollered, "Hey, was that a bald angel?"

Someone else yelled back, "I didn't know there were bald angels."

A third cried out, "That can't be a bald angel."

Shiny hollered out, "Oh, yes it is, and Shiny is my name!"

For the first time in the little bald angel's life, he was proud to be who God had created him to be.

Shiny thought, *God made me bald to stand out so people would notice me.* With a thud, Shiny landed. His feet touched down firmly on the ground called earth. "Wow! That's was amazing!"

The little bald angel felt different, entirely different, strong and confident. The message for the blind man burned in his heart, but how would he find Third Street, and how would he find the blind man's house? Shiny found himself standing at the corner of Main Street and Center Avenue. As he stared up at the street sign, a little girl walked up to him and tugged on his pant leg.

"Hi, my name is Lucy. Are you lost?"

Shiny knelt down and answered, "I don't think so. Well, maybe. Yes, I believe I am."

Confused, Lucy asked, "What's your name?"

"My name? A-ah, my name is Shiny."

"Sam. I like that name. where are you from?"

Now Shiny was confused. He had clearly told Lucy his name was Shiny, but she called him Sam. The little bald angel would soon discover God communicates His messages at His appointed time. He uses every opportunity to accomplish His will.

"I said my name is Shiny."

The little girl responded again, "I know your name is Sam, but where are you from?"

"From heaven. I've come to give the blind man on Third Street a message."

Just then Lucy's mom walked up. "Sir, can I help you?"

Before Shiny could respond, Lucy tried to explain to her mother. "Mommy, this is Sam, and he's come all the way from California to visit Mr. Blake, the blind man who lives on Third Street."

Shiny stood up, and with a blank look stared at Lucy's mom. He thought, *California? I've never been outside of heaven.*

"Well, Mr. Sam, or whatever your name is, do you always to talk to little children? Lucy, I told you, never talk to strangers."

Shiny stood silently as Lucy's mom grabbed her hand and stormed off. As they walked away, Shiny heard Lucy's mom reprimanding her. "I told you never talk to strangers. Ever, ever, ever! Especially big, bald bikers."

Sometimes God allows people to see things quite differently. Lucy and her mom saw Sam the big bald biker, but Shiny was still his adorable little self.

Shiny stood there staring at the Main Street and Center Avenue signs. Still confused, he thought, *Big bald biker? What is she talking about? I'm just a little bald angel with a message from God for a blind man. I wish someone were here to help me. I feel so alone. Earth is not how I thought it would be.*

It smells terrible. The colors here are so dull compared to heaven. Now I understand why people are so excited when they come home to heaven. Shiny sat down on the curb and put his little bald head in his hands. "I knew I couldn't do this. All the other angels are going to make fun of me when I get back. If I ever do get back."

Suddenly—yes, suddenly happens on earth too when God wants to get something done—a little roly-poly bug looked up at Shiny from the curb. "Hey, hey you! Flap your wings!"

The little roly-poly bug saw Shiny as the little bald angel. All God's creations see each other as they really are. Shiny obeyed the roly-poly bug and flapped his wings.

Then God spoke. "Friend, don't be afraid; be strong. I have given you strength, and I will be with you. Trust Me and keep walking forward. I will lead you."

Shiny responded, "Which way is forward? Do I go down Main Street or Center Avenue? I don't know which way to go. I'm afraid I'll go the wrong way."

God smiled and said, "Don't be afraid. Just go, and I will lead you. Remember I will never leave you alone. I hear all your thoughts, even when you think you're alone. I sent the roly-poly bug to help you out. Don't you just love those little guys? I like to touch them and make them ball up. They're some of my best handiwork. Go now. I'm with you."

Shiny stood up, and God vanished. "Why is it every time God says he will be with me, suddenly He disappears?"

There was a clap from heaven. "I'm always with you, even when you don't see me."

Shiny felt strength surge through his arms. He took a step toward Main Street and heard from heaven, "If I were you, I'd go down Center Avenue."

So the little bald angel turned around and walked down Center Avenue.

CHAPTER 3

Shiny to the Rescue

Shiny found himself at the corner of Center Avenue and First Street. While he was staring at the sign, three men ran past Shiny and almost knocked him over. Another man came running out of a store and yelled at Shiny. "Did you see which way they went?"

Shiny stood stunned. He was getting his first taste of earth, and it wasn't pretty.

Again the man yelled, "Did you see which way they went?"

Shiny asked, "Did *I* see which way they went?"

"Who else would I be asking? You're the only one around."

Shiny gazed at the man and said, "They ran that way," as he pointed down First Street.

"Thanks!" the man yelled as he ran back into the store to call the police.

Shiny began to walk down Center Avenue when the man from the market came back out and asked, "Sir, what's your name, in case the police need to ask you any questions?"

"My name? My name is Shiny."

"Sam, it's a pleasure to meet you. My name is Murph, short for Murphy. Would you like to come in and have a glass of soda while we wait for the police?"

Shiny thought, *He thinks my name is Sam too? I wonder what God is up to.* Again, Shiny was learning that God can make people on earth see and hear things to accomplish His plans. "Are you a stranger?" Shiny asked.

15

Murph laughed. "I certainly don't think so. Everyone in this town knows me. Why do you ask?"

"Lucy's mom said never talk to strangers."

Shiny's response drew more laughter from Murph, and he asked again, "Well, are you coming in?"

Shiny wanted to go into the store and help Murph, but he knew he had to get to Third Street and find Mr. Blake, the blind man. Shiny was about to learn that sometimes God gives assignments along the way.

Murph motioned him in. Shiny nodded and followed behind. "Welcome to Murphy's Corner Market. My store is the oldest store in town. I've never seen you around here."

"I've come to deliver a message from heaven to the blind man who lives on Third Street."

Murph looked stunned. "You know, Sam, I've always wanted to go to California. Someday I hope to go to Disneyland and see the Pacific Ocean too. Now, about Mr. Blake: he comes into my store almost every day. Wouldn't be surprised if he stopped by any minute. He loves drinking sodas and listening to me tell stories about the good old days."

Shiny felt more courage as Murph spoke. In a peculiar way, he felt like he was right where he was supposed to be. "What kind of soda would you like, Sam?"

Shiny stared at Murph with a blank look.

"Sam, you look like a root beer man to me. How about an ice-cold root beer?"

Shiny nodded.

"Here you go. I bet they don't have root beer like that in California. So how do you know Mr. Blake?"

As Shiny sipped the root beer, he thought, *This tastes heavenly.* "I don't know Mr. Blake; I'm just the messenger God has chosen to share the good news."

Murph had the strangest look on his face. Dumbfounded, Murph responded, "What you just said didn't make any sense, but it makes me want to cry for some reason. I haven't cried since Nelly passed away over twenty years ago."

"Was Nelly your wife?" asked Shiny.

"No, Sam, Nelly was my horse that I used to deliver groceries. Nelly was a real workhorse. Couldn't get her to stop even when I'd say, who-o-o-a, Nelly, she just kept going. Well, enough about Nelly. So what kind of bike are you riding?"

"Bike?"

Murph looked at Shiny and said, "Well sure, you must have a motorcycle, dressed like that. Biker boots, leather pants, and that vest with Bald Angels written on the back. That's clever, Bald Angels, I like that. I just assumed a big, strong man like you must have quite a bike."

Shiny didn't know what to say; he couldn't lie.

Murph rescued Shiny. "I guess I ask too many questions. It's just been a while since we've had anyone new pass through town. Now tell me, can you identify those three men who tried to rob my store?"

"They tried to rob you?" Shiny was innocent to the ways of a fallen world. It broke his heart to think that people would steal from each other. It didn't line up with the ways of heaven.

"Why, yes! If it wasn't for you showing up, they would've taken all my money."

"What do you mean?" asked Shiny.

"Well, just as they were demanding me to give them my money, a flash of light pierced through the window, right there!"

Murph frantically pointed to a spot on the window and then continued. "The three men and I turned and looked at the flash, and there you were. I don't mean to be rude, but it was as if the sunlight bounced off your head and caromed right through the window. It was blinding. When they saw how big and strong you were, they took off running right out of my store. I guess I'm lucky you were walking by. I'm lucky you're bald."

Shiny realized that God pays attention to every detail. God allowed Shiny to appear like a big, bald biker so Murph wouldn't get robbed. He would soon find out that God had another purpose for Shiny's disguise.

Shiny stared at Murph and scratched his head as he drank more root beer. As he sipped the heavenly liquid through a straw, he realized, *I guess I'm right where I'm supposed to be. I'll trust God to get me to Mr. Blake at the appointed time.*

Just then, the small corner market shook, and Shiny heard from heaven, "You're doing fine. Just relax, and I will lead you."

Murph reacted to the quake. "Don't worry, Sam. California isn't the only place that has earthquakes. We get some shakes of our own from time to time. That was a good little jolt."

Shiny grinned as he took another sip of root beer. Murph went on about how Shiny had saved him from the robbers. Shiny wondered, *How is it that everyone sees me so different here on earth? I wonder what they mean by a big, bald biker. I wonder what I look like.*

God whispered, "Remember I'm with you, and by the way, have a good look in the mirror. Enjoy My creativity."

More courage surged through Shiny. He sat up and looked in the mirror behind the soda fountain. For a moment, God allowed Shiny to see how people on earth saw him. He was stunned when he saw his reflection in the mirror. There sat an enormous bald biker with massive arms. Shiny raised his arms, and his muscles popped out of his shirt.

Just then two police officers walked through the front door. Murph called out, "Hey, Benny, Lenny, come on in. I want you to meet someone. This here is Sam."

The police officers introduced themselves to Shiny and shook his hand.

Murph continued, "If it wasn't for Sam walking by, those guys would've taken every cent I had."

Officer Benny asked Shiny if he had seen any of the men's faces as they ran by. Shiny was confused when he looked at the officers. They appeared identical. He couldn't tell who was Benny and who was Lenny.

God whispered again. "They're identical twins. I made them that way. I love making twins. It's a double blessing kind of thing."

Shiny thought, *I've never seen twins before; very cool.* He answered the officer. "No, I didn't see their faces, but one did run with a limp."

Officer Benny asked. "Right leg or left leg?"

"It was definitely his left leg."

Benny glanced at Lenny. "Sounds like Limp Leg Lefty and his boys are at it again."

Lenny joined the conversation. "Yep."

Shiny would soon learn that Benny was the twin who did all the talking and Lenny was a man of few words. The only word Lenny ever said was *yep.*

Benny continued. "Thanks for your help, Sam. We've been trying to catch Lefty and his boys for quite a while."

In rhythm, Officer Lenny added, "Yep."

Officer Benny asked Shiny, "Are you going to be in town for a few days in case we need your help? We may ask you to come down to the station to identify the robbers once we catch them."

Shiny wasn't quite sure what to say. He didn't know how long he would be on earth, and he couldn't lie. He didn't know how long it would take to find Mr. Blake and deliver God's message. He didn't want to take the chance of failing God and being the laughingstock of heaven.

"Well, I think I'll be here for a few days," was Shiny's response as he glanced up at the ceiling and shrugged.

Shiny didn't hear anything from heaven but continued to trust. "Where are you staying, and do you have a phone number we can call?" As Shiny was trying to figure out what to tell Officer Benny, a call came in on the officer's radio.

Officer Benny interrupted. "Excuse me, Sam, but we have another call to answer, so just leave your information with Murph." The twin police officers scurried out of the store while Shiny was left staring at Murph.

"I can't thank you enough for what you did today. If you ever need anything from me, just come by the store, and I'll help you out."

Shiny couldn't believe his ears. Maybe Murph could give him directions to the blind man's house. "There is one thing you can do for me. Would you be able to give me directions to Mr. Blake's house?" Shiny hoped Murph would help.

"Sam, I can tell you right where Mr. Blake lives. That's the least I can do for saving me from Lefty and his boys."

Shiny felt like a lightbulb turned on in his head. *"God put me here to help Murph so he could direct me to Mr. Blake."* God smiled down on Shiny.

Murph continued, "Now, are you walking, or are you going to ride your motorcycle?"

"I think I'll walk."

"The only reason I ask is downtown has all one-way streets. If you're going to ride your motorcycle, it's a little confusing. Since you're going to walk, go straight down Center Avenue. When you get to Third Street, which is two blocks down, make a left, and Mr. Blake's house is the fourth house on the left."

"Thanks, Mr. Murphy, you've been a great help. When I get back to heaven, I'll be sure to put a good word in for you to our heavenly Father."

Murph gave Shiny a puzzled look and then responded, "Sam, please call me Murph, and tell your boss in California he's welcome at Murph's Corner Market anytime, and the root beer's on me."

The little bald angel shook his head as he walked out of the corner market.

And Shiny is his name, not Sam.

CHAPTER 4

Robe of Confidence

As Shiny walked down Center Avenue, he wondered how he would approach Mr. Blake.

How would he get Mr. Blake to come to the door? While he was pondering this in his heart, Shiny saw a sign that read Third Street. He turned left and walked down the street. When he arrived at the fourth house on the left, he stopped. He stood there thinking. "Now what do I do? I don't want to make a mistake."

So Shiny just stood still and waited. Suddenly and unexpectedly, thunder roared from heaven. "Walk up to the door and knock on it."

Shiny looked up. "Thanks, Father, and I didn't even have to flap my wings. I knew you would help me."

Another bolt of lightning flashed across the sky. "I'm here to help, little friend. Go up and knock on the door. Don't worry, just open your mouth, and I will fill it with the right words to say. Be confident. I'm with you."

As Shiny approached the door, he could feel confidence rush through his body. Every time God spoke, Shiny could feel his confidence grow. Shiny was learning the importance of trusting God to help him in every situation he faced. As Shiny inched toward the front door, a thought crossed his mind: *I wonder if Mr. Blake will see me as an angel or as the biker? If he does see me as the biker, I wonder if he'll be afraid and not open the door, or will he let me in if he sees me as an angel?*

Again, the heavens thundered. "Little friend, Mr. Blake is blind. He can't see you. That's why I've sent you to bring him the message of My healing power, so he will see again."

"Oh yeah, sorry about that. I was just—hey, you heard my thoughts again!"

"Just knock on the door, brave one, and remember I'm with you. All you have to do is open your mouth, and I will fill it."

Shiny stepped up to the door, took a deep breath, and knocked. He waited. It seemed like he waited for the longest time. Then, from behind the door, he heard a man's voice. "Who is it?"

Shiny spoke up. "My name is Shiny, and I've come to give you a message from God."

There was a long pause, a very long pause, like when God is getting ready to do something big.

The door opened, and there stood Mr. Blake. Tears were streaming down his face from behind his dark glasses. "Come in."

The blind man turned and walked back into the darkness of the house. Shiny stood there and didn't know what to do. He quickly decided to follow the blind man into the house. Everywhere he looked, the room was dark or dimly lit at best. Everywhere Shiny went, the room would light up. The blind man found his way to a big easy chair and sat down.

Mr. Blake began to sob. Shiny knelt down next to him and patiently listened to his sobbing. "Why are you crying, sir?"

The words rolled off Shiny's lips before he even thought about what to say. The blind man turned in Shiny's direction. "Are you an angel? Please tell me. I hope this isn't just another cruel trick being played on a blind man."

"What do you mean, sir?" Shiny was confused by the question. He felt more courage surge through him. He felt confident God was at work to heal Mr. Blake. For the first time, Shiny believed God would open Mr. Blake's eyes so he could see.

Still sobbing, Mr. Blake spoke. "Well, you said your name is Shiny, and you came from heaven to give me a message from God. I've been praying for years that God would give me my sight. So please tell me, are you really from heaven? How can I believe you?"

God interrupted. "Shiny, tell Mr. Blake I was there when the accident to his eyes happened that day at work in the lab. Tell him I allow some things to happen, but I have sent you to let him know I am healing him for My glory. Encourage him to believe."

Shiny was gaining insight into the ways of God. All day long, every time he spoke, people heard something entirely different, but now the blind man heard exactly what he had said. When God wants to get a message to someone, He has the power to open their ears and have them understand what He says.

As Shiny began to share God's message with Mr. Blake, he heard a crashing sound from the back of the house. The blind man jumped up and grabbed a baseball bat that was next to his chair and started moving toward the sound in the back of the house.

Shiny followed right behind. When they approached the back bedroom, the blind man flung open the door, and there was Limp Leg Lefty and his buddies, trying to open a safe. Lefty and his boys were stunned by what they saw. There was the big, bald biker again, standing right behind Mr. Blake.

Lefty screamed, "Please, no! Please, sir, don't hurt us! Please! We give up."

Mr. Blake shouted at them. "Hurt you? I'm going to beat the tar out of you! You've been stealing from me long enough, and it's time you paid for it."

Mr. Blake began swinging his bat blindly in the direction of Lefty's voice. Shiny raised one hand and stopped the momentum of the bat.

Lefty got down on his knees and looked up at the big, bald biker. "Please, sir, please don't hurt us. We'll turn ourselves in. Just don't hurt us."

Shiny didn't know what to do, so he started flapping his wings. He waved and flapped with all his might, and the next thing he knew, he was back in heaven. All the angels greeted Shiny with their usual laughter.

Rufus met him first. "Hey, Shiny, when are you going to get some real wings that work?"

The bald angel dropped his head and walked down the Street of Gold to his apartment.

Suddenly God appeared to Shiny as he was walking down the Street of Gold.

"What's wrong, little friend? You seem downcast."

Shiny looked up at God. "I don't know what to say. You gave me one message to deliver, and I couldn't even do that right. I failed! I couldn't even protect Mr. Blake from Lefty and his boys. How can you ever trust me again?"

God knelt down next to Shiny. "Whoa, little bald buddy. Come here and jump up on My knee. Let Me share something with you."

Shiny couldn't believe the kindness of God; he didn't seem angry at all. Shiny jumped up on God's knee and was surprised how warm and cozy God felt. Shiny was amazed how good it felt to be sitting on God's lap. He felt a love he didn't know existed, a love that makes everything all right. The kind of love that makes you confident that God is good.

Shiny noticed that God's warmth made him feel safe and secure. The heat radiating from God made Shiny forget all about what had happened on earth. Even when God called Shiny bald, it felt like a compliment. Being in the presence of God tends to do that.

God pulled Shiny close to Him. "Brave one, I want you to know one thing: everything I wanted to get accomplished was done. You did great! You stopped the burglars from robbing Murph's Market. You saved Mr. Blake from being stolen from again. The words you spoke to Mr. Blake have given him faith to believe his eyes will be opened Christmas Eve, and his eyes will be opened, trust me. It sure was fun making you look like a big, bald biker. You see, My little one, I have many reasons for making you bald. I love creating something out of nothing."

God smiled and held Shiny close to Him. Shiny was amazed at what he heard. He thought God would be angry with him for failing. He thought God would punish him and never let him go to earth again. He even thought God would never speak to him. God never said anything about failing, and He wasn't upset at all. He was proud of Shiny's courage and obedience.

If anything, God seemed pleased with Shiny. All He did was tell Shiny what a great job he had done and that Mr. Blake was going to see again. Being held by God gave the little bald angel an enormous boost in confidence. With every God encounter, Shiny was growing in confidence. He asked God, "You mean Mr. Blake is going to see again?"

"That's right, brave one, Mr. Blake is going to see again. I love to do miracles, especially on Christmas Eve, and thanks to you, Mr. Blake will see. Not only that but Lefty and his boys are going to go to church for the first time in quite a while. I might add they are going to ask My Son, Jesus, to be their Savior. How cool is that?"

Shiny looked up at God puzzled, "You say *cool*?"

"I'm the inventor of cool." God smiled.

For the first time, Shiny felt joy welling up inside. He felt so much joy he began to jump up and down on God's knee. Shiny and God laughed and laughed because of the joy Shiny was experiencing.

"Can I do more? I want to do so much more. What can I do next?"

God affirmed, "Brave one, I have so much more for you to do; this is just the beginning. I'm sending you to the crippled boy on Adams Way. Be brave and be of good courage when you go. I want you to let him know that I am going to make him walk again. All he has to do is believe."

Shiny jumped down off God's knee. "When do I get to go? When?" While Shiny was looking up at God, waiting for an answer, God disappeared into a cloud of glory. Thunder rang through heaven.

"When your new wings sprout, go!"

As Shiny was walking home down the Street of Gold, he thought, *New wings? I already have wings.*

Up ahead were Rufus and the angels, hanging out at Diamond way. As Shiny approached the crowd of angels, something seemed very different. Shiny felt like he was wearing a robe of confidence. Rufus looked different to him. He didn't seem as intimidating. He appeared to be less daunting.

"Hey, Shiny, is it true what we heard happened to you?" asked Rufus.

"Happened to me? What do you mean?"

"Did you get to sit on God's knee? Is it true? Where did you get that robe of confidence?"

Shiny looked down and couldn't believe his eyes. Sure enough, he was wearing the robe of confidence that angels who bring good tidings get to wear. It was a robe you couldn't earn through works only by obedience. God freely gave it to Shiny so he would know his confidence came from God.

When Shiny looked up at Rufus, he perceived a newly acquired respect that he hadn't experienced before. Having had the opportunity to sit on God's knee and spend time with Him gave Shiny favor with the other angels. The angels continued to ask Shiny questions about what it was like to sit on God's knee. They spent the rest of the afternoon asking Shiny what it felt like to be that close to God.

One angel asked, "Were you afraid to sit on God's knee?"

"No, I had the most wonderful time of my life. God is gentle and accepting. He's an excellent listener and makes you feel very comfortable in His presence. You feel like you're the most important person in the world when you're with Him. The best part of being with God is He has all the answers to everything you ask."

Shiny was going out of his way to make every angel feel a part of the whole God experience. He did everything possible to share that God is available to everyone.

Another angel asked, "How big is God?"

Shiny stopped and thought for a moment. "He is bigger than you could ever imagine. I really can't describe how big He is because the more time you spend with Him, He seems to be right there with you. You know He can put the whole world in His hand. In your head, you understand that heaven is His throne and earth is His footstool, but He's right there with you. It sounds crazy trying to describe Him."

Shiny paused to collect his thoughts. "You know, being in God's presence gives you confidence that nothing is too big for God, nor anything too small."

All the angels hung on Shiny's every word. They saw Shiny in a new light, the light of God's glory. Spending time on God's knee released an authority that brought instant promotion. He seemed shinier to the other angels.

Rufus broke the silence. "Shiny, thank you for sharing your experience with our heavenly Father. You've made us feel as though we were right there with you. If it's okay, may we walk you home so we can ask more questions?"

Shiny found it hard to believe Rufus was asking to spend time with him. "I would be delighted to spend more time with all of you. It would be an honor."

All the angels followed behind Rufus and Shiny as they walked him home. As they approached the steps to Shiny's apartment, Rufus whispered in Shiny's ear, "Would you be my friend?"

Shiny smiled, and without hesitation he answered, "I thought we were friends."

Rufus smiled back. "For sure."

Shiny walked up the steps to his apartment, turned back to his new friends, and proclaimed, "Thanks for making my day even more special. Hope to see you tomorrow. May God bless you and keep you and make His face shine upon you."

CHAPTER 5

Doctor Shiny

I t was a new day. Shiny put on his robe of confidence and opened the front door. Rufus and the host of angels were waiting. A speechless Rufus gawked at Shiny's new robe. Finally Rufus drummed up the courage to ask Shiny if he could feel his robe.

"Sure, you could try it on if you'd like."

When Shiny took off his robe, the other angels fell back and couldn't believe what they saw.

Shiny had sprouted the most powerful set of wings. They were wings like those of a young eagle. Shiny was unaware of his new wings. He thought, *I feel different; everything in my life seems right. I have confidence that God will be with me no matter what happens.*

Shiny wondered why the other angels were reacting so dramatically. As he looked around, he saw angels pointing and covering their mouths in awe. Some had tears running down their faces.

Rufus handed the robe of confidence back to Shiny. "Are you aware only archangels sit on God's knee, and those look like archangel wings to me."

Shiny had no response as he thought, *Archangels speak with a voice of authority by God for a particular mission or purpose.* He didn't know what to say, so he didn't say anything. He wondered if Rufus was getting ready to play another joke and make fun of him in front of the other angels. Shiny was still learning how to trust and understand when others were being sincere.

Rufus continued, "Those wings have a purpose; God doesn't just give out wings like that. All of heaven will rejoice when God fulfills His plans in you. Shiny, go and do whatever it is God has for you. Be brave. God is with you."

Louie, one of God's trumpeting angels, tooted his horn, proclaiming, "Shiny, today is a new day, and God is preparing you to fly with wings of an eagle. You will spend eternity bringing messages of hope to people who need to be encouraged. Always be careful not to toot your own horn. Give God the glory."

Suddenly a mighty wind rose from the east and blew under Shiny's new wings. The wind lifted Shiny, and he took off toward the earth tunnel. Flying on the wings of the wind was becoming more and more comfortable for the bald angel. He was learning to trust in God.

"I can go anywhere with these wings. I like flying; it speeds up what I can get done for God."

Shiny felt the wind catapult him into the earth tunnel. He felt much stronger and faster. He thought, *When God blows the wind under these wings, nothing can stop me.* As Shiny was soaring through the earth tunnel, he noticed the faces of people who were coming home to heaven.

People from every country were racing to heaven. The tunnel was reverberating with shouts of joy and people singing God's praise. The sound caused the wind under Shiny's wings to blow stronger.

One man cried out, "Look at those wings. I've never seen such beautiful wings."

Shiny shouted back, "Wait until you get to heaven and see King Jesus on His throne."

A woman cried out, "I've never seen wings like that."

Shiny winked at her and said, "God gave me these wings. Aren't they beautiful?"

Finally, a little boy screeched, "Do I get wings like that?"

"You won't need wings in heaven, friend."

When Shiny finished speaking, he found himself standing at the corner of Main Street and Center Avenue. Yes, Shiny was back on earth. The smell of earth was still offensive to Shiny. He could feel hopelessness in the air. He thought, *No one in the earth tunnel mentioned anything about my bald head. All they were talking about were my new wings.*

Shiny strolled down Main Street, searching for clues that would help him find the crippled boy. He was still adjusting to how earth looked and smelled compared to heaven. He thought how sad it was that people on earth hadn't experienced the glorious beauty of heaven. He wondered how people put up with the lack of color and that stinky stench of hopelessness.

Shiny came upon an office building. He read the sign on the wall: Main Street Children's Clinic.

"Children's Clinic? I wonder if someone inside this office could tell me where the crippled boy lives. Should I just walk in? I wonder how they will see me. I wonder if they will see me as the bald biker."

Shiny was starting another *I wonder* when suddenly there was a clap from heaven. "Brave one, you don't have to wonder how they will see you. I've got it covered. Let's just have some fun. Go in and enjoy what I'm about to do. Remember I will always be with you. Be confident."

Shiny looked up to the heavens and thanked God for being so faithful, always showing up right when he needed Him to be there. He was beginning to learn how remarkably fun God was, especially when He was getting ready to perform a miracle. Shiny realized when he wondered about things, God always had the answer.

Shiny thought, *I guess that's why He is the God of wonder.*

With his increased confidence, Shiny opened the door and walked in. When he crossed the threshold, he recognized a familiar fluttery feeling inside, the feeling that comes over him when God changes his appearance. *How cool,* he thought. *I wonder how I look.*

A young woman sitting behind the front desk greeted him. "Hello, are you the new doctor from Summerville?"

"No, my name is Shiny, and I've come to deliver a message to the crippled boy who lives on Adams Way. Do you happen to know where I might find this boy?"

The young woman looked at Shiny with amazement. "Mr. Steward, do you mean Billy Smith?"

Shiny chuckled to himself. *Oh boy, here we go. Now I'm Mr. Steward. I guess God was right, this is going to be fun. I'll just play along.*

"Is Billy Smith the crippled boy who lives on Adams Way?"

"Yes he is, and this must be your lucky day, Mr. Steward, because Billy has an appointment with us in fifteen minutes."

Again Shiny had a good chuckle. *No such thing as luck when you have God on your side.*

The young woman continued, "Excuse me for not introducing myself. My name is Amy. I'm Dr. White's assistant. Would you like to sit down and have a cup of tea or coffee while you wait for Billy?"

Shiny thought, *I wonder if tea or coffee is as good as root beer. I guess I'll ask for a cup of coffee.* When he opened his mouth, God filled it. "A cup of cold water would be heavenly."

Why did I say that? he thought.

God whispered to Shiny, "Trust me—you don't want to start drinking coffee. It tastes like mud compared to root beer."

Mud? That doesn't sound good.

Again God whispered, "Trust me—it's not."

Shiny took a seat in the waiting room.

Amy continued, "You know, Mr. Steward, you look just like how the new doctor described himself on the phone. He's coming in for an interview today."

"Really, and how did he describe himself?"

Shiny thought, *This will be interesting to see how God disguised me this time.*

Amy appeared embarrassed. "Well, the gentleman said he would be in a suit like what you have on, and he's bald. So, as you can see, when you walked in I thought you were the new doctor. I'm sure you understand how I could have made a mistake like that."

"Oh sure, not a problem, Amy. I love that I'm bald; it makes me unique where I come from."

Shiny was learning to embrace who God had created him to be. His new authority was causing his self-esteem to grow.

Amy quickly responded with relief, "Where you're from, what do you mean? Are there not many bald men in California?"

Shiny thought, *I hope I get to go to California sometime. California sounds like its heaven on earth.*

A small, thin man with glasses, a white coat, and a red tie came from the back office. "Well, this must be the new doctor. I'm Dr. White. Pleasure to meet you. Why don't you come on back, and we'll have a chat?"

Dr. White invited Shiny to follow him to the back. Amy tried to explain to Dr. White that Shiny was not the new doctor. Dr. White interrupted her. "Don't worry, Amy. I'll take care of our new doctor. Come on back. What would you prefer I call you?"

Shiny looked to Amy for help when the phone rang. Amy picked up the phone and shrugged her shoulders. Shiny shrugged back and followed Dr. White.

"Tell me Doctor what medical school did you attend?"

Shiny answered Dr. White. "I'm not a doctor. I've come to bring a message from heaven to the crippled boy who lives on Adams way."

Dr. White responded. "That's an outstanding school. Now please tell me what do you prefer I call you?"

Shiny shook his head and thought, *I'm not fighting this anymore.* "Everyone calls me Shiny, so you can call me Dr. Shiny."

Dr. White laughed. "I love that, Dr. Shiny, I think you will fit in perfect around here."

He laughed again as he continued. "We need someone who will make the children laugh and give them hope. Maybe the kids in this town will look forward to coming to the doctor."

Suddenly! Yes, suddenly happens in children's clinic when Dr. Shiny around. Suddenly there was an announcement on the loudspeaker.

"Our next patient is here for his appointment."

The door opened, and Amy wheeled Billy Smith to the back. Dr. White directed his attention to Shiny. "Why don't you take this patient. Just throw on a lab coat and have at it."

Shiny tried on one of Dr. White's lab coats. It was way too small. He attempted to push his arms through. He pushed and pushed. While he was struggling to make the coat fit, God spoke from heaven.

"Shiny just follow my lead. We're going to have some fun now! Remember brave one, I'm with you and contrary to popular belief I love to have fun."

Dr. White stepped in and rescued Shiny from the coat. "I don't think that's going to fit a big guy like you, Dr. Shiny."

God had again caused Shiny to appear much larger than his cuddly Shiny self.

"Billy, I have a real treat for you today. This is Dr. Shiny, and he's going to do your examination. Come on over, Dr. Shiny, and let me introduce you to Billy Smith."

Shiny stepped toward Billy's chair, and with each step, he felt God's power moving through him like a rushing river. If he didn't know better, he was sure he could hear God chuckling in the background. Shiny smiled and addressed Billy. "Hello, Billy. My name is Shiny, and I've come to bring you a message from God."

Billy looked up at Shiny from his wheelchair. "I've never seen a bald doctor before."

"Me either," responded Shiny.

Billy and Dr. White laughed. "See, I told you, Billy—Dr. Shiny is a funny doctor."

Shiny thought, *What's so funny about that? It's the truth. God, You've got to help me here because I don't know what to do. I haven't a clue of what to do next. Can You please help me?*

God whispered to Shiny, "Ask for a tongue depressor, and ask Billy to open his mouth. Look in it, and just have fun with it. Pretend you're a doctor."

"Billy, why don't you open your mouth for me, and let's have a look?"

Billy opened his mouth wide and looked up at Shiny.

"What a big mouth you have for such a little boy! Well, everything appears to be fine from what I see."

Dr. White and Billy laughed again. Through the laughter, Dr. White forced out, "You are quite the comedian, aren't you?"

Another whisper came from heaven. "Shiny, bend down and examine his legs. Tell Billy his legs have not lost any more strength. Take your time and look at both legs. Dr. White will be very impressed with you."

Shiny followed God's lead, and Dr. White was very impressed.

"I must say, Dr. Shiny, you have a way with kids. I'll leave you here with Billy to finish up. After the exam, meet me in my office. I want to hear more about your medical school experience back in California."

Shiny stared at Dr. White as he walked away. Looking up, Shiny hoped for some heavenly help. *Father, I hope you're having fun, 'cause frankly, I feel a bit awkward. Now what do I do?*

Again God spoke into Shiny's heart. "Now we're going to have some fun. Shiny, we're going to surprise Billy with the truth that will set him free. My truth will release faith in Billy to believe he will walk again. I will fill your mouth with words of life so Billy will believe Me for the miracle of healing."

Shiny was so excited he felt like singing out "Holy, Holy, Holy." He started to hum the tune when Billy interrupted. "Excuse me, Dr. Shiny, but are you going to finish my exam? I have to get back to school."

"A-ah, yes, I will finish the exam. What would you like me to do next?"

"You're the doctor. You tell me."

"Okay, let's finish this examination. Watch this."

Shiny began to flap his arms up and down in hopes of getting some direction from God.

A frustrated Billy quizzed Shiny once more. "What are you doing?"

God announced, "Here we go, My little bald friend. Open your mouth and let Me fill it."

Shiny opened his mouth. "I've come to bring you a message from God, and I'm waiting for Him to tell me what to say."

Billy giggled. "Dr. Shiny, you're the silliest doctor I've ever seen, and I have seen plenty of them. So do you have a message from God?"

Now Shiny was excited. Billy had heard what Shiny said. The crippled boy looked up from his wheelchair. "Well, flap those arms and tell me what God has to say."

This excited Shiny even more. "O-O-kay!"

Shiny started flapping his arms with all his might; then suddenly God opened Billy's eyes. Shiny's new wings appeared, and Billy's mouth dropped wide open as he sat completely stunned by what he was witnessing. God allowed a heavenly pause for Billy to soak it all in and to release an extra measure of faith to Billy.

Shiny had to struggle to keep his feet on the ground. He could feel his mouth filling with words.

He tried to contain himself and then finally gave way. He began to hover over Billy as he opened his mouth. "God wants you to know He sent me to here today so you'll believe that on Christmas Eve, our heavenly Father will make you walk again. He is going to perform this miracle in your life to proclaim His goodness to the entire known world. You will become famous, and God will use you to bring glory and honor to His name."

Tears rushed down Billy's face as he laughed with immeasurable joy.

Shiny continued to proclaim. "This joy will stay with you as a sign that God is going to do what He sent me here to tell you. This joy will be the strength which will cause you to rise up out of your chair for the glory of God. Daily you will feel this joy bringing increased strength to your legs, and on Christmas Eve you will rise out of that nasty old chair."

Billy broke out into shouts of joy. "Thank You, God. You've heard my prayers! Thank You, Thank You!"

Through Billy's tears of joy, he watched Shiny's wings lift him up higher, and you guessed it.

Suddenly Shiny was gone.

Shiny was sitting on God's knee again. God was looking down at Shiny with a big smile. For the longest time, God stared at Shiny with a big grin on his face. He just kept smiling at the little bald angel.

No words were necessary. The little bald angel and the God of all creation just enjoyed sharing the moment together. Shiny's eyes began to fill with tears, and his heart was bursting with joy. He was sure his heart would pop from the joyful pressure.

Shiny couldn't contain himself any longer. "That was the coolest! Thank You, Thank You, Thank You! I want to do more, Father. Please give me more to do. I want to spend the rest of my life taking messages of hope to earth. Can I bring Your kingdom to earth? You know, let Your kingdom come on earth as it is in heaven."

God gazed at Shiny with a puzzled look. "The rest of your life? Shiny, I've created you to live forever. You are here for all eternity."

Shiny busted up laughing. "I was just so excited about delivering Your messages. Father, I want to do this for all eternity. I want to be Your messenger. It feels so good to see people finding hope in You. People do want to believe You're real."

God smiled again. "I know, brave one, when you're doing what I made you for, it feels good. I have so much more for you to do. The best is yet to come."

"How can it get any better than seeing little Billy believing that You will heal his crippled legs?"

God responded, "What I have for you is even better."

Shiny looked up at God. "How do you always know what I'm thinking?"

God just smiled. Shiny returned the smile and nestled in a little closer.

Meanwhile, back at Main Street Children's Clinic, Billy sat stunned in his wheelchair. Amy came over and asked, "Billy, are you okay? Where's Mr. Steward?"

"Mr. Steward?"

"Yes, the bald-headed man in the suit."

"You mean Dr. Shiny?"

Just then Dr. White walked up. "Where's Dr. Shiny? He should know better than to leave a patient alone."

"I don't think Dr. Shiny will be back soon," declared Billy.

Dr. White said, "What do you mean he won't be back soon?"

Amy walked back to the front mumbling, "Dr. Shiny, who's Dr. Shiny?" As she opened the door, she was met by a bald man in a suit.

"Hello, my name is Dr. Red Davis. I'm the new pediatrician"

CHAPTER 6

The E-Max Theater

Shiny was skipping down the Street of Gold back to his apartment. All he could think about was how good God was and what his next assignment would be. He hoped he would have the opportunity to deliver the good news of God's eternal life through His Son, Jesus Christ.

Shiny broke out into his version of "Jesus Loves the Little Children." He sang, "Jesus loves the little children, all the children of the world. Red and yellow, black and white; they are precious in His sight. Jesus loves the little children of the world."

Shiny was becoming quite the singer. He sang and skipped all the way home. It seemed like an eternity since the other angels had made fun of him. Life had been very good since Shiny had been spending time with God. He loved partnering with God on earthly assignments.

When Shiny arrived home, he broke into the most beautiful rendition of "Holy, Holy, Holy Is the Lord God Almighty." He walked by the large mirror that hung over his dining room table and couldn't believe what he saw. He found himself staring at the most incredible pair of angel wings he had ever seen. He turned his back toward the mirror and looked over his shoulder. Staring at his wings in the mirror, he thought, *God must be in the business of creating new for His glory.*

Shiny was becoming the new creation God had promised. As Shiny was pondering the beauty of his new wings, he was interrupted by the thought, *Hey, I wasn't supposed to get my wings until I delivered three messages.*

He heard what sounded like the crashing of cymbals. "Shiny, your wings are developing each time you bring a message to earth. You're becoming the messenger I created you to be, even as I speak. I have one last message for you to bring to earth before you become one of My chosen messengers of good tidings. Rest now, and when it's time for the third message you'll know."

The cymbals silenced, and Shiny was alone again. As he looked in the mirror, he noticed his whole countenance was different. He walked toward his bedroom. That's right, angels have wonderful bedrooms where they rest in the presence of God while they wait for new assignments. Real angels look forward to taking their naps. As he walked into his bedroom, he found himself wondering when he would be going back to earth to deliver another message.

Serving God was becoming Shiny's passion. Just the thought of going back to earth put a smile on the little bald angel's face. Shiny found himself smiling quite a bit since experiencing lap time with God.

As he entered his bedroom, it seemed brighter than normal. Shiny would discover his new confidence caused God's glory to shine brighter everywhere he went. He hung his robe of confidence on a hook next to his bedroom door. He was getting ready to lie down on his big featherbed when he heard what would soon become a very familiar sound.

Knock, knock, knock. *What's that noise?* thought Shiny.

Knock, knock, knock. *I've never heard that noise before.*

KNOCK, KNOCK, KNOCK! *Wow, that's loud. What is that?*

God spoke. "Brave one, someone is knocking on your door. You might want to go see who's there."

Shiny responded, "Someone is knocking on my door? No one has ever knocked on my door. No one has ever come to visit me."

Shiny opened his front door, and there was Rufus with the angels. Rufus stood in silence, shaking his head as he stared at Shiny's wings. Louie, one of the trumpeting angels, broke the silence. "What beautiful wings you have!"

Rufus joined in. "They're beyond beautiful. Shiny, you're becoming what God designed you to be. Come with us, so we can prepare you for what's next."

Shiny asked Rufus, "What's next? Am I in trouble?"

"No, Shiny, just the opposite! What you are about to experience will cause praises to spring forth from deep within you. Come now and follow us."

Rufus motioned Shiny to follow him. Shiny grabbed his robe of confidence and followed Rufus and the angels down the Street of Gold.

"Where are we going?" asked Shiny. "I've never gone this way before."

Louie the trumpeter proclaimed, "We're taking you to the E-Max theater."

Shiny questioned, "E-Max theater, what's that? Is that like the IMAX theater where they show movies in 3-D?"

Louie responded, "Better, it's the Earth-Max theater, where angels watch what's happening on earth. Everything you watch is in 4-D."

Shiny asked, "What's 4-D?"

"I don't know, but it's better than 3-D."

When the angels arrived, they stopped at the concession stand and got some popcorn with M&M candy. In heaven, all popcorn comes with M&M candy already mixed in. It's the way God intended it. When they entered the theater, Rufus called to Shiny, "Come sit with me, big guy, and watch how magnificent God is."

Shiny was amazed at how much respect Rufus was showing him. He took a seat next to Rufus and couldn't believe how beautiful the E-Max theater was. Shiny was amazed how good M&Ms and popcorn tasted. He was surprised how much life had changed since he was called to serve God.

The beauty of the theater took Shiny's breath away. Everywhere he looked, the bald angel saw the incredible splendor of God's creation. The ceiling was the open heavens filled with stars.

It appeared to be galaxies upon galaxies for as far as the eye could see. The screen was a large, billowy cloud below. It was as if the entire theater was a balcony suspended in the air overlooking the cloud. There wasn't just one balcony, but balcony upon balcony. The balconies reached farther into the heavens than any human could comprehend. The balconies were filled with God's angel army. It was as if the angels were encamped all around, looking down on earth in anticipation of specific assignments from God.

Suddenly the most majestic anthem began to play. It was heavenly. The angel army rose in unison as the anthem increased in volume. As the music filled the heavenly expanse, the cloud below rolled away. Right before their eyes, the heavens opened, and there was earth. They were watching earthly events unfold right before their eyes. What they were viewing was better than any man-made movie. The events on earth were the angel army's entertainment, provided by none other than God Himself.

Shiny was speechless as he watched the lives of Mr. Blake and Billy Smith. It was hard for him to comprehend that what seemed like just moments before, he had been interacting with both of them on earth.

Shiny was beginning to understand how magnificent God had designed heaven and earth to work together. He was in awe of how God had total control over time and yet was not bound by it. He realized in a moment that God was in complete control of heaven and earth. Shiny watched the events unfold before him with his host of new friends. He marveled at the reality: when God wants to get something done, He does make it happen suddenly.

Rufus interrupted Shiny's daydream. "Hey Shiny, check out what Mr. Blake is doing. Listen to his prayers."

Mr. Blake was at home on his knees, praying and thanking God for what was about to happen. He kept thanking God for sending Shiny. Mr Blake's faith had moved him from a place of asking and hoping to seeking and praising God for what He promised. In heaven, you could hear Mr. Blake's prayers knocking on heaven's door.

"Thank You for hearing the cry of my heart. Thank You for sending Your heavenly host to encourage me. I give You glory for what You are going to do in my life. I dedicate the rest of my life telling people that You are alive and still do miracles."

Shiny was very excited to hear what Mr. Blake was praying. He glanced at Rufus and saw his new friend smiling back at him. "Pretty cool, isn't it, Shiny? There's nothing better than being used by God."

Shiny smiled as tears of joy ran down his face. As he turned his attention back to earth, he saw Billy Smith in his bedroom. Billy's father was lifting him out of his wheelchair and placing him in bed.

Shiny listened to Billy. "Dad, I'm telling you God is going to heal me on Christmas Eve. The bald angel said so."

His father looked at him with compassion. "Son, we must trust that God knows what's best for us."

Billy and his father prayed together, and then his father turned off the lights and left the room.

Shiny was amazed at what he was witnessing. He could see Billy's prayers rising into the heavens, but when Billy's father prayed, his prayers never reached the ceiling of the bedroom.

Rufus leaned over and whispered to Shiny, "Want to have some fun?"

Shiny sat up and without hesitation responded, "Yes!"

Rufus smiled again and encouraged Shiny. "Put your popcorn down and flap your wings. God is with you."

Shiny flapped his wings, and the next thing he knew, Shiny was standing in Billy's bedroom. Billy lay there speechless with eyes wide open, staring at Shiny. The glory of God reflecting off Shiny's head lit up Billy's room. Before Shiny could even think of what to say, he found himself proclaiming, "Billy, God will do what God has promised. Don't let your faith waver. No man can stop God's glory from coming upon you. Christmas Eve will be like none you've ever experienced. You will rise and walk. This town will be changed forever because of the miracle that God is going to do for you. You will be their hero for many years to come. God has chosen you to be His ambassador of baseball. Billy, I have come to bring you good tidings of great joy. See you on Christmas Eve!"

When Shiny finished, he was shocked at what came out of his mouth. Billy continued to lie still and stare straight into Shiny's eyes. Then the craziest thing happened: Billy looked at Shiny and blurted out, "When God heals me, you'll never be the same either. God is going to do the same for you as He is for me. Your name will shine forever in heaven, bringing glory to God." Billy looked at Shiny more intently and shouted, "Shine on, amigo!"

Shiny and Billy broke into uncontrollable laughter. Through his laughter, Shiny replied, "Shine on, amigo!"

Shiny and Billy would become friends for life and into eternity.

Billy's father opened the bedroom door. "Billy, are you okay?"

"Oh yes, Father, I am more than okay."

Billy's father turned as he was closing the door and said, "Go to sleep now. You need your rest."

Shiny and Billy laughed some more. Billy asked Shiny, "What's your name?"

Through his laughter, the angelic visitor quietly announced, "Shiny is my name."

Billy had an inquisitive look on his face. "Shiny, are those chocolate stains on your robe?"

Shiny looked down at his robe and laughed louder. Before he could look back up, he found himself sitting next to Rufus at the E-Max theater.

"What did you think of that, Shiny?"

"That was more than cool! The words just flew out of my mouth! I love to deliver God's messages to my friends on earth."

Rufus explained that's how God's plans for our lives work. "Shiny, this is what God made you for, and when you're doing what God created you for, life just flows."

They spent the rest of the afternoon watching people on earth. Shiny was so excited to see what God was doing and what He was planning to do for those He loves. Shiny went home that evening and washed the M&Ms out of his robe of confidence.

Chapter 7

The Chubby Little Cherub

S hiny finished his evening chores and prepared himself for bed. As he laid his head on his pillow, he found himself pondering how different life was. He had incredible new wings, a host of new friends, including Rufus. Most of all, he was experiencing the joy of the Lord doing God's work. With God in control, Shiny felt confident he could do just about anything.

Shiny closed his eyes and thanked God for using him in the lives of Mr. Blake and Billy Smith. In the middle of his prayer, he drifted off into a deep sleep.

Shiny had a dream. In the dream, God had put him in charge of a host of angels who were assigned to bring messages of hope to people who were desperately in need of miracles. Shiny was training angels how to share messages to hopeless people by being attentive to God's divine direction. He shared with the angels how important it was to flow with the Spirit of God when on earth. Shiny taught the trainees to be dependent on God alone and not look to their abilities. He shared with them how good and loving God is and that He desires to restore all things to their original purpose.

One angel in particular was a little angel named Hercules, and he was the tiniest angel of all. In the dream, Shiny took Hercules under his wings and was teaching him to do God's work. The dream ended with Hercules growing in courage and strength in the Lord. He became an angel of high authority. Even though he was tiny, Hercules became bold, proclaiming the truth of God.

Shiny woke up the next morning and pondered the dream in his heart. He lay in bed wondering, *Could that be a dream from God?* He decided to get up and start his day. Shiny made his bed like all good angels do. He made breakfast for himself and washed the dishes like all good angels do. Shiny put the rest of his dirty robes in the washer—that's right, like all good angels do.

You see, angels love to do their chores. That's why they're angels.

Shiny opened his front door and was welcomed by the singing of birds. "Good morning, all of God's creation! This is the day the Lord has made, and I'm going to rejoice and be glad in it."

He started down the Street of Gold and ran into Rufus and a host of angels. Shiny thought, *I wonder how many is a host of angels.*

God immediately answered, "That's a great question, little friend. Ten thousand times ten thousand, which would be one hundred million."

"Wow! That's a lot of angels."

God responded, "Yes, I created them all to be unique; they're not all with Rufus."

Rufus greeted Shiny first. "Good morning, Shiny. How are you doing today?"

Shiny greeted the other angels and then answered Rufus. "I'm so excited about what's going to happen today."

Rufus was stunned by Shiny's response. "You've heard what's going to happen today?"

Shiny didn't know what Rufus meant. "I just feel good about the day the Lord has made, and I'm excited."

"So you haven't heard?" Rufus asked.

"No."

All the angels gathered around Shiny and collectively began to talk and sing all at once. The noise of the clamoring angel army caused heaven to shake. Louie blew his horn and declared, "Shiny, God has announced today, yes today, He's giving you your final assignment before he promotes you. You are going to take on hopelessness in the name of the Lord."

Shiny looked at Louie. "Promote me?"

Louie blew his horn again. "Yes, God has announced you're going to train the host of angels how to bring messages to people of every nation on earth who are in need of miracles. He's going to have you take little Hercules with you on your next assignment, so you can start training him."

Shiny had a faraway look in his eyes as Louie was blowing his horn. When angels have a faraway look in heaven. Believe me—it's a faraway look. Louie stopped talking when he realized Shiny wasn't listening. Shiny was distracted by his thoughts, realizing his dream was exactly the same as what Louie had just described.

The goodness of God touched Shiny's heart. He had always known God was good, even back when he was without wings and alone. Now he was experiencing God's goodness firsthand, but he was struggling to accept that he was worthy to benefit from this indescribable goodness.

"Shiny, did you hear what Louie said?" asked Rufus.

"Yes, I heard him, but it almost sounds too good to be true."

"What do you mean too good to be true? Nothing with God is too good to be true, Shiny," exhorted Rufus.

Shiny quickly responded, "No, no, I didn't mean it that way." After collecting his thoughts, he continued. "It's just that I had a dream last night, and everything Louie was talking about was in it. I even saw Hercules in my dream, and I've never met him before. Now Louie is telling me that there is a real Hercules, and everything in my dream is about to come true. Can God get any better?"

Rufus whistled, and from behind the host of angels stepped Hercules. Yes, that's right, his name is Hercules, and he is cute.

Rufus directed his attention to Shiny. "I'd like you to meet Hercules. Boys, get yourselves ready for the ride of your life."

Shiny looked down at Hercules and thought, *I've never seen anything as cute as him in all my life.*

God thundered from the east, "Hercules is one of My cutest angels."

Hercules had bright-red curly hair and big blue eyes. He had big dimples in both his rosy-red cheeks. He stood just a hair under three feet tall and was a little on the chubby side, for an angel, that is. He just kept looking up at Shiny with the innocence that would melt the hardest of hearts. God created Hercules to soften the hardness of men's hearts and prepare them to receive the good news. God gifted Hercules with His favor.

Hercules broke the silence. "My, you have amazing wings, and your head is very shiny. You're quite beautiful. Would you be my friend?"

Shiny again was being asked for the precious gift of friendship. He was humbled by the request and frankly was a bit embarrassed at how Hercules was going on and on about how beautiful Shiny was. Shiny thought, *Who in their right mind could ever deny a request of friendship from this adorable little cherub?*

The chubby little cherub spoke up. "May I call you Shiny?"
Shiny nodded.

Hercules said, "I want to be just like you someday. Can I go where you go and do what you do?"

Shiny's heart overflowed with joy as he responded. "Hercules, I would be honored to be your friend, and where I go you will go. Everything I've learned I'll share with you, and you will be strong and courageous as you become a mighty messenger of God. You will go throughout the earth, ushering in the power and worship of God, so miracles can take place. Oh, and God wants you to know that you will enjoy the good-tasting things of His creation. Enjoy!"

Shiny paused and thought, *Good-tasting things? I wonder what that means.* He continued,

"God will give you a voice that few will be able to match. God will send you to the most distraught, discouraged, and downtrodden people on earth. God will give you boldness. His favor will go before you. You will share a message of hope, which will bring life to those who have given up. The most hopeless people will cry out to know Jesus, the Son of God."

Hercules looked up at Shiny with big tears running down his face. "But I'm from the host of little angels. I'm just a chubby little cherub."

Shiny encouraged Hercules. "Remember in God's kingdom, the least will be the greatest. Remember David was the youngest in his family, and God used him to take down Goliath, and don't forget Gideon's army. Come now, little buddy, jump up on my wings, and let's get ready for the ride of our lives."

Hercules climbed on Shiny and crawled under his wings. Shiny giggled as Hercules nestled underneath his wings. Shiny spread his wings so Hercules could get comfortable for the ride. As Shiny was pulling his wings down over Hercules, suddenly lightning shot across the eastern sky.

God declared, "It is time to conquer the most difficult of all. I'm sending you to defeat the voice of hopelessness. There's a man who lives in the center of town who has lost all hope. Go, share My message of hope with him. Tell him that I love him. No matter what he says, tell him that I love him."

Shiny and Hercules stood in the stillness left from when God stopped speaking. It was beyond quiet. It was quieter than they had ever heard in heaven. Maybe not heard, because it was quiet. You can't hear quiet, right? Well, it was quieter than what you could imagine.

Suddenly Hercules broke the silence with a whisper. "Shiny, what was that?"

Shiny lifted his wing ever so slightly and whispered, "That was God."

It was silent again. Shiny could feel Hercules shaking under his wings.

"Have no fear, little buddy. God is for us, and if God is for us, who in heaven or on earth could be against us? We're going to conquer hopelessness in God's strength."

After a moment of silence, Shiny heard from underneath his wings, "That's cool."

Shiny laughed as he made his way to the earth tunnel. As he was walking, he had a thought:

How am I going to know who this hopeless man is? All God said was he lived in the center of town. I don't know his name or where he lives.

Suddenly God broke into Shiny's thoughts. "You will know him by his level of hopelessness."

Shiny continued to walk ever so slowly toward the earth tunnel. When Shiny arrived, he was amazed at what he saw. Rufus and the angel army were all there to cheer on Shiny and Hercules. Louie was blowing his trumpet with all his might. Herald was leading a choir of angels. Some angels were clanging cymbals, while Rufus was leading cheers through a megaphone. It was quite the celebration to send Shiny and his new cherub chum off to conquer hopelessness.

Hope flooded Shiny's heart. From under Shiny's wings, Hercules asked, "Shiny, why is your heart beating so loud?"

Shiny flapped his wings and proclaimed, "It's hope, Hercules; it's hope!"

When he let out the second shout of hope, Shiny found himself standing right in front of Murph's Corner Market. Hercules peeked out from underneath Shiny's wing and looked around. "Where are we? It smells awful out here."

Shiny responded with one word: "Earth."

"How did we get here?"

"Suddenly, Hercules, suddenly."

Shiny went on to explain to Hercules that when God wants to get something done, everything happens suddenly. Hercules jumped down from underneath Shiny's wings and took a look around.

"Well, what do you think of earth so far, Hercules?"

Hercules stood there for a moment and then offered his opinion. "To be honest, Shiny, I'm disappointed. I thought earth would be full of color, like heaven. I thought it would be much brighter and the sounds would be alive. All I hear are the whispers of hopelessness, sadness, and defeat. The smell is terrible. I never knew anything could smell so bad."

Hercules tried to continue, but tears began to roll down his chubby cheeks.

Shiny put his arm around the little cherub and explained, "It wasn't always like this. God created it to be just like heaven, a real paradise. You know heaven on earth, but then came the apple and the serpent, and you know the rest of the story. Hercules, it's not the end of the story. On Christmas, everything gets turned around, and God wins. Jesus, God as man, comes and conquers death. Jesus gave His life so man could be made right with the Father. He wins every time. For all eternity God wins. It's that simple."

Shiny was giving Hercules some firsthand on-the-job training. Shiny would teach Hercules that boldness is most active when sharing the simple yet profound message of Christ's death and resurrection.

Hercules would become quite bold with the love of God. The chubby little cherub looked up at Shiny with a big grin on his face. "I love God so much." More tears streamed down the chubby cherub's cheeks.

Shiny looked at Hercules. "Let's take this place for God and kick the hopelessness out of here once and for all."

Stepping out in faith, Hercules looked at Shiny and with all his might yelled, "Let's do it!"

48

The two angels broke out laughing. As they tried to gather themselves for their assignment, Murph came out of his store and asked if he could be of help. "Are you two lost?"

Shiny wondered if Murph recognized him as he responded, "Yes, we are lost. Can you direct us to the center of town?"

"Center of town? Why would you want to go there? That's a very dangerous place." Tom Murphy continued to question them. "What business do you have in the center of town? Is there someone in particular you're looking for?"

Shiny could tell Mr. Murphy didn't recognize him as the big, bald biker. Shiny decided to sidestep his questions by introducing Hercules and himself. "Sir, my name is Shiny, and this is my good friend Hercules. We've come to bring a message of hope from heaven to a man who lives in the center of town."

"Pleasure to meet you, Saul, and you too, Henry. My name is Tom Murphy, but everyone calls me Murph. I'm sorry to tell you, but the only people who live in the center of town are a few homeless sorts. Would you two like to come in and have a cold soda?"

Shiny just smiled and thought, *Hmm, now I'm Saul, and little Hercules is Henry.*

Experience told Shiny not to fight it but just play along and have some fun. He could hear God's words echoing in his head from his last visit to earth.

Just have fun and follow my lead. "Murph, we would love to come in and have some soda. Do you have root beer, by any chance?"

"Root beer! I have the best root beer this side of the Mississippi. Come on in, and I'll treat you two to the best root beer you've ever had."

Hercules looked up at Shiny as they followed Murph into his store. "Root beer? Who's Saul and Henry? Why does this man think we've come from California?"

The two heavenly messengers followed Murph into the store. For now we'll just call them Saul and Henry.

Murph invited Shiny and Hercules to grab a couple of stools at the soda fountain as he poured two root beers. "So tell me again why are two young men like you wanting to go to the center of town?"

Shiny answered, "We have a message to deliver to a hopeless man. We're here to let him know how much God loves him. Do you know who he might be and where we can find him?"

Hercules took his first sip of root beer and discovered the first of the many good-tasting things God had waiting for him.

The Smell of Hopelessness

Murph announced, "Saul, there's only one man who fits that description, and yes I do know where he is, but I don't think he will talk to you. He's hasn't spoken to anyone for a very long time. He's like Job in the Bible. He too has lost everything, but unlike Job, he has turned his back on God."

Shiny wondered what Murph heard to give such a response. The man he described sounded very hopeless. He sounded like someone who was in desperate need of God's help. Shiny felt a rush of excitement as he thought of God stepping in and sending His love to turn around a life gone bad.

Psalm 23 came to Shiny's mind. "Your rod and Your staff will comfort me."

Shiny thought, *This sounds like a soul who needs to find comfort in the Good Shepherd's love.*

Shiny and Hercules listened as Murph explained. "About ten years ago, the mayor of our fine town, Mr. Thomas, lost everything. I mean everything. His wife passed away. He lost the election after being mayor for twenty years. On top of that, he lost his home in a fire. Mr. Thomas was the choir director at church. When he lost everything, he turned his back on God.

"He now lives on the streets with the homeless and doesn't talk to anyone. The children call him doubting Thomas. The poor man has nothing left to live for. You want to see a hopeless soul, Mr. Thomas is your guy. To be honest with you, Saul, I don't think he'll talk to you. He hasn't spoken to anyone for the past five years."

Murph paused and got lost in the moment. Then he started in again as if a thought triggered the response. "You know, boys, Mr. Thomas stopped by the store years ago when I was a bit discouraged. He told me, 'Don't forget, Murph, the Lord is your shepherd and a good one at that.' I remember he said Psalm 23 was his favorite psalm."

Murph paused again, collected his thoughts, and then continued, "I've never forgotten those words. They still come back from time to time and encourage me right when I need it. Mr. Thomas is a good man, one of the most encouraging men I've ever known. He's just lost his way."

Shiny and Hercules sat there sipping root beers as Murph continued. "Just maybe you two have something that will renew hope in Mr. Thomas. Saul and Henry, there was a time when everyone in town would go to Mr. Thomas if they needed a word of encouragement. Now all hope is gone. If you boys are serious about meeting with him, you can find Mr. Thomas in the center of town, more than likely sleeping on a bench in Central Park. I wish you luck. Our community needs to see a miracle, and Mr. Thomas would be a big one, believe me."

Shiny glanced at Hercules and then back to Murph. The three smiled as Shiny and Hercules sipped their root beers. Just as they were finishing their last sips, police officers Benny and Lenny walked in.

"Hey, Murph, how are you doing today?"

"Just fine, Benny. How are you two doing? Keeping crime off our streets?"

Everyone laughed as Benny responded, "Oh yes, we have soo-o much crime in this town. We just picked up Mr. Thomas from Central Park and dropped him off at the station so he could grab a shower and have a meal. We'll let him out tomorrow after he's had a good night's sleep."

Lenny offered his patented "Yep."

Hercules blurted out, "Is that *our* Mr. Thomas?"

Office Benny gave Hercules his police officer glare and inquired, "What do you mean *your* Mr. Thomas?"

Shiny jumped in. "Excuse me, officer, but did you say you picked up Mr. Thomas?"

Officer Benny gave Shiny a quick once-over. Murph joined in and rescued Shiny and Hercules.

"Benny, this here is Saul and his friend Henry."

Hercules boldly interrupted. "You can call me Hank," followed by a dimply smile. Hercules directed his cherub grin, dimples and all, in Shiny's direction.

Shiny shook his head and thought, *Hercules is a real natural with this earth stuff. He fits right in.*

Murph smiled at Hercules and then continued, "These two young men have come all the way from California to share with Mr. Thomas a message of hope."

Officer Benny directed his attention to Shiny and Hercules. "A pleasure to meet you. If you'd like, we'll give you a ride to the station, and you can try to talk with Mr. Thomas, but I doubt he'll speak to you. He doesn't talk to anyone."

Hercules spoke up again. "We get to ride in a police car? How fun is that!"

Officer Lenny affirmed Hercules with another "Yep."

Officer Benny responded to Hercules. "I'm sure you two have never been in a police car before. You both look like law-abiding citizens. Why don't you finish your root beers. Then we'll drive you to the station."

Officer Lenny joined the conversation one last time. "Yep."

Hercules boldly asked Murph, "May I have another root beer for the road?"

Shiny was impressed with Hercules's bold request, and so was Murph. "I don't see why not. Hank, you may become my best customer. Let me pour you one more for the road."

Shiny and Hercules took their final sips and thanked Murph for being so friendly.

Hercules jumped down off the stool and with sheer delight grabbed his root beer to go. Shiny and Hercules followed the officers out to the police car. When they arrived at the police station, there was Mr. Thomas, asleep in the only jail cell in the station. He appeared to be quite old, and his clothes were tattered and dirty. The two angelic messengers could smell him as they approached the bars of the jail cell.

Hercules whispered, "I've never smelled anything like that."

Shiny whispered back, "That's the smell of hopelessness, and we've come to rid Mr. Thomas of it."

Hercules smiled his dimpled grin and confidently followed Shiny to the jail cell bars with his root beer in hand. The two heavenly hosts stood quietly watching Mr. Thomas sleep.

Officer Benny gave them some final instructions. "You're welcome to stay as long as you'd like. Just know that Mr. Thomas hasn't spoken to anyone for quite some time. Good luck, Hank."

Officer Lenny patted Hercules on the shoulder and then left them with Mr. Thomas.

"What do we do now?" whispered Hercules as he sipped root beer.

Shiny quietly tutored his heavenly companion. "We wait for Mr. Thomas to wake up, and when he does, God will fill our mouths with just the right words to say."

So they waited—almost five hours. As they were waiting, they could hear the angel army in heaven singing "Holy, Holy, Holy," which helped pass the time. When angels worship, it moves God's heart in heaven, time speeds up, and everything happens faster.

What Shiny and Hercules weren't aware of was the dream Mr. Thomas was having. In his dream, he went to church for the first time in years on Christmas Eve. During the service, he saw Mr. Blake stand up and share that God healed his eyes, seeing for the first time since the accident that made him blind. He saw Billy Smith get up out of his wheelchair and walk in the middle of the service. Finally, he saw two angels hovering above the congregation, singing beautiful songs over the people. One angel was bald, and the other had red, flowing, curly hair, resembling Cupid.

In the dream, Mr. Thomas stood up and spoke for the first time in years. He gave a testimony of hope, sharing God's love and forgiveness. Mr. Thomas shared how much God loved him and had forgiven his bitter heart. The dream ended with Mr. Thomas seeing his wife in heaven, rejoicing with the host of angels. They were dancing with all their might and shouting for joy. He knew she was in heaven rejoicing with the host of angels over what God was about to do on Christmas Eve for Mr. Blake, Billy, and her husband.

Meanwhile, Shiny and Hercules were patiently waiting for Mr. Thomas to wake up. They had no idea about the dream. God was washing away all doubt and hopelessness from Mr. Thomas with this dream. It was so peaceful that Shiny and Hercules fell asleep while they were waiting for Mr. Thomas to wake up.

Suddenly Mr. Thomas woke up and found Shiny and Hercules asleep in his jail cell. When he sat up, God caused Shiny and Hercules to wake up. The two angelic hosts looked around and couldn't believe their eyes. While they were asleep, God had somehow moved them *into* the jail cell with Mr. Thomas. The three sat stunned, trying to figure out what in the world had happened while they were sleeping.

Mr. Thomas stared at the two messengers from heaven. He kept rubbing his eyes but never said a word. He was trying to figure out how the two angels he saw in his dream on Christmas Eve had ended up in the jail cell with him. He couldn't tell if he was having a vision or if the two angels were literally with him in the cell.

Shiny and Hercules silently stared back. Shiny was trying to figure out what to say to give Mr. Thomas hope, while Hercules was wondering what was going to happen next and thinking how much fun he was having.

Hercules's thoughts were running wild: *root beer, police car rides, and now I get to see the inside of a jail cell, just like the angel in the book of Acts who helped Peter escape from prison.* Hercules wondered if they were going to help Mr. Thomas escape. *I wonder if God is going to have us bust Mr. Thomas out of here.*

As the three were caught up in their thoughts, Mr. Thomas began to weep. He cried for the longest time, not speaking a word. Shiny and Hercules began to cry with Mr. Thomas, but they never spoke.

Shiny remembered if he flapped his wings, God would be faithful to tell him what to do or say, so he began flapping with all his might. As Shiny was flapping his wings, Hercules sat there thinking, *Okay, God, how are we going to bust Mr. Thomas out of here? Come on, God, bust those doors wide open, just like you did for Peter in the Bible.*

God whispered into Hercules's ears, "Watch this, little one. I'm going to do one better. I'm going to break the chains of hopelessness off Mr. Thomas once and for all."

More tears rolled down the chubby cherub's cheeks. Shiny flapped and flapped his wings. The harder he flapped, the more Mr. Thomas sobbed. Shiny flapped so hard he began to hover over Mr. Thomas in the jail cell. Hercules looked up at Shiny hovering over him.

"Hey, where do you think you're going? Wait for me!" Hercules left his cup of root beer behind and jumped with all his might, landing right in the crook of Shiny's wing.

Mr. Thomas was stunned by what he was witnessing. While Mr. Thomas watched with amazement, God sang to him, "I love you, I love you, I love you with an everlasting love."

Suddenly Shiny and Hercules were standing at the entrance of the earth tunnel and were greeted by the cheering of Rufus and the host angels. The cheers rang throughout heaven.

Rufus greeted Shiny with a big angel hug. As Rufus clung to Shiny, jumping up and down, he exclaimed, "I've never seen anything like that in all my life, and I've been around for a long time!"

Shiny wasn't quite sure what Rufus was referring to. "What do you mean?"

Rufus let go of Shiny and answered, "I've never seen so much of God's love poured out on one person since Jesus looked at Peter after he denied Christ three times. Remember before the cock crowed? Man, Jesus really must have loved Peter."

Rufus continued, "God poured His love all over Mr. Thomas, and there's no doubt God used you and Hercules to bring His love down to Mr. Thomas."

Chapter 9

Hope Restored

"**Y**ou mean we didn't blow it?" Shiny couldn't believe what he was hearing.

Respectfully Rufus replied, "Shiny, you're the man, I mean the angel. You brought it, big guy. You brought God's love to Mr. Thomas, just like God planned. No more doubting for Mr. Thomas; he'll never be the same. He's so full of God's love that he won't be able to contain himself."

Shiny was still confused as he questioned Rufus. "But Mr. Thomas didn't say anything, and Hercules and I didn't say anything either. What happened to change his life, Rufus?"

"While you and Hercules were waiting for Mr. Thomas to wake up, God gave him the most beautiful dream. It was a dream that even Mr. Thomas couldn't doubt. Everything God promised was in the dream. Mr. Blake could see again, Billy could walk, and Mr. Thomas regained hope. His life was restored, just like Job in the Bible. Shiny, everything God sent you to do is going to be done on Christmas Eve!"

When Rufus finished, the host of angels picked up Shiny and started tossing him up and down.

They were all shouting, "Hip, hip, hooray, hip, hip, hooray!" Then Rufus led them in a cheer. "And Shiny is his name, and Shiny is his name!"

The cheers grew louder and louder with each toss of Shiny. The cheers reached the east side of heaven, where God lives. When God heard the cheering in the distance, He smiled. As God smiled down on the activities of the day, His glory lit up Shiny's head. The glory of God was so bright the hosts of angels were struck by the reflection.

God's glory caused all of heaven to break out into laughter, as the angel army sang the most beautiful renditon of "Joy to the World."

The singing ushered in another Christmas season. The appointed time had come for God to perform His miracles. People around the world began pulling down boxes filled with Christmas decorations from their attics. Christmas tree stands were being set up, and the first snow in many parts of the world began to fall. The smells of cinnamon and eggnog filled the air.

It seemed like Thanksgiving would never arrive; now the autumn leaves were being covered by snow. Winter had come, and snowmen were being built.

Shiny and the angels spent the season hanging out at the E-Max, watching the beauty of Christmas unveiled. Herald loved leading the host of angels in Christmas carols as they watched the holiday events from their vantage point.

Every so often a small contingent of angels would take off through the earth tunnel disguised as carolers and surprise a local neighborhood with a visitation of the most beautiful Christmas carols.

Angels love to sing for a cup of eggnog or hot chocolate. That's why when an unfamiliar group of carolers comes knocking on your door, always be ready to give them a drink. You never know when you might be entertaining angels in disguise.

Hercules displayed a new enthusiasm, having had the experience of visiting earth with Shiny.

He was always quick to point out all the people on earth he had met and would share his stories with any nearby angel who had a listening ear.

Herald loved this time of year. He would go around singing his cause at every opportunity.

His favorite Christmas carol was "Hark, the Herald Angels Sing." He would always joke about how God allowed that song to be written just for him.

Many of the other angels were given special Christmas assignments to go to earth and bring good tidings of great joy.

Angels covered the earth disguised as people of all occupations— some as police officers, some as doctors and nurses, and even some masquerading as big bald bikers, bringing hope to people who needed a word of encouragement.

Christmas was the time of the year when God loved to draw attention to his Son, Jesus, who came to take his place in history as the Savior of the world.

It's time to celebrate Emmanuel, the Son of God, Jesus Christ, God with us! The name Emmanuel declares the plan of God to reunite Himself with a lost world.

God came down from heaven as a man to be with us, and His name is Jesus. He became a baby in the Virgin Mary's womb and entered the world just like any of us.

The most surprising part of the story is that Jesus gave up His throne in heaven and took on the cross and died for the sins of the world so they could have eternal life with Him. He was willing to die so humanity could have life.

That has to be the greatest story ever told. The best part of this story is that God's salvation through Christ is a gift!

Well, Christmas came suddenly. Gifts were given and received. The greatest gifts were yet to come.

Mr. Blake now works at Murph's Corner Market with Tom Murphy. He can see again! The entire town is alive with hope.

Billy Smith got up and walked! Not only does he walk, he can run! He's captain of his Little League baseball team. The town is ignited with more hope each time Billy gets a hit and runs the bases.

Mr. Thomas just won the recent election for mayor, and his campaign slogan was "Hope Restored."

Oh, yeah, I almost forgot. Lefty and his boys now sing in the church choir, led by none other than Mr. Thomas.

Yes, Christmas Eve was one to remember, and you know what? This Christmas, when you go to bed, if you get real quiet and listen very carefully, in the distance, you just might hear the host of angels cheering, "And Shiny is his name, and Shiny is his name!"

So the next time you see a falling star, it may be Shiny flying through the earth tunnel to bring messages of hope to people who need to hear about God's love.

The good news is that God sent us Jesus, His Son, who came to become the Savior of the world, to free us from sin and death. Jesus gave

His life on the cross so we could have life and spend eternity in heaven with God, our heavenly Father.

The Christmas story of Jesus is Shiny's favorite story to share with people who are in need of hope.

Shiny now lives in a neighborhood in heaven called New Heights. From Shiny's home, he has an excellent view of heaven and earth. He appears to have grown in stature. Some say when God's glory shines on him, he does look a lot taller, but truly Shiny still is the same lovable little bald angel God intended him to be.

Remember God loves to take little and do great things with it.

Shiny does like to spread his mighty eagle wings and fly around heaven singing, "Holy, Holy, Holy." Shiny is free of all shame and sings out God's praises. Oh, and his head is as shiny as ever, especially when God's glory shines in heaven.

He loves being the only bald angel. Shiny spends most of his days training angels so they can bring the good news to earth. He especially enjoys teaching the host of little angels.

Remember the least in God's kingdom will become the greatest.

I almost forgot Hercules has become the angel God intended him to be. Hercules speaks with great boldness and loves to boost about how loving and kind God is.

Rufus leads the angels in cheering on those who are coming home to heaven by way of the earth tunnel. Rufus loves cheering for people who have believed in Jesus, the Son of God. He has a special podium at the Reception Stadium where he leads the crowds.

Shiny, Rufus, and Hercules have become great friends. In their spare time, they love to watch earthly events at the E-Max, while eating M&Ms and Popcorn of course.

Hercules recently put in a bold request to have root beer served at the E-Max.

I think I just saw a flash of light across the sky. You know what that means.

More Shiny to come!

A CHRISTMAS LULLABY

Mr. Thomas Goes Home

Knock, knock, knock!

"Shiny, are you home? Open up, it's me, Roof."

"Be right there."

Shiny grabbed his robe and opened the door. Hi Roof, come on in. What's the good news?"

"Shiny, that's exactly it, God's calling you to eternity past to help usher the Good News into history."

"What?"

Shiny was perplexed. He had no idea about what Rufus was talking about, nor did he have any clue that God was going to use him to usher in the single most significant event in all of history.

Shiny challenged Rufus. "I thought I was going to train a new group of messengers from the host of little angels. I was supposed to meet Hercules for breakfast, and then we were going to start teaching the little angels."

"All I know is our heavenly Father spoke to me at the Earth tunnel and told me to get you ready. Shiny let's get moving. We're going to the garden."

Shiny was completely stunned by Rufus declaration. "The garden!"

"Yes, Shiny you heard me correctly, the garden." Rufus motioned to follow him as Shiny shut the door behind him.

Shiny was struggling. "Are you sure about this Roof?"

"Absolutely, Now let's get moving."

Shiny hurried to catch up to Rufus as he called out. "Roof, have you ever been to the garden?"

Rufus hollered back. "One time. A long time ago. I think it was before Noah and the flood."

"Before the flood?" Echoed Shiny.

"You know in the book of Genesis when God decided to destroy the earth and all creation. Sin was out of control, so God chose Noah to build an ark and take two of each animal into the ark. For forty days, God the Father brought rain on the earth. God saved Noah, his family, and all the animals in the ark. Then He started everything over."

Shiny interrupted. "I know the story, Roof, but did you get to meet Jesus when you went to the garden?"

"Well, I stood at the gate and watched as He prayed for Noah so he would remain faithful to follow through with building the ark."

Rufus continued as he picked up his pace. "Shiny, our Father wants us to experience His wonder, so we can be filled with stories of hope to share with those who need to hear a message that will change their lives forever. God just wants His children to turn toward Him."

Shiny started jogging to catch up to Rufus. "Why me, Roof? Why would God the Father choose me for this assignment?"

"Shiny, it's not for us to question God when he calls. All you can do is trust and obey. There's no other way to be happy but to trust and obey."

Rufus smiled at Shiny and said, "Buddy, this is going to be a special season in your life, and remember—Ol' Roof will be cheering you on."

Shiny and Rufus spent the afternoon walking and leaping and praising God as they made their way to the garden on the east side of heaven. "Hey, is that who I think it is?"

Rufus answered, "Yep, that's him."

Shiny yelled out, "Hercules, what are you doing here?"

"Well, I was on my way to meet you for breakfast, and suddenly God thundered, and the east wind blew me over here. Next thing I knew, I saw you and Rufus walking down the garden path. What are you guys doing out here? I thought we were going to have breakfast and train a new group of little angels."

The three heavenly hosts continued walking down the garden path, enjoying the pleasant fragrance that was coming from the garden. With each step, Shiny found his heart being flooded with faith for something huge. He began to thank God for the opportunity waiting for him in the garden.

Hercules broke the silence with more questions. "Rufus, If God has an assignment for Shiny in the garden, then who's going to train the host of little angels?"

Rufus gave Hercules a coy grin, and before he could answer him, the chubby little cherub objected.

"No, Roof, I'm not ready to do the training by myself. You know I'm not ready, right?"

Hercules continued. "Rufus, how can God expect me to do the training on my own? I've only watched Shiny do the training, and half the time I was daydreaming about root beer."

Suddenly God spoke, and His glory filled the garden path like a cloud. The three heavenly hosts stood still, recognizing God's voice.

From out of the cloud, God sang to Hercules. "I have called you to do great and mighty things in My power. I have prepared you to rise above your thoughts and limitations. I will be with you. I will be with you."

The glory of God filled the whole garden and created a fog bank that enveloped the chubby little cherub. Everywhere they looked, they saw nothing but God's glory.

As God continued to sing the chorus over them, "I will be with you," Shiny and Rufus watched as Hercules began to rise off the garden path and hover over them. Hercules rose higher and higher, and he began to shout. "I will obey, and I will go in the strength of the Lord. I will go. Nothing can stop me now because God is with me."

Filled with courage, Hercules's feet touched down on the path. God's glory had lifted him.

Rufus and Shiny stood there for a moment and then busted up laughing, which seemed to give Hercules even more confidence. As joy showered down on Hercules, he began twirling around, spinning hilariously like a skillful ballerina. Overcome by joy, Rufus and Shiny buckled at the waist, hunching over and grabbing their thighs to try to catch their breath from the laughter.

Hercules came to a spinning halt. Rufus composed himself and encouraged Hercules. "Well, I guess we all know who God has chosen to do the training in place of Shiny."

The three laughed as they continued down the garden path.

"Hey, isn't that Mr. Thomas and his wife up ahead?"

Approaching the couple, they could hear the woman trying to get her husband to slow down.

"Would you slow down? You're moving so fast! Let's try to make this morning last."

The three angels stopped and greeted Mr. and Mrs. Thomas. Hercules boldly spoke up. "Excuse me, but you don't have to worry about the morning lasting. You're in eternity now. Everything is new every morning, and everything lasts forever."

Mrs. Thomas gave Hercules a welcoming smile. "You're right, I forgot where I was since my husband came home."

Shiny looked on with amazement.

Mr. Thomas addressed Shiny. "I'm home; this is incredible. I was lost, but now I'm found."

He continued, "Shiny, why I ever doubted God is beyond me." The once-hopeless soul paused and then took a big leap into Shiny's arms. Shiny caught him in midair as Mr. Thomas yelled out, "Shiny, I'm home, I'm finally home! It so is wonderful!"

The five of them all spun around, dancing and celebrating Mr. Thomas's homecoming to heaven. Shiny introduced Mr. Thomas to Rufus and then asked Mr. Thomas, "Do you remember Hercules?"

"Why sure, he was there the day you visited me in jail. I'll never forget that day as long as I live."

Hercules quickly informed Mr. Thomas that he would remember it for a very long time now that he had entered eternity. Hercules formally introduced himself to Mr. Thomas. "Hello, Mr. Thomas. It's sure good to see you again. It's great to see you up here. Oh, by the way, what were you thinking about, that day in jail?"

Mr. Thomas thought intently for a moment then gave his response. "I was completely awestruck. I must say, when I saw the two of you in jail, any doubts I had about God were washed away immediately. I realized God loved me more at that moment than I could ever love Him in a lifetime. From that day forward, I trusted God with my whole heart. Your visit changed my life forever. I experienced God's faithfulness. Oh, please forgive me. I forgot to introduce my wife. Millie, these are the angels who visited me in jail."

Rufus introduced himself. "Hi, I'm Rufus, but all my friends call me Roof. It's a pleasure to meet you."

The Thomases walked with the three heavenly hosts as they continued their journey to the garden. Mr. and Mrs. Thomas enjoyed the stories of hope that Shiny and his friends shared with them along the way. He found it difficult to believe that Shiny had been the laughingstock of all the angels in heaven. "I never would have imagined that angels could be so big and powerful. When I saw you in the jail cell, you seemed so large. Now seeing all the other angels, you don't look as big to me. Shiny, you may not be the most prominent angel in heaven, but God used you in the greatest way in my life."

In comparison to God, Shiny explained that all the angels in heaven were quite small and that it's God's glory shining on creation that magnifies everything to honor Him. Shiny went on to explain that God isn't concerned about outward appearances; all He cares about is our hearts.

Mr. Thomas shared with his new heavenly friends about his outrageous journey to heaven through the earth tunnel. "It was so incredible; all I remember was hearing Pastor Andrews's shoes shuffling across the cold hospital room floor as he approached my bed. I didn't have the strength to open my eyes. I felt the warmth of his hand grasp mine and heard him say, 'It's time to go be with Millie.'"

Mr. Thomas paused for a moment and then continued. "You know, Shiny, I never felt any fear; an ocean of peace washed over me. I thought the nurse had come in and poured warm water over me. It started on the top of my head and ran all the way down to my feet. Then it happened."

Hercules interrupted enthusiastically. "What happened?"

Mr. Thomas looked straight at Hercules. "Suddenly there was Jesus, standing at the foot of my bed, smiling at me. His grin increased as He addressed me, saying, 'Well done, my good and faithful servant.'"

The heavenly hosts and Millie all began crying and laughing at the same time. The joy caused them to break into dance, and I mean breakdance. Hercules was spinning around on his head, Shiny was stepping out, Rufus was doing a series of jumps and spins, and Millie even joined in.

Mr. Thomas shouted out to them, "Hey, I'm not finished with my story!"

They stopped the dancing celebration. As they wiped the tears of joy off their faces, Mr. Thomas continued. "Jesus extended his hand to me and said, 'Let's go home.' The next thing I knew, I was flying through the most beautiful tunnel I'd ever seen. The walls were glowing stones of all colors. The sound was indescribable. It was a harmony I've never heard. People were racing alongside me, singing and rejoicing. As far as I could see, people were on both sides of me.

"I looked to my left, and I saw what appeared to be a host of angels racing past me, flying toward earth. The next thing I knew, there was Millie, with other family members and a ton of lifelong friends. I saw people I hadn't seen in decades. It all happened so suddenly, yet it seemed like an eternity. Then I touched down on a gold-dust path, and there I was in the middle of this enormous stadium at the throne of Jesus."

Rufus spoke up. "Mr. Thomas, get used to it. In heaven, time lasts forever, yet everything seems to happen suddenly. I guess what I'm trying to say is time just doesn't exist like you know the time on earth. Our Father has made eternity seem like everything is in the present. I guess you might say God makes time last forever, while 'suddenly' is happening all around. You'll find the seasons and days are very different here."

The five continued walking together, each sharing stories of God's goodness. They spoke of Jesus, the one who gave it all so people could come to heaven and be with Him for eternity. They even shared with Mr. Thomas about the magnificent work that was ahead for him. Not labor like on earth, but eternal work that God designs to fulfill His destiny throughout all of eternity.

When they arrived at the still waters, Mr. Thomas announced that he and Millie were going to lie down in the green pasture and be still for a while. The angel comrades said their good-byes and continued down the garden path.

Hercules skipped ahead of Shiny and Rufus.

CHAPTER 2

The Garden

Hercules had skipped quite a distance ahead of Shiny and Rufus, when suddenly he was forced to stop in his tracks. He stood awestruck by what he saw and heard coming from the garden. Trying to communicate to Shiny and Rufus was futile. His five senses were being stimulated simultaneously by the beauty he observed in the garden.

Hercules reverently whispered to Shiny and Rufus, "Do you sense what I sense up ahead? Could it be?"

Shiny and Rufus caught up to Hercules.

Rufus explained, "Hercules, you're exactly right—it's Him. He loves to spend time in the garden alone with our Father. He's waiting to meet up with Shiny to take him on an adventure into eternity past."

In unison Hercules and Shiny responded, "Eternity past?"

"Yes, this is part of your training. Our Father wants you to experience the Son so you can share with the hosts of angels and people on earth just how much hope there is in Jesus."

Rufus encouraged Shiny and Hercules to continue to press in toward the beauty up ahead. "Come on, let's experience the beauty of His Holiness."

As they approached the entrance to the garden, Shiny began to sing praises to God like never before. His praises caused creation to expand around him. The birds were multiplying around him. Colors burst forth. The trees began to dance, and flowers sprouted up all over the hills on either side of the path. Shiny's singing moved the heart of God to create. It was truly incredible.

Rufus explained, "Everything that happens in heaven is truly amazing. The wondrous things of God will continue through all eternity. Together when we praise God, it moves His heart, and He brings forth beautiful creations for us to enjoy with Him."

The three angels were standing at the entrance of the garden. Shiny peered through the gates, fixing his gaze on a tree in the center of the garden. Two seraphim stood guarding the gate with worship.

The seraphim made an impression on Hercules. "Look, they have six wings!"

Rufus continued to explain, "Yes, two to cover their faces from the holiness of God, two to cover their feet, and they fly with the other two. They worship God for all eternity, singing 'Holy, Holy, Holy.'"

"Why do they need to cover their feet?"

"Herc, I think to show humility and honor to God. A holy act of reverence."

Hercules paused as he absorbed all that Rufus had shared. "I guess that makes sense."

Shiny made an attempt to look up at the seraphim as they hovered over the gate, but the fiery glow from the six-winged angels was blinding.

Rufus handed Shiny some sunglasses. "Here, try these. You have to see how beautiful they are."

Shiny put the sunglasses on and couldn't believe his eyes. The seraphim had flames glowing from them, and the sound was more than his angel ears could take in.

"Hey, Rufus, I didn't know we had sunglasses in heaven."

"Herc, These aren't just any sunglasses, these are S-o-n-glasses."

Shiny asked Rufus, "What are those flames shooting out from the seraphim?"

"It's God's eternal glory reflecting off His servants."

Hercules added, "Cool."

Shiny handed the sunglasses back to Rufus and returned his gaze to the garden. He was awestruck by the beauty of the tree planted in the middle of the garden. He continued to study the beauty of the leaves and the brilliant colors of the fruit hanging from the tree as a man suddenly appeared standing under the tree. The three angels fell to the ground at the appearance of the man. Lying flat on his back, Hercules had the courage to whisper, "I can't move."

Rufus parroted back, "I can't move either."

The weight of God's glory pinned the three angels to the ground as they lay still at the entrance gates.

Shiny spoke up. "Rufus, is that who I think it is?"

"Who else could have this effect on us?"

Hercules whispered again, "I wish we could lay here forever. This feels heavenly; it feels so peaceful and energizing at the same time."

Reverently the three angels listened to the seraphim as they sang out, 'Holy, Holy, Holy.' A beautiful shower of warm rain fell on the angel trio as the seraphim serenaded. The warm rain fell ever so gently, penetrating their spirits. It was refreshing after such a long journey. The serenading seraphim continued to sing over them, providing a live worship concert.

The rain was providing preparation for something special. The raindrops penetrated through their robes while going deep into their spirits without getting their robes wet. Their senses were being affected by this heavenly downpour.

From their position on the ground, they would look around and simultaneously hear and taste what they were observing. The flowers in the garden were blooming right before their eyes, and they could smell and taste the flowers. As the rain came down, it had a creative effect on everything it touched.

Shiny, Rufus, and Hercules enjoyed quite a show as they lay in the garden, under the power of God's presence.

Suddenly the east wind blew open the gate, and the man from under the tree called, "Come to me."

Shiny glanced at his buddies for confirmation. Rufus responded with a reverent nod. The bald angel stepped first and then Rufus, while Hercules crept low behind the two of them.

They approached the center of the garden as the sounds grew around them. All they could hear was the sound of glory, a sound they'd never heard before. They had experienced the light of God's glory reflecting off Shiny's bald head. They had felt the wind of His glory, but they had never *heard* God's glory like they did at that moment. The glory sound seemed to envelop them. They felt as though the sound of God's glory wrapped them like a garment. It sounded like a strong, warm breeze blowing through a dense forest.

Suddenly the man under the tree turned and spoke. The angels fell at the man's feet. The sound of his voice was like warm honey dripping in their ears. They could hear the sounds of what he was saying, but no words were understood. The sound of his voice was like fire in their hearts. It was a heavenly language of love.

They were unable to move; the joyful fire was burning a message in their hearts.

The three angels lay under the tree in the center of the garden, listening to the voice of Jesus. His voice was giving them a sense of direction and purpose like they'd never experienced. His spoken words were like a melody to a song, leading them in a new direction.

Then it was silent. There was no sound, no movement. Just stillness.

CHAPTER 3

Three Bells

The three heavenly hosts found themselves back at New Heights, where Shiny lived. They were silent as they walked side by side.

"How did we get here, Rufus? We were just laying in the garden."

"Herc, I think God translated us, just like Philip in the book of Acts."

Hercules questioned, "Translated?"

Rufus explained to his cuddly little friend, "Yes, God suddenly got us where He wanted us to be, like in the Bible when God translated Philip from the Ethiopian eunuch after Philip told him about Jesus. You know, translate, like to move from one place to another."

Hercules exclaimed, "Wow! God can do anything."

Then Shiny joined in. "You've got that right."

The three were silent as they walked some distance together. Then Hercules asked, "What just happened?"

Rufus answered, "We met Jesus. His voice touched our hearts."

Shiny spoke up. "I think He's still touching mine."

Rufus and Hercules stared at Shiny, waiting for more. Shiny just kept walking.

"What do you mean He's still touching your heart?" asked Hercules.

"His words are reverberating inside of me. Every word is like the beat of my heart."

"What is He saying?"

Shiny explained, "I keep hearing, 'Go with Me to eternity past. Go with Me to eternity past.' I keep hearing it over and over. Those words are going deep into my soul."

Rufus prodded Shiny. "Is He speaking anything else to you? Is He telling you when to go?"

"Yes, tomorrow, but I don't know when tomorrow will come."

Rufus counseled Shiny. "The Lord will tell you when tomorrow is."

Shiny said good-bye to Rufus and Hercules as he silently turned to walked home.

Hercules called out, "Wait a minute. How can there be a tomorrow in eternity? I thought there wasn't time or any days in eternity. You know, God is the same yesterday, today, and forever."

Rufus sat down and explained to his friends, "The Bible does say the elders come before God's throne and serve Him day and night. So somehow time will be measured. I think this is how it works in eternity. Today is the same as yesterday, and tomorrow is the same as today. So when God says tomorrow, He is choosing an appointed time in eternity, because yesterday, today, and tomorrow are all the same but different."

Hercules pondered Rufus's words and then said, "That doesn't make any sense."

"I know, but when tomorrow comes, it will make sense, because then today is yesterday and tomorrow is today, so that becomes God's appointed time."

Rufus paused to let Hercules take in his explanation.

Hercules responded, "Now that makes sense."

Rufus continued, "Yeah, I think that's kind of how eternity works—you're always in the present, whether it was yesterday, today, or tomorrow. It's all about faith and trusting God to tell you when the appointed time is. You see, that's how God can be the same yesterday, today, and forever. Get it?"

An impatient Hercules responded, "Totally. So will God tell Shiny when tomorrow was … or is?"

Patiently Rufus explained, "Well, He didn't tell Shiny today when tomorrow is, but Shiny will know tomorrow when the appointed time comes."

Shiny shook his head as he waved to his two pals and went home. That evening he rested in the presence of God. He fell asleep and had a another dream.

In the dream, God shared the Christmas story with Shiny. He shared how He would send His Son, Jesus, to earth. God the Father would ask His Son to leave His throne in heaven, which is at the right hand of the Father's throne. God explained that Jesus would be born of a virgin named Mary, whose husband would be Joseph.

Now this is where the dream gets really exciting. In the dream, God spoke directly to Shiny.

"When I ring the bell three times, you will go with My Son, Jesus, to earth and spend time with Joseph. He will need a friend. I want you to be his friend while Jesus is on earth. I'm calling you to eternity past with an important assignment. I'm assigning you to be the one who brings hope to My servant Joseph. He is a faithful servant, but I am calling him to trust Me like I have asked no man to trust before. He will be called to endure much ridicule. I will use his experience to prepare him to train My Son for what Jesus will have to endure. Shiny, you will be a friend to Joseph in his greatest time of need."

Suddenly Shiny woke up to the ringing of a bell.

As he opened his eyes and looked around, he was startled by the realization that he was lying under the tree in the middle of the garden. He stood up and looked around for the longest time. Never did he question how he had arrived in the garden. Shiny had learned when you rest in the presence of God, things happen suddenly. God can accomplish more when we rest in Him than if we try to wrestle with Him to get our way.

Shiny soaked in all the garden had to offer. Everywhere he looked, he could hear, smell, and touch the eternal beauty of the garden.

Then God spoke. "Get ready, because things are going to begin to happen suddenly from here on. Are you ready?"

Before Shiny could even reply yes, suddenly Jesus was with Shiny.

Shiny gazed into his eyes and experienced a love beyond measure. He looked at Jesus's hands and saw the holes from the nails. He looked down at His feet and saw the same. As he was looking down at His feet, Jesus placed His hand under Shiny's chin and slowly raised Shiny's gaze and looked into his eyes.

Then Jesus spoke. "Shiny, come and walk with Me in the garden."

Shiny obeyed and walked with Jesus toward two gates at the back of the garden.

Jesus spoke. "Do you see those gates?"

Shiny nodded.

Jesus explained, "That is the Eastgate. The gate over there is the Westgate. The Eastgate will lead us to eternity past, the Westgate to future opportunity. Shiny, when you hear the third bell, we will walk through the Eastgate into eternity past. Everything will suddenly be very different for both of us."

Shiny finally had the courage to speak. "Lord, when the third bell rings, do I meet you here? I don't want to be late. I don't want to blow it."

Jesus put his arm around Shiny's shoulders. "Friend, don't worry about a thing. When you hear the third bell, you will be right where you're supposed to be. Our Father will make sure of that. He's the God of details."

"Can I stay with you? I don't ever want to leave your presence."

Shiny couldn't believe how bold he was with Jesus, the Son of God. He discovered being with Jesus caused confidence to flow effortlessly.

"Shiny, I'm always with you, even to the end of the age. Now go get some rest. Our Father has much for you to do in eternity past. My earthly father, Joseph, needs your friendship."

Jesus turned and walked back toward the tree in the center of the garden. Shiny watched as Jesus walked away. Jesus turned back toward Shiny and gave him a thumbs-up and called out, "Hey, Shiny, hope on, amigo!"

Jesus grinned at Shiny, and suddenly, Shiny was back at his house, lying in his bed.

Shiny asked Jesus, "Did I hear you right? Did you really say *amigo*?"

Jesus responded, "Yep, I can speak every language known to man and then some."

Shiny thought, *I guess that makes sense. He is the creator of all things.*

Jesus declared, "You got that right," and smiled.

Shiny spent the rest of the day jumping up and down on his bed, rejoicing in the strength he received from being with Jesus. He thought, *I've got to find Rufus and Hercules and tell them what happened.*

Shiny grabbed his robe and bolted out the door. On his way to the E-Max theater, Shiny ran into Mr. Thomas and almost ran past him.

"Shiny, where are you running off to?"

"Come on, Mr. Thomas, follow me to the E-Max."

Mr. Thomas asked the age-old question, "Is that like the IMAX theater?"

Shiny answered on the run. "Better, you'll see, come on!"

Mr. Thomas took off running and was amazed at how quickly he caught up to Shiny. "I haven't run like this in years. I'm running and not getting tired or feeling faint. I feel like my youth has been renewed. I feel like I could fly like an eagle."

As they ran stride for stride, Shiny explained to Mr. Thomas, "This is just the beginning of eternity for you. You are going to find there is nothing you can't accomplish in heaven. The truth of who God is in you will only cause you to grow in confidence. You'll discover that nothing is impossible, because you are always in God's presence."

Mr. Thomas glanced at Shiny as they ran side by side. "You know, Shiny, I think I'm going to stay here for a while."

They laughed all the way to the E-Max.

Arriving at the theater, they stopped at the concession stand and grabbed some popcorn and M&Ms and then found their way to where Rufus and Hercules were sitting, enjoying the afternoon activities. Mr. Thomas was very impressed that the M&Ms were already mixed into the popcorn. He kept staring at the popcorn box in utter amazement. Shiny sat down next to Rufus and couldn't believe what he was watching. Rufus and the gang were watching Shiny and Jesus in the garden. It was like an eternal replay. Joy flooded Shiny and Mr. Thomas as they watched the replay of Shiny and Jesus in the garden.

Shiny was confused to observe what had just happened as if it were happening right now.

Then God explained, "In heaven, everything is as if it were happening for the first time. That, My friend, is the beauty of suddenly. When things happen suddenly, they seem to last forever, even though it seems like it just happened at that very moment."

"Wow! That's heavy." Shiny sat and pondered the wisdom of God.

Rufus leaned over to Mr. Thomas and whispered, "Hey, Mr. T, is it okay if I call you Mr. T?"

"Absolutely, Roof."

Everyone laughed when Mr. Thomas called Rufus *Roof.*

Rufus chuckled along with everyone and then continued. "Okay, Mr. T, you want to see something really cool?"

"Sure."

Rufus turned to Shiny. "You ready to roll?"

"You betcha!"

Rufus declared, "You know the drill, Shiny. Go for it."

Shiny knew exactly what Rufus was referring to. With all his might, he began to flap his beautiful eagle wings. Mr. Thomas's eyes almost popped out of his head at the splendor of Shiny's wings in full span, creating a whirlwind that almost lifted everyone around him off the ground.

Suddenly Shiny was back on earth, and Mr. Thomas was watching everything Shiny was doing.

Shiny found himself sitting in the bleachers at a Little League baseball field near the edge of town. The bald angel surveyed the baseball field, and there was young Billy Smith, positioning himself between second and third base. Billy took his position with his glove low to the ground.

Suddenly God opened Billy's eyes, giving him a supernatural recognition of the bald onlooker in the stands.

From his shortstop position, Billy yelled at the top of his lungs, "Hey, Shiny, shine on, amigo!"

Waving to Billy, Shiny yelled back, "Shine on, amigo!"

Suddenly the ball was hit like a rocket straight at Billy.

He fielded the ball with ease and flipped it to his teammate Eric Swan at second base, who stepped on the bag for a force out to end the inning. Billy and his teammates ran into the dugout as the small crowd in the bleachers cheered them on.

Billy shouted to Shiny from his spot in the dugout. "Hey, Shiny, what are you doing here?"

Shiny hollered back, "Just checking in to see how you're doing. Looks from here like you're having another great game. I watch all your games from heaven."

Grabbing his bat and helmet, Billy responded, "You watch me from heaven?" as he approached the on-deck circle.

"Yes, with all my angel friends. We love watching you play baseball. We're all proud of you."

From the on-deck circle, Billy shared, "I'm giving it my best, Shiny. I thank God every day for healing my legs and giving me the chance to play the game I love. Please thank God for me when you see Him."

"I know God is so proud of you, Billy. Keep shining for Him."

The bald angel stopped talking and watched with excitement as Billy approached the plate to take his turn at bat. As Shiny sat there waiting, he heard a familiar sound from heaven. All the angels at the E-Max were cheering with all their might for Billy to get a hit. Shiny thought this is what it must feel like to be a father. He was very proud of the young man Billy Smith was becoming.

Billy stepped into the batter's box and took his stance, ready to take on the first pitch. The young pitcher looked toward home plate to receive the catcher's signal. He nodded and delivered the ball to the plate. Billy threw his hands back and stepped into the pitch and swung with a fury.

Shiny got very excited. "Swing, amigo!"

The E-Max theater was full of anticipation as the angelic hosts along with Mr. Thomas watched Billy Smith take a mighty swing at the pitch. It was the bottom of the fifth inning, and Billy's team was behind four to three. There were two outs with runners on second and third. The pitcher delivered another fastball, and with one mighty swing, Billy Smith drove the ball to right center.

The ball hit the outfield fence on a bounce. Both runners scored, and Billy found himself standing on second base with a double. His team now had the lead five to four. Billy looked up at the crowd and saw Shiny hovering above everyone. Shiny then flew right over to Billy and stood next to him. It looked like Billy's eyes were going to pop out of his head.

"Shiny, what are you doing?"

"I'm so proud of you, and so is our heavenly Father. Keep giving it your best, and God will get the glory. He has big plans for your life. He healed you so you can fulfill His plans. By the way, I liked the way you pulled that ball to right field so both your teammates could score. Your swing looks splendid."

Billy and Shiny had a good chuckle. Then the second bell rang.

The E-Max theater was silent as they watched the interaction between Billy and Shiny. Rufus looked at Mr. Thomas and gave him a wink. "Isn't this a great place to enjoy a ballgame?"

Mr. Thomas answered with glee, "I never knew how incredible heaven would be. Do we get to do this forever?

Just as Mr. Thomas was finishing his question, Shiny appeared next to him in the E-Max. He joined the conversation as if he had never left. "Yes, you get to do this and a lot more. Our Father has an entire eternity filled will plans and purposes for you. The most important lesson to learn is to rest and enjoy the beauty of what God has created for us."

Mr. Thomas stared at Shiny. "How did you get back here?"

"Suddenly, Mr. Thomas, suddenly. Get used to it. Everything with God happens suddenly here."

Mr. Thomas shook his head and smiled as he sat forward in his chair and watched Billy lead his team to a championship season. As Mr. Thomas reclined in his chair, he realized he had the best seat in the house to watch Billy play baseball. "God is marvelous!"

Shiny yelled downed to Billy from his seat in the E-Max theater, "Hope on, amigo. Hope on!"

The angelic hosts along with Mr. Thomas looked at Shiny with a puzzled look. As Shiny rose from his seat to give it a go, the entire host of angels and Mr. T stood up and joined Shiny in unison.

"Hope on, amigo. Hope on!"

They stayed standing as a line drive was hit just to Billy's left. As the ball was just about to fly by, Billy dove and stuck out his glove to make a stabbing catch in midair. Billy quickly jumped to his feet and delivered a strike to the first baseman to throw out the runner trying to going back to first for a double play to end the game.

The third bell rang out across heaven.

The angels were rejoicing over the play Billy made. They sang and gave God the glory for healing Billy's legs, allowing him to play baseball. Rufus led the host of angels in a chorus of "For He's a Jolly Good Fellow." The angels and Mr. Thomas were filled with joy and laughter as they continued to watch the events on earth unfold.

Billy and his teammates celebrated their championship season at a local pizza parlor. Trophies were handed out and a whole lot of pizza was eaten that afternoon. Billy went home with his parents, and after removing the dust of the game with a good shower, he spent some time on his knees next to his bed, thanking God. The angels and Mr. Thomas joined in with

Billy thanking God for the miracle of healing and the joy of seeing a life fulfilled.

Billy looked to the heavens and thanked God for allowing him to see what he called his guardian angel. "Dear God, would You let me see Shiny many times over the course of my life? I really get a boost of faith when Shiny visits. He really knows how to encourage me and lift my spirits."

Back at the E-Max, Mr. Thomas took a look around. "Where's Shiny?"

Hercules surveyed the theater. "Hey Roof, where is Shiny?"

Rufus answered Mr. Thomas and Hercules. "Shiny is in eternity past."

Mr. Thomas gave Rufus an inquisitive look. "Eternity past? Where's that? What's that?"

"Mr. T, you'll find the longer you're here, the more eternity will make sense to you. Shiny has been commissioned with a greater work in eternity that will bring us all hope in a way that will be used to bring many home to Jesus. In eternity, hope, faith, and love are magnified to a greater degree than what could ever be known on earth. All I can tell you is keep the faith and hope on. The next time we see Shiny, we will all be rejoicing like never before."

CHAPTER 4

Eternity Past

Joseph knelt at his workbench in his carpentry shop.

"Heavenly Father, I don't understand, but I will trust You. I trust You with Mary. What do You want me to do? Father, I feel so alone. There's no one to talk to. No one understands, but I know You understand. Please, Father, help me through this time. I feel desparate, I feel lost."

In the stillness, Joseph placed his faith in God alone. He drifted off to sleep. While he was sleeping, Shiny suddenly appeared. Shiny was standing in Joseph's carpentry shop. He spoke to Joseph as he lay fast asleep next to his workbench.

"Joseph, son of David, don't hesitate to get married. Mary's pregnancy is Spirit-conceived. God's Holy Spirit has made her pregnant. She will bring a son to birth, and when she does, you Joseph, will name Him Jesus—'God saves'—because He will save His people from their sins."

Shiny had become quite comfortable delivering messages of hope to people, trusting God would fill his mouth. Still Shiny was amazed at the words that came out. When Shiny was done speaking, Joseph woke up. Rubbing his eyes, he kept staring up at Shiny. He couldn't believe what he was seeing.

Shiny appeared to Joseph in all God's splendor. His eagle wings folded soldierlike at his side. His robe of confidence draped entirely around what appeared to be a developing muscular silhouette. His beautiful bald head reflected God's glory, lighting up the carpenter's shop.

Joseph found the courage to address Shiny. "Who are you? Where have you come from?"

Without hesitation, Shiny answered, "I am a friend of God, chosen to walk with you through life's journey. Along the way, we will have some good laughs doing it. Our Father told me you need a friend. Can I be your friend?"

Shiny found his confidence in the Lord. Joseph absorbed what Shiny offered and then responded, "What shall I call you?"

Without hesitation, the heavenly host responded, "Shiny is my name."

"Are you an angel?"

"Reporting for duty."

The rest of the evening, Shiny informed Joseph that he was to stay with Mary through her pregnancy. Once she delivered the baby Jesus, Joseph was to marry her. Shiny continued to share with him how God had chosen Joseph to raise His Son, Jesus. Joseph would train him in righteousness and model for Jesus the truth found in the law of Moses. Shiny finished his counsel with the declaration of a unique high calling.

"God has honored you to be the earthly father to the Son of God."

Joseph offered Shiny drink and food. They shared their first of many meals together.

Shiny would find his friendship with Joseph a unique, special gift from God. After dinner, Joseph turned in for the evening to prepare for another rigorous day building furniture in his carpentry shop.

Shiny rested in the presence of God.

The next morning, Joseph woke up early to feed the livestock and get ready for the new day. After feeding all the animals, Joseph entered his shop to be greeted by the bald angel.

"Joseph, how did you sleep last night?"

"I felt God's peace throughout the evening, and I had a sense when I woke up this morning that everything would work out. If you don't mind, I'm going to spend some time in prayer before I continue my day."

Shiny asked if he could watch over Joseph as he prayed. "I would be honored if you would watch over me while I pray."

Joseph prayed while Shiny listened. God's glory appeared and reflected off Shiny's bald head and filled the workshop.

Then God spoke to Joseph. "Joseph, do not be afraid. I will protect you and Mary. I will guard over My Son, Jesus. Go to Bethlehem and register for the census. Don't be afraid, for I am with you. This trip is the fulfillment of My prophecy that My Son, Jesus, would be born in Bethlehem, so have a blast. Shiny will be with you. He knows how to have fun. I love you."

When Joseph was done praying, he looked up at Shiny.

In full angelic fashion, Shiny spread his wings over Joseph, and the glory of God came like a cloud cover. Joseph fell to the ground and started laughing hilariously. Shiny joined in. He spread his wings and lay down next to Joseph. Shiny had learned how to lie on his back with his wings spread so he wouldn't wrinkle his beautiful set of eagle wings.

Through the laughter, Joseph cried out to Shiny, "I get to be Jesus's papa. What an honor."

More laughter erupted from the two as they lay flat on their backs in the carpenter's workshop.

Joseph and Shiny would find through the years their friendship would be bonded by a joy that comes from obeying to the Father. They would look back over eternity and reminisce about God's faithfulness and how it brought them everlasting joy.

Joseph and Shiny would become inseparable, except when God called Shiny back to heaven.

Suddenly a calm breeze blew across Joseph and Shiny as they lay still.

Joseph whispered to Shiny out of the stillness, "Shiny, what is that?"

"That, my friend, is the Spirit of the Lord, God's Holy Spirit. He is every bit God, just like the Father and the Son. Remember in the book of Genesis when it says, in the beginning before there was anything created, the Spirit of Lord was hovering over the waters. Well, the same Spirit, the Holy Spirit is hovering over us. He is here to prepare you for the journey ahead."

When Shiny finished, Joseph lay still, soaking in the presence of the Holy Spirit. Joseph felt courage rising up inside of him. He felt peace deep in his soul. He felt incredible joy. He felt a deep love welling up inside of him for Mary and his newborn son, who they would give the name Jesus.

The doubts he had about Mary were being washed away. He didn't care what people were saying. As he was pondering Shiny's words, he blurted out one word: "Cool!"

The two friends enjoyed the rest of the day together.

From the E-Max theater, Hercules said, "Wait a minute—Joseph, the father of Jesus, said *cool*?"

Rufus explained to Hercules and the other angels who were looking on, "Well, it's a loose translation of the Aramaic language Joseph spoke."

Hercules asked again, "Oh, so you don't know for sure that he said *cool*?"

Rufus declared, "We don't know anything for sure. Only what our Father reveals to us."

Meanwhile, back on earth, the next morning—shortly after the Holy Spirit had visited—Joseph packed up his donkey and prepared for the trip to Bethlehem.

Again Hercules interrupted from his seat at the E-Max as he watched Joseph and Shiny below. "How far was it between Nazareth and Bethlehem?"

Then God spoke. "Well, I'm glad you asked, because I was just getting ready to tell you about this dangerous journey."

Hercules asked, "Father, what do you mean *dangerous journey*?"

"The journey was an eighty-mile trek on foot. First they traveled along the coast and then up and over mountains. It was typical for robbers to be hiding in the mountains to rob people who traveled alone."

Joseph planned his trip in such a way that they would go in a group with other Nazarenes, who were making the journey to register for the census. Mary would be spending most of her days walking, because riding on the donkey would be too uncomfortable for her.

Again the inquisitive little cherub asked Rufus, "Why would riding the donkey be uncomfortable?"

Rufus simply said, "Mary was nine months pregnant. Have you ever tried to ride a donkey when you're nine months pregnant?"

Hercules answered, "I've never been pregnant or had to ride a donkey for eighty miles over mountains."

"Well, there you go."

The angels at the E-Max all erupted with laughter at Rufus's response.

Mary and Joseph started on their journey to Bethlehem, where baby Jesus would be born in a manger, just like the Bible says. The trip would take about a week. Joseph was very considerate of Mary's condition. He would frequently ask Mary if she wanted to stop to rest so he could give her a foot massage.

Hercules chimed in from heaven, "That was sweet of him."

Then God spoke. "Yes, Joseph is a good man. That is why I chose him to raise My Son, Jesus."

Hercules responded, "Really?"

On the fifth day of the trip, the three of them got separated from the caravan of Nazarenes they had been traveling with the first four days.

Shiny, Joesph, and Mary were on their own, going through a dangerous mountain range known for where robbers hid, waiting for travelers. As they made their way through the mountains on the fifth day, suddenly Dottie stopped dead in her tracks.

Hercules whispered from heaven, "Dottie, who's Dottie?"

Rufus whispered back, "That's the name of the donkey. Dottie the donkey."

Hercules whispered again, "The donkey had a name?"

Rufus gave his best Lenny impersonation. "Yep."

Dottie the donkey stopped and called out to Shiny. "Shiny, right around that bend are where thieves usually hang out and catch travelers by surprise. I smell something foul in the air."

Shiny whispered, "Are you sure? Maybe we should ask God."

Dottie whispered back, "God already spoke to me and said there are robbers around the bend. Plus I've made this trip hundreds of times over the past thirty years."

Shiny spoke up with confidence. "Joseph, I think we need to pray right now."

Then Joseph prayed. "Lord, what is it You want us to do? Show us, Father."

Shiny added, "Amen."

Dottie chimed in, "Amen."

Hercules blurted out from heaven, "Wait a minute. This Dottie the donkey talked?"

Rufus expounded, "Sure, in the Bible, God made Balaam's donkey talk."

Hercules asked, "Where in the Bible is that?"

"That would be Numbers 22:28, off the top of my head." Rufus continued to expound. "Here's some other fun facts about donkeys. They can live up to fifty years, and they aren't stubborn. They are really smart and can sense danger, just like Dottie."

Dottie began walking again, taking the lead. Joseph, Mary, and Shiny followed just behind. Sure enough, a band of thieves was lying in wait. The leader of this band of thieves had a severe limp. His buddies called him Lou-gangly.

Hercules couldn't contain himself. "Lou-gangly? What does that mean?"

Rufus joked, "I think in Aramaic it means Limp Leg Lefty."

"Oh, come on!" Hercules then reached in and took a handful of popcorn and M&Ms from Rufus's box and continued to look on with anticipation.

Lou-gangly and his boys were lying in wait. As Joseph and Mary made the turn, there was the band of thieves, standing with knives threatening to take everything they had.

Without hesitation, Joseph stepped forward, full of courage. "I have come in the strength of the Lord, and you have no right to stop us here. I command you to step aside, or you will regret it. If you think David was tough on Goliath, watch what I will do in the strength of the Lord!"

Before the thieves could respond, the glory of God reflected off Shiny's bald head, blinding them. The glory was so bright it carved a path directly through the thieves, leading Joseph and Mary to safety. The three thieves were never to be seen again.

Joseph, Mary, and Shiny walked the rest of the day in silence, rejoicing in their hearts for what God had done. That evening as they lay down to rest, Mary asked Joseph, "What was that bright light that led us to safety today?"

"Shiny," was all Joseph said as he closed his eyes.

Mary asked for clarification. "You mean the shekinah glory of God?"

Shiny whispered in Joseph's ear. "Say yes, Joseph. Tell her she's exactly right. That was God's Glory shining down on us."

Joseph responded, "Thank God you're bald."

Mary sternly looked at Joseph. "Excuse me?"

"Not you, dear. Shiny, my angel, is bald. You know the angel I told you about. Good night, dear. May God give you sound sleep and refresh you for our long journey tomorrow."

Mary kissed Joseph on the forehead and smiled. "Okay, old man, let's get our rest."

Hercules stopped chomping on his popcorn and M&Ms and asked, "So Mary can't see Shiny?"

"Only Joseph can see Shiny. I told you Joseph and Shiny would develop a special friendship."

As Joseph was trying to drift off to sleep, Shiny whispered, "Hey, Joseph?"

"What?"

"Hope on, amigo, hope on."

Joseph responded as he rolled over, "Excuse me?"

Shiny chuckled as Joseph turned over and fell asleep.

Shiny woke up and found himself back in his bed in heaven. The day seemed extra bright, full of God's light. Shiny was thankful for God using him in Joseph's life. He got up and started his day. After completing his morning chores, Shiny stepped outside, and there were Rufus and Hercules, sitting at his steps, waiting for him.

Shiny greeted them with "Good morning" and then asked, "Do you guys ever sleep?"

Hercules and Rufus laughed, and Hercules answered, "Yes, we sleep, but when God calls, we respond, and here we are."

"God called?"

"God has a new assignment for you and me. We need to get ready to spread some hope on earth."

"Hercules, I'm ready. What's the assignment?"

Hercules looked at Rufus for help. "Shiny, our Father wants you and Hercules to go introduce Mr. Blake to his new wife."

Shiny jumped up and down with glee. "Mr. Blake is getting married?"

"Isn't that cool?" Hercules replied as he joined Shiny in the jumping celebration.

Rufus filled in the details. "Mr. Blake has always desired to be married but never thought anyone would want to marry a blind man. God has not only healed his eyes, but He's giving him the desires of his heart. Wait until he sees how beautiful the woman is that God has chosen for him."

Shiny asked, "When do we get to go?"

"Soon and very soon," was Rufus's response.

Hercules asked, "What do you mean by soon and very soon?"

"It's another way to say *suddenly*. When God is ready, it will be soon or very soon. Not long. You know what I mean. It will happen suddenly."

Hercules confronted Rufus. "Then why didn't you just say *suddenly*?"

"That's a great question."

The three amigos bolted for the earth tunnel. On their way, they ran into Louie the trumpeter and Herald.

Herald sang out, "Have you heard the good news? Jesus is being born in Bethlehem. He's going to fulfill the prophecy of Isaiah and be born of a virgin. He will usher in a whole new season of salvation. Anyone who believes in Him will be saved from death and spend eternity here in heaven."

Rufus asked Herald, "Has he already been born?"

"No, I'm just announcing the good news that Shiny will be there at the birth of Christ."

Shiny didn't know what to say. Hercules slapped Shiny on the back. "That's my buddy!"

Louie the trumpeter joined the conversation by tooting, "Where are you guys off to?"

Shiny spoke up. "Hercules and I are going to earth to introduce Mr. Blake to his new wife."

Herald sang out, "I heard God was up to something special for Mr. Blake. First He heals his blind eyes, now He gives him a wife. God, You are so good!"

The angels walked together, singing of God's goodness.

CHAPTER 5

The Reception Stadium

"**L**isten to that. The sound of people cheering loved ones home never gets old." Rufus stopped speaking and stared at the half-moon-shaped stadium filled with saints cheering home their loved ones.

At the entrance of the earth tunnel was the reception stadium, where people waited for their friends and family members to come home to heaven. In the center of this enormous edifice was the throne where Jesus sat and greeted the new arrivals with rewards for a life having served Him. The mouth of the earth tunnel was met by a landing pad made of gold dust. People would come flying out of the tunnel, hitting the landing pad in full stride, which led straight to the throne of King Jesus. Saints were always emptying out of the stands to greet their loved ones and watch them receive rewards from the King of kings.

Rufus turned to the other angels. "Is there any better sound or sight than this?"

A jubilant Hercules answered, "Nope."

The other angels chuckled and gave Hercules a loving rub on his curly red head. Each angel passed by Hercules and would follow in line, ruffling his curls.

Shiny walked up to Hercules and put his arm around his shoulders. "Come on, little buddy, let's go make Mr. Blake's day."

"Okay!"

Hercules and Shiny followed behind as Rufus, Louie, and Herald led them to the entrance of the earth tunnel.

Shiny called out to a familiar friend. "Hey, Freddy, what are you up to?"

Freddy the fly loved to hang out at the entrance of the earth tunnel to greet newcomers. Watching the faces of people coming home brought the tiny fly great joy. Being at the entrance was the perfect spot for the little fly to greet new arrivals.

Freddy welcomed the angels and then answered Shiny. "You know me, Shiny—I love watching the faces of people coming home. The excitement and amazement in their eyes always brings me joy. I like to greet people and let them know Jesus is waiting with arms wide open."

Shiny acknowledged the friendly fly. "Freddy, you have such a big heart. You bless me, my friend."

Freddy quickly corrected Shiny. "Actually, I have nine hearts. One main heart and eight other hearts. My main heart is a one-millimeter-long tube with the other smaller hearts running alongside of it. So really I have tiny hearts, but they do allow me to have 370 heartbeats per minute. Maybe that's why I'm always excited, because my heart is beating so fast."

Hercules observed, "Wow, Freddy, you're really smart."

God spoke. "Funny you should say that. Flies can process a vast amount of information. They process information about proper motion and movement in their environment in real time, a feat that no computer, and certainly none the size of Freddy's brain, could hope to match. It's the way I created flies. That's your science lesson for the day, My little messengers."

Stunned by all this information, Shiny only had one response: "Freddy, you're one of God's most incredible creations. I love you, little friend. Got to go. See you soon."

Freddy fluttered his wings, said good-bye, and flew off toward the reception stadium.

Shiny waved back and then called out to Hercules, "Let's get going. We're going to deliver some good news to the man who was blind but now can see."

Hercules yelled, "Let's do it!"

Rufus, Louie, and Herald cheered them on as Hercules took his place under Shiny's wings and the two took flight into the cavernous tunnel. Shiny and Hercules were met again by a horde of newcomers flying home.

On their left were all ages and colors of people from every nation, speeding by them.

"Look, Hercules, they have the appearance of a rainbow!" As Shiny exclaimed, he pointed to a bald man and shouted, "Herc, a bald man just like me!"

The bald man waved to Shiny as he raced past them. Hercules pointed out a chubby little man with curly red hair. "Shiny, look at that. I can't believe it."

The chubby little man yelled, "What's your name?"

"I'm Hercules!"

The cherub lookalike appeared puzzled as he raced by. "Really?"

"I'm a chubby little cherub!"

The chubby little man laughed and said, "I guess I am too."

Shiny and Hercules floated to a soft landing and found themselves standing outside of Murph's Corner Market. Hercules took a quick look around and proclaimed, "Shiny, I don't know if I will ever get used to this smell."

"I know, little buddy, the smell of hopelessness is awful."

The two heavenly messengers took another quick look around, anticipating Murph to come out of his market to greet them.

Shiny spoke up. "Herc, When Jesus comes back on His white horse, this stench will be gone forever. Until then it's our job to bring hope to the hopeless."

"Jesus is coming back on a white horse?"

"Yes, Herc, King Jesus will come back on a white horse, conquering everything once and for all. The Bible tells me so."

Hercules asked Shiny, "Do we get to ride white horses?"

"No, the saints in heaven will ride with Jesus like an army to stop hopelessness. We will be cheering them on."

Suddenly Mr. Blake stepped out of Murph's market. "Can I help you?"

Hercules looked up at Shiny in disbelief, realizing Mr. Blake was standing right in front of them.

Without flinching, Shiny answered Mr. Blake. "Good afternoon, sir. My name is Shiny, and this is my good friend Hercules. We've come all the way from heaven to bring you some good news. I was wondering if our friend Murph is around?"

Mr. Blake had a look of shock on his face as he listened to Shiny.

"Is something wrong?" asked Hercules.

Mr. Blake spoke up. "Boys, you won't believe this, but Murph is on vacation in California. He has always wanted to visit Disneyland and see the Pacific Ocean. He had hoped he might run into the two of you. Saul and Henry, Murph is going to be so disappointed he missed you. He said he couldn't wait to see what root beer tastes like in California. He's sure our root beer is better. He says it's the water."

Shiny and Hercules didn't know what to say. They stood there silently waiting for Mr. Blake to speak up, hoping that maybe God would break in and give them some divine help. The awkward pause was cut short when Mr. Blake asked the two angels if they wanted to come in and have a root beer.

Shiny answered Mr. Blake. "We would love to come in and have a root beer."

Hercules spoke up. "Mr. Blake, please call me Hank, and I love root beer! I love getting to do God's business here on earth! Could I have a root beer float?"

Hercules thought, *Float? What's a root beer float, and why did I say that?*

Then God interrupted. "My chubby little cherub, you're going to think you're back in heaven when you taste a root beer float."

Hercules looked up. "God, You're so good! A root beer float it is!"

Hercules was getting ready to follow Shiny into the market when suddenly the little roly-poly bug spoke up. "Hey, chubby little cherub, come over here."

Hercules looked back at the curb and eyed the small crustacean. "What can I do for you, little friend?"

The roly-poly bug quickly replied, "You can call me BB, short for Blueblood. What's God up to now? I know He sent you here for a magnificent reason."

"We've come to introduce Mr. Blake to his new bride. God is preparing him for an incredible future."

"Really? That's exciting. I have watched the once-blind man pray for a wife. God is so good!"

Hercules asked Shiny, "Why did you call the pill bug a little crustacean? I thought crustaceans were crabs and shrimp."

"The pill bug or roly-poly is actually not a bug but a crustacean that comes from the shrimp family."

Hercules processed. "So then he's a shrimp bug."

Shiny laughed. "Brilliant. Let's get our root beer floats."

Hercules stopped. "Wait! Why is his name Blueblood?"

"Pill bugs' blood really is blue, not red."

"Really?"

"Really. Now let's go get a root beer float."

Again Hercules stopped Shiny and asked, "How do you know all this stuff about pill bugs?"

Shiny looked back at Hercules and said, "Spending time on God's lap has many benefits."

Shiny walked into the store, leaving Hercules with the roly-poly bug. Hercules bent down and addressed BB. "What do you mean Mr. Blake has prayed for a wife?"

"Since Mr. Blake started working for Murph, he comes out here and takes a break. He walks back and forth, praising God and thanking Him for giving his eyesight back. Then he prays and asks God if He would give him a wife to love and walk with through life."

Hercules was surprised at what Blueblood had to say. "You mean the desire of Mr. Blake's heart is to be married?"

"Yep!"

Meanwhile, inside the store, Shiny was having quite the conversation with Mr. Blake.

William Blake was sharing with Shiny how God had sent an angel to tell him that his eyes were going to be healed on Christmas Eve. He continued to share that everything happened just the way God promised, through the words of the angel who visited him. Shiny was so moved by Mr. Blake's sharing of God's faithfulness that tears welled up in his eyes. Shiny wondered if God would open heaven and let Mr. Blake's see Shiny and Hercules as the angel messengers He had sent.

Then something unusual happened. The door opened, and in walked Hercules with a woman.

Hercules greeted Shiny and Mr. Blake with a big grin.

"Mr. Blake, Saul, could one of you help this lovely woman? She just moved into town and is looking for some help with where to go to buy furniture for her new apartment. This is Miriam; she's a journalist who has been hired to write articles for the paper in town. Miriam, I would like you to meet Mr. Blake, and this is my good friend Saul from California."

Shiny looked at Hercules with amazement, thinking, *Boy, he really does take to this earth stuff. Now he's calling me Saul from California.* Shiny smiled at Hercules while turning his attention to Mr. Blake and Miriam, who were apparently making a connection.

Mr. Blake nervously spoke up. "Yes, I am Mr. Blake, but you can call me William. I could help you find furniture. I could assist you in any way you need. I could help you find your way around town. Yes, I could help."

There was an uncomfortable pause. Then Hercules spoke. "Yes, Mr. Blake could help you for sure. He is an upstanding man, with excellent qualities. He has a wonderful home, and I didn't know your name was William, what a …"

"Wonderful name." Miriam interrupted, with a coy smile.

Shiny repeated, "William, a wonderful name it is. Hercules, we better get going and let William here be of service to Miriam. We have some important business to attend to, right Hank?"

Shiny smiled his big, shiny grin as he called Hercules *Hank.*

Hercules quickly asked, "What about my root beer float?"

Mr. Blake excused himself and attended to Hercules question. "Saul, you and Hank must stay long enough to have a float."

Shiny simply said, "Absolutely."

Hercules grinned, exposing his dimples.

The four new friends hung out for much of the afternoon, drinking root beer floats and sharing stories. Miriam shared the circumstances that brought her to town. She told of her desire to move to the Midwest and experience a slower lifestyle. The fast pace of New York had not been as satisfying as expected. She shared how the glamour of New York had tarnished quickly and left her feeling empty inside. Miriam talked about how excited she was to meet new people and get settled.

William Blake shared his compelling story of how God healed his blind eyes. Miriam was astonished as she listened to William share the wild story of how an angel came to visit him at his home and told him God was going to heal his eyes on Christmas Eve. He continued to explain how his eyes were opened for the first time in twenty years, exactly the way God had promised through the visiting angel.

With tears running down her face, Miriam interrupted Mr. Blake. "So are you telling me you were really blind, and you went to church, and God healed your eyes?"

"That's exactly right! That's just how it happened."

Hercules took a break from devouring a second root beer float. "Miss Sanders—it is *Miss*, isn't it?"

"Oh, no, I'm not married," she responded, "and please call me Miriam."

Hercules gave Shiny a thumbs-up and then continued. "Miriam, isn't it wonderful that God healed Mr. Blake so he could see again? Mr. Blake, isn't it wonderful to be able to see all of God's beautiful creation?"

Hercules gave Mr. Blake a wink and went back to devouring his root beer float. William Blake was obviously embarrassed, realizing Hercules was referring to Miriam when he made the comment about God's beautiful creation.

William blushed ten shades of red as he responded, "Yes, Henry, it's wonderful to be able to see again."

Miriam asked for confirmation. "So you believe there really is a God who loves enough to heal?"

William looked straight into Miriam's brown eyes and affirmed, "Miriam, I know there's a God who loves and heals. His name is Jesus. He loves us so much that He's willing to forgive all our sins."

The room went silent, except for the slurping noise coming from Hercules's straw as he polished off his second float of the afternoon. Hercules kept glancing back and forth between Miriam and William like he was watching a tennis match. He was trying to see how God would bring them together. He enjoyed watching a real live love connection.

Miriam had a faraway look in her eyes as she pondered William's words.

Shiny interrupted the moment. "Miriam, God loves you just as much as He loves Mr. Blake. He loves you so much that He sent His Son, Jesus Christ, to die on a cross for your sins so you could receive His free gift of forgiveness, just like William received his sight. Heck, it's easier for God to heal blind eyes than it is to forgive sin. All you have to do is believe

Jesus is the Son of God and that He died for your sins, and you could have eternal life."

Silence flooded the store.

Miriam fixed her attention on Shiny while tears streamed down her face. "You know, Saul, maybe God is what I was looking for. I thought moving here I could find a slower lifestyle and find some peace."

Hercules whispered to Shiny, "God's not the only thing she's going to find here," as he glanced at Mr. Blake.

Shiny gave Hercules an affectionate pat on the top of his curly head as he addressed Miriam. "Miriam, it's no accident that we're all here today. God has allowed us to meet and spend the afternoon together so you could hear the good news about how God healed Mr. Blake and how much He loves you. Miriam, that peace you're looking for can only be found in Jesus."

"What do I need to do?"

William shared with Miriam, "When I was ten years old, I went to church. The minister shared the same good news that Saul just shared with you. As the pastor finished speaking, he said, 'If anyone would like to receive Jesus Christ as Savior, just bow your head and pray this prayer with me.' Miriam, I prayed the minister's simple prayer. I didn't feel any different, but I can tell you my life was changed forever. I knew when I went home and told my parents that I had prayed and asked Jesus into my life, somehow things were different. I know God is always with me, and not once have I ever felt Him abandon me. Even when I had the accident that took my sight, I had peace deep down inside that God would take care of me. He loves you, Miriam, and all you have to do is pray and ask God to come into your life and be your Savior and Lord."

William Blake paused for a moment as he waited for Miriam to raise her head and make eye contact with him. "Miriam, would you like to pray with me to ask Jesus to come into your life?"

"Yes."

The four bowed their heads together as William led Miriam in the simple prayer. "Dear Lord Jesus, I repent of my sins. Come into my heart. I receive Your free gift of forgiveness, and I ask You to be my Lord and Savior. Amen."

As they lifted their heads in unison, William explained how Miriam's name was now written in the book of life and that her eternal life was sealed by the work Jesus had performed on the cross. He went on to explain how Jesus rose from the dead on the third day so everyone could have the security of knowing God conquered death once and for all.

Hercules boldly entered the conversation. "Would you like us to pray that God will give you a husband also?"

Murphy's Corner Market had never been as silent as it was at that moment. William broke the silence and asked Hercules if he was ready for another root beer float.

Hercules jubilantly responded with a resounding "Yes!"

Over the loud slurping of a third root beer float, William drummed up the courage to ask Miriam if she would like to attend church on Sunday.

Shiny and Hercules said their good-byes and let Miriam know what an honor it was to meet her and share their best friend, Jesus, with her.

All eyes were filled with joyful tears as the four hugged one another.

As Shiny and Hercules were leaving the store, William called out, "You know, Saul, I feel like I know you from somewhere. Your voice sounds really familiar to me."

Shiny smiled at William. "Mr. Blake, my name is Shiny, and I bring God's messages of hope to people who need to have their eyes opened."

Suddenly God opened heaven and allowed William Blake to see Shiny and Hercules as the angel messengers. Mr. Blake's eyes almost popped out of his head as he stood speechless in the little corner store. The angels left the store and immediately found themselves back at the E-Max, being greeted with shouts of joy from the angel army. The entire theater, balcony upon balcony for as far as the eye could see, was filled with angels jumping up and down, rejoicing and singing God's praise. Some were jumping up and down on their seats, others were dancing in the aisles, and some were flying back and forth across the theater, singing the heavenly chorus.

Yes, another name had been written in the book of life. Miriam Sanders, daughter of the Most High God.

Hercules said, "That's so wonderful, but did Miriam agree to go to church with William Blake?"

Rufus responded, "What do you think?"

By the way, the finger of God pierced through the sky, gently poking Hercules in the tummy, ridding him of a bellyache caused by one too many root beer floats.

CHAPTER 6

Two Cherries on Top

Shiny spent the evening with the angel army, praising God for bringing salvation to Miriam Sanders. Angels flew from the reception stadium to the E-Max theater and back. Anticipation flooded the atmosphere. Something big was brewing.

God's praises were escalating in volume. In one voice, the angel army sang out one of their favorite worship songs, "Faith Is Rising," releasing greater hope than at any time in history. A thick faith cloud was rolling in, filling heaven.

Rufus flew past Shiny and Hercules bellowing, "Faith is rising; hope is climbing. Can you feel it in the air? Faith is rising; hope is climbing. God is everywhere. Do you see God's glory? Faith is rising. Something special's in the air!"

Hercules and Shiny took a leap of faith and joined Rufus.

Freedom to fly was very exhilarating for Shiny. He remembered back to when he'd had no wings. He was reminded what it felt like to be grounded and about how he longed to be God's messenger of hope. Then his thoughts turned to the glorious day on earth. Shiny's heart was filled with thanksgiving to God for using him in the lives of Mr. Blake and Miriam.

Hercules shot past Shiny. "Watch this!"

Hercules performed a series of rolls and spins as he flew around singing, "Praise God from whom all blessings flow." Hercules couldn't control the jubilant joy as he pulled off a few more rolls and spins just for fun. As Shiny was cruising along, he scanned the heavens, and as far as his eyes could see, there were angels flooding the sky, flying and singing. The angels' song caused the faith cloud to rise even higher. Not one angel slept that night. The praise party continued throughout the evening, extending into the early-morning hours.

Then God opened the heavens and declared, "Let Emmanuel come forth! Let the Son of man be born. Let the whole earth receive the blessing of My perfect gift."

The heavens were hushed, but only for a moment.

"Hey, what does Emmanuel mean again?" asked Hercules.

The heavens declared, "God with us."

"Oh yeah."

The angels in heaven erupted with jubilation. Heaven was going crazy with the announcement of the coming of baby Jesus, the Son of God. God in the flesh.

Rufus and the angels greeted Shiny coming out of his high-rise apartment. "Shiny, this is so exciting! Let's get to the garden."

Shiny affirmed Rufus. "My heart is beating out of my chest. I can't hold the excitement in any longer. I have to sing God's praise." Shiny erupted with singing, "Holy, holy, holy, is the Lord God Almighty."

Rufus was stunned as he listened to Shiny leading the angels in praise. Tears streamed down Rufus's cheeks as he watched Shiny coming of age. His heart filled with joy as he realized how far along God had brought Shiny. Shiny stopped singing and asked Rufus if he was okay.

With big tears rolling down his face, Rufus answered, "That was the most beautiful singing I've ever heard. I'm so honored to be your friend. God is so pleased with you."

Shiny blushed ten shades of red. Rufus wrapped his arms around Shiny. "Come on, buddy, let's go meet your appointment with destiny."

A large crowd of angels followed behind Shiny, Rufus, and Hercules as they made their way down the garden path. As they were walking, they heard trumpets blasting from the east.

God announced, "Shiny, I have an assignment for you before I send you to eternity past. Take Hercules with you to visit little Lucy. Her mother just received some dreadful news from the doctor. Make a bold declaration to her that I am the Great Physician. Let her know everything will be okay. Explain to her that I am turning this around so they can give glory to My

Son." Trumpets blew again. All the angels came to attention at the sound of the blast.

God continued, "Let Hercules take the lead on this assignment. I'm sending you on to eternity past. Hercules will stay to encourage Lucy. Be brave, My friend. I'm about to rock the world with the greatest miracle of all."

Shiny inquired, "Father, is the greatest miracle the birth of Christ?"

"Yes, and you will be there rejoicing with all the witnesses. Go and celebrate; the King is coming!"

When God finished speaking, the heavens opened wide. The crisp blue sky was filled with creation rejoicing. Birds were singing, cows were lowing, and sheep were baaing (or whatever sound sheep make). The angels didn't hold back either. They were dancing, singing, and shouting at the expectation of the coming King.

Hercules asked, "Wait, don't sheep bleat? Weren't they bleating?"

God responded, "Bleating means crying or whining. Baaing sounds more joyful."

Hercules thought, *But baaing isn't a word.*

Then God declared, "It is now. The sheep were so excited they were baaing."

Hercules boldly asked, "Why weren't the cows mooing?"

God responded to the chubby little cherub, "Lowing is the sound a cow makes when it moos."

"Why didn't you say that?"

The heavens thundered, "I did."

Hercules was silent. Shiny explained to Hercules and Rufus what God had shared with him about visiting Lucy and her mom. Hercules was very excited about the news of him taking the lead.

"How will I know what to say to Lucy and her mom? What if I say the wrong thing? Oh my, I wouldn't want to say the wrong thing."

Rufus consoled Hercules. "Don't worry, Herc. God will be sure to tell you what to say. Right, Shiny?"

"Oh yes, God is always faithful to give you the perfect words to speak, and they come out at just the right time. If God doesn't want you to say anything, just be still and trust He is God."

Hercules experienced a boost of confidence from the encouraging words of his friends. "Cool, then let's get a move on. We need to go help Lucy and her mom believe in the God of miracles."

Rufus and Shiny stood there while Hercules walked ahead. Hercules stopped and looked back. "Are you two coming?"

Rufus called out to Hercules, "Don't you think we should wait for God to give the go-ahead?"

"Oh, I thought He did."

The chubby little cherub took the lead, giggling all the way.

Rufus and Shiny shook their heads and chuckled as they attempted to catch up to the ambitious little angel. At the earth tunnel, Shiny and Hercules said their good-byes to Rufus and the angels.

Rufus grabbed his megaphone and led the angel army in a rendition of "Hip, hip, hooray, Shiny and Herc are on their way. Hip, hip, hooray, God will light the way."

Shiny and Hercules heaved themselves into the earth tunnel with an enthusiastic leap of faith. It was as if heaven was a springboard propelling the two messengers of hope into the tunnel. The excitement of baby Jesus's birth had heaven pounding like a bass drum.

Rufus gave one last shout out to his two angel buddies. "Tell Lucy God is good and His mercies endure forever. Tell Lucy's mom Jesus is coming with healing in His wings. It's all going to be okay!"

Rufus's voice trailed off in the distance as Shiny and Hercules raced down the earth tunnel.

The chubby little cherub pulled his wings tight to his sides and shot ahead like a bullet, leaving Shiny behind.

"Hey, where do you think you're going?" Shiny shouted.

Hercules hollered back through the howling wind, "I'm so excited I just want to share the good news with Lucy and her mom. I can't wait to get there."

Shiny tucked his wings tight to his sides, and in seconds he pulled up alongside Hercules.

The two angels were experiencing the fullness of who God created them to be, and it was exhilarating.

Shiny flew over the top of Hercules, smiled, and yelled through the wind, "Hope on, amigo. Hope on!"

Hercules performed a masterful 360-degree roll and smiled back at Shiny. The two angels were becoming quite good at delivering messages to earth. Hercules flew underneath Shiny, flying on his back as he looked up at him. "I can almost taste the root beer float."

Shiny exhorted the chubby little cherub, "You better go easy on those root beer floats. You don't want another bellyache."

They laughed all the way to earth. As they softly touched down, Shiny commented, "I didn't notice anyone coming home to heaven."

Hercules responded, "Neither did I."

Then God whispered from heaven, "Dear ones, you were having so much fun you didn't realize how many saints were enjoying watching you. You put on quite a show. People were being entertained as they raced past you. You see, when your focus is on what I've called you to, your joy blesses others. I'm so proud of you. Now get yourselves ready to bless Jane and Lucy."

Hercules drew his attention upward and asked, "Who's Jane?"

Shiny answered, "That must be Lucy's mom."

Hercules looked at Shiny and said, "Why didn't I think of that?"

God smiled. Shiny wrapped his arm around Hercules's shoulders. "Come on, buddy. I know where we can get you a root beer float."

"Okay! Let's do it!"

They walked in the direction of Murph's Corner Market. As they turned the corner to Main Street, there was little Lucy with her father, walking into the market.

Hercules suggested, "Hey, Shiny, maybe that little girl and her father would know where we could find Lucy and her mom."

"That *is* Lucy."

Hercules was surprised by Shiny's response. He shook his head and followed behind Shiny as they walked up to the little corner market. Just as Shiny was getting ready to open the door, he heard a familiar voice call out from the street, "Saul, Hank, what are you two doing in town?"

The visiting angels turned toward the voice, and there were the twin police officers, Benny and Lenny, getting out of their squad car. Benny continued, "I can't believe you guys are back in town. We wondered what happened to you the day you visited Mr. Thomas in jail. We came back, and you were gone. I have to say, whatever you said to Mr. Thomas changed his life forever. I'm so glad to see you. You'll never know how much you contributed to bringing hope back to our little town."

Lenny joined the conversation. "Yep."

Shiny wasn't quite sure how to respond. Before he could open his mouth, Hercules jumped in. "Hey, Officer Benny, maybe we could get another ride in your squad car."

Benny deferred to Lenny. "Yep."

Hercules broke out his patented dimpled grin as he glanced at Shiny for affirmation.

Benny asked Shiny, "Saul, are you and Hank here to see someone special?"

Hercules again was quick to interrupt. "We are. Do you know little Lucy and her mom, Jane?"

"Hank, we know everyone in town. We know the Coopers."

Lenny confirmed, "Yep."

Benny offered, "Why don't we head into Murph's. If I remember right, don't you boys like root beer?"

"Root beer floats!" Hercules was sure to make his request known.

"Come on, boys, the floats are on us."

Benny opened the door to Murph's for the two visiting angels. The four walked into the market and were greeted by William Blake. Upon seeing Shiny and Hercules, Mr. Blake was moved to tears. God opened his eyes to see the two angels as the heavenly messengers.

Benny and Lenny were totally unaware of what Mr. Blake was witnessing. William Blake looked at Shiny and asked, "Are you the angel who brought me the message that God spoke about healing my blind eyes?"

Shiny smiled. "That would be me. God sent me to bring you hope. He's so good."

Totally unaware of Shiny and William's interaction, Officer Benny interrupted. "William, you remember Saul and Hank from California? They are the young men who encouraged Mr. Thomas to turn his life around."

William responded, "I remember them quite well. I'm sorry to say Murph still isn't back from California. He decided to extend his stay. He wanted me to be sure to take care of you. He hopes to see you next time you visit. He also wanted you know that California is even better than what he imagined, but the root beer definitely isn't as good as what we have here at home. Murph said it's the water."

Hercules jumped in right on cue. "Speaking of root beer, could I have a float?"

William smiled and turned to start making a root beer float for Hercules. Hercules jumped up on one of the bar stools and asked, "Could you put some whipped cream and a cherry on top?"

William's smile grew broader. "Why not? That's the least I can do for you, my friend."

"Make that two cherries, please." Hercules rested his chin on the palm of his hands as he intently watched William Blake create yet another root beer float.

Hercules turned to Shiny. "This is the next-best thing to heaven."

William served up the root beer float with two cherries on top. Shiny surveyed the store to see if he could locate Lucy and her dad. As Shiny was looking around the store, he heard little Lucy. "Daddy, can I have an ice-cream cone before we go?"

Lucy and her father appeared from behind of one of the aisles. "Yes, dear, you can have an ice cream. Why don't we make it a double today, and we'll share?"

"Okay, Daddy. Chocolate chip and strawberry?"

Lucy's father smiled at his little girl as they approached the soda fountain.

Officer Benny addressed Shiny. "This must be your lucky day, boys."

Lenny agreed. "Yep."

Lucy's father had a puzzled look on his face as he listened to Officer Benny address Shiny.

Benny greeted Lucy's father. "Hello, Mr. Cooper, Lucy. How are you two doing today, and how is Mrs. Cooper getting along?"

Mr. Cooper politely greeted the twin officers and William and then responded, "We are getting along just fine under the circumstances. We're still hoping for the best."

He glanced down at Lucy and smiled and then picked her up and plopped her on a stool next to Hercules. "Mr. Cooper, I'd like to introduce you to my good friends from California. This is Saul, and that young man at the soda fountain is Hank."

Lucy asked Hercules, "Do you know Sam the bald biker? He lives in California."

Hercules smiled. "He's one of my best friends back home. He really is one of the nicest guys you could ever know. He just looks like a big, bad dude, but he really has an enormous heart."

Lucy addressed Shiny. "Sam looks a lot like you but with big muscles."

Shiny quipped, "All us bald guys look alike."

Mr. Cooper extended his hand. Shiny reached out and shook it. As they were shaking hands, Hercules blurted out, "We've come all the way from heaven to bring your wife the good news that God is going to heal her and strengthen her faith in God."

Mr. Cooper respectfully responded, "It's a pleasure to meet both of you. So you're from California, and you want to visit my wife so you can pray for her to get well?"

His response didn't surprise Shiny at all; he was used to people on earth hearing something completely different than what was said. Hercules, on the other hand, was quite confused.

Shiny affirmed Hercules with a loving pat on his curly top. He then answered Mr. Cooper. "Yes, Mr. Cooper, we are visiting for a few days and would love to bring some hope to your wife."

William joined the conversation as he refilled Hercules's glass to the brim with root beer. "Mr. Cooper, I can tell you these are extraordinary young men who will be completely respectful of your wife's situation. Saul was the one who gave me hope to believe God was going to heal my eyes on Christmas Eve."

"Really?" was all Mr. Cooper said as he weighed William Blake's words.

Lucy gazed up at her father as she took another lick from her ice cream. "Daddy, can we invite Saul and Hank to our house so they can pray for Mommy?"

Mr. Cooper affectionately smiled at his little girl and then addressed the small crowd of concerned onlookers. "You have to understand, Jane is down, discouraged, and depressed right now. She really hasn't been up to having many people come visit her, not even family. I'm not sure this is a good time."

"With all due respect, Mr. Cooper, Saul and I are just what your wife needs right now. I'm confident we can bring her hope like no family member could. God has commissioned us to carry the message of hope everywhere we go."

Stunned by what came out of his mouth, Hercules looked to Shiny for help.

Suddenly God counseled Shiny. "Tell Mr. Cooper, 'It's now or never, and if I were you, I would choose now.'"

Shiny was surprised by God's directness. "Little one, you've got to trust me with this. Take courage. I am with you, and I do know what I'm talking about." Then God went silent.

Immediately Shiny opened his mouth, and the very words God had whispered shot out like a rapid-fire machine gun. Mr. Cooper's eyes teared up. William asked Mr. Cooper if everything was okay.

"Yes, I just can't believe Saul's words. Last night Jane said to me, 'It's now or never. God is either going to heal me or not. I hope it's now.' It's as if you were right there listening to our conversation."

Wiping the tears from his eyes, Mr. Cooper continued to address the small crowd. "We know God healed your eyes, William, and we know he healed little Billy Smith, but our faith right now has really been challenged. Saul, when you spoke those words, 'it's now or never,' something inside of me screamed *yes, now!* God can heal Jane just like he healed others in our town."

Smiling at Shiny, William encouraged Mr. Cooper. "Ben, I believe it is now. I know God will use these two men as instruments, just like when he healed my eyes."

Lucy asked William Blake, "Were you really blind and God healed your eyes so you could see again?"

William tenderly addressed Lucy. "I can tell you for sure—I was blind, but now I see. God did it on Christmas Eve, and it happened suddenly."

Lucy squeezed her eyes tight and looked around. "So is being blind like having your eyes shut all the time? Everything is dark?

William smiled at Ben Cooper as he addressed his inquisitive little girl. "Yes, it's like having your eyes closed all the time, but God is so good that He decided to open my eyes. Now I can see everything."

"Well, Daddy, what do you think?"

Ben Cooper declared, "Lucy, I think the time is now for us to invite Saul and Hank to visit Mommy. What do you say?"

A big smile filled Lucy's face. "Daddy, can I finish my ice cream before we go?"

Another timely *yep* from Lenny brought laughter and lightened the mood in the little corner store.

William went on to share with Ben and Lucy about the faithfulness of God and how wonderful it was to have his sight restored. He also shared about his new relationship with Miriam Sanders. He told Ben how it was Hercules who introduced them.

Hercules added, "Well, I was just at the right place at the right time. My father taught me the importance of always making myself available."

Hercules continued to explain that it wasn't ability God was looking for but *availability*. Hercules preached quite the little sermon that afternoon. Mr. Cooper and Lucy were all ears. You could feel that faith was rising in the small corner store. Shiny was proud to see how God was raising up Hercules to deliver messages of hope. When Hercules finished encouraging the Coopers, Lucy asked Shiny, "Could I ride with you and Hank in your car to visit Mommy?"

Hercules looked at Shiny to see what he would say. Shiny waited, hoping for some wisdom from above so he could give Lucy an answer. Mr. Cooper saved the visiting angels. "Lucy, I think we should offer to give them a ride in *our* car. Don't you think that would be a polite thing to do?"

"Okay, Daddy, but I've waited my whole life to ride in a car from California."

Hercules was puzzled. "Your whole life? How old are you, Lucy?"

"I will be six on January 14."

Mr. Cooper proudly smiled as Hercules responded, "I guess that is a long time to wait, isn't it?"

"It's a lifetime for me," Lucy quipped.

Again laughter filled the little corner store, lightening the load from the weight of Jane Cooper's illness.

CHAPTER 7

Snow Angels

Meanwhile, in heaven, Rufus was intently watching from his seat at the E-Max theater.

He delivered play-by-play to the other angels as they looked on. Rufus provided details of how God would heal Jane Cooper and the impact it would have on little Lucy's life. Watching Shiny and Hercules from above, Rufus called out in anticipation their every move. All the angels in heaven listened with the expectation of God doing great and mighty things. Rufus prophesied that William Blake and Miriam Sanders would wed sometime during the holiday season.

Rufus was on quite the oratory roll when suddenly, bolts of lightning flashed across the sky, canvassing the E-Max theater.

Rufus was silent. All the angels bowed as God declared, "Rufus, my faithful servant, how would you like to make a cameo appearance and encourage Jane and Lucy?"

"Father, that would be like dying and going to heaven."

God paused.

Rufus made an attempt to redeem himself. "Father, I guess that didn't make any sense since I'm already in heaven, and I don't have to die to get here. I was just so excited. What I meant to say was that I would love to go to earth and surprise Shiny and Hercules and have the opportunity to encourage Lucy and her mom. I know that I am ready to go in Your strength."

God encouraged Rufus. "My faithful servant, I knew what you meant. I love your enthusiasm, and I am so pleased how you have been such a good friend to Shiny. It's time for you to experience the joy of bringing good tidings of great joy."

Rufus asked, "What do I do when I get there?"

"Trust Me, and follow My lead. I will direct your path, I want to encourage you to loosen up and have some fun. Relax and bring some heaven down to earth."

The sky cleared, and Rufus found himself uncharacteristically quiet as he sat watching earthly events from his perch at the E-Max. Thoughts flooded his mind, and the wonder of God caused Rufus to ruminate.

"I hope I can please God and not let Him down. I just need to loosen up, like He said. I've got to relax and enjoy the ride."

Rufus was finishing his self-induced pep talk when he felt Louie elbow him. Louie, the trumpeting angel, leaned over to Rufus and said, "You okay, buddy?"

"I'm going to earth to bring some good news to Lucy and her mom."

Louie tooted his horn. "Rufus, I'm so excited for you! When are you going?"

"I guess whenever God says go."

No sooner had Rufus finished speaking those words when suddenly he found himself standing in the Coopers' house. In the living room was a beautifully decorated Christmas tree. The house was well adorned with the finest furniture and many tasteful accessories. Rufus walked down the hallway and opened what appeared to be a bedroom door. When he reached to open the door, he heard a weak voice call from the bedroom, "Ben, is that you?"

Suddenly a car pulled into the driveway. Shiny, Hercules, Lucy, and her father exited the car as a gentle breeze caused snowflakes to drift down on their heads.

Lucy cried out, "Daddy, maybe it will snow for Christmas!"

Hercules boldly proclaimed, "I bet if you ask God, He will make it snow on Christmas. He loves to answer prayers, He's such a good God."

From heaven, God sang out, "Let it snow, let it snow, let it snow."

They scurried to the front door and dusted the fresh snowflakes off their clothes.

Mr. Cooper opened the door and invited Shiny and Hercules in. They stepped through the door and were greeted by Lucy's cat, Aspen.

111

Aspen looked up at Shiny and exclaimed, "More angels! Something special must be going on."

Shiny knelt down and was getting ready to address Aspen when he looked up. There was Rufus—as big as life—smiling at Shiny and Hercules.

Shiny gasped, "Rufus?"

Lucy corrected Shiny. "No, my cat's name is Aspen. He's a lilac lynx— see the hair on the tip of his ears? That makes him special. Besides, *Rufus* is a dog's name."

Hercules chuckled, and Rufus frowned.

Aspen asked, "Who's Rufus?"

Rufus loomed over the cat. "I'm Rufus."

Aspen loudly proclaimed, "You're beautiful!"

Rufus blushed and returned the compliment. "So are you. All of God's creations are beautiful in their own way."

Mr. Cooper invited Shiny and Hercules to make themselves comfortable in the living room.

"Saul and Hank, why don't you have a seat here? Lucy and I will let Jane know we have some guests."

Lucy and her father made their way down the hall, leaving Shiny and Hercules in the living room.

Hercules erupted. "Boy, do they have guests! Rufus, what in the world are you doing here?"

"God sent me. Can you believe it? I'm as shocked as you are. I was hanging out with the angel army watching you guys at the E-Max. Then God spoke to me, and the next thing I knew, I was here."

"How cool is that?" Hercules continued. "Rufus, what are you going to do? What's your assignment?"

"I don't know. God said to trust Him and have fun."

Shiny laughed and said, "Don't worry, Roof; God will be faithful. Believe me—it will be more fun than you've ever had."

Hercules wondered, "You think they have root beer here? I would love for Rufus to experience the heavenly taste of root beer."

The angel messengers chuckled.

Aspen jumped up on Shiny's lap, looked up, and said, "What a beautiful head you have. How did your head get so shiny?"

Shiny blushed. "Thank you. God made my head shiny."

Just then, Mr. Cooper appeared from the darkened hallway. "Boys, I'm sorry, but Jane says she's really not up for visitors. She is very discouraged right now. She said she is too tired to see anyone, but she did want me to thank you both for coming."

Hercules rose up. "Mr. Cooper, it's now or never! We've got to seize this opportunity. You know *carpe diem*, seize the day, and all that jazz? Listen, God is with us! I can feel His Spirit in the room. Maybe you can remind her of what she said last night. I'm telling you it's now and not never."

Mr. Cooper was frozen with fear.

Then God whispered a command. "Go, Rufus!"

"Go? Go where?"

God commanded again, "Go follow Mr. Cooper."

Mr. Cooper stood up. "You're right. I will let Jane know that the time is now. Just like she said last night. I'll be right back."

Mr. Cooper walked back down the hallway and entered the bedroom, completely unaware that Rufus was right behind him.

"Jane, I really believe the time is now. We need to step out in faith and trust that God can do for us what He's done for others."

Mr. Cooper waited for his wife to respond. Rufus silently stood soldierlike behind Ben Cooper.

Jane Cooper lay still on her bed, staring straight at the powerful angelic being standing behind her husband. Lucy was cuddled up asleep next to her as Jane continued to stare at the heavenly visitor.

Rufus was too tall to stand up in the bedroom, so he hunched down to clear the ceiling. He spread out his wings to cover the Coopers like an umbrella. Clinging to Lucy, Jane continued to stare at the heavenly sight.

Ben tried patiently to wait for his wife to respond, but he grew impatient. "Jane, are you okay?"

Holding Lucy ever so tight, Jane nodded, affirming her husband.

"Does that mean you're okay with me bringing back our guests to pray for you?"

Still frozen at the sight of Rufus, Jane nodded.

Ben addressed his wife. "So you're sure you're okay with this? You look like you've just seen a ghost. Is everything all right?"

Rufus bent a little lower, spread his wings, smiled, and winked at Jane Cooper.

Jane weakly nodded to her loving husband one last time, while she squeaked out a feeble reply. "Yes, it's okay."

Mr. Cooper shook his head in confusion, turned, and walked out of the bedroom.

Rufus waved to Jane as he followed Mr. Cooper out the door. Still stunned, Jane waved back.

"Boys, my wife has agreed to have you come back and visit her."

Hercules blurted out his pleasure. "Oh, good! Let's see what God will do! *Carpe diem*, baby!"

Mr. Cooper muttered, "I just hope whatever He does, it will be now and not never. We need a miracle."

Shiny said, "My God is able to do immeasurably more than all we ask or imagine, according to His power that is at work within us. To God be the glory."

Hercules did his best impersonation of Lenny. "Yep!"

Ben Cooper opened the bedroom door and ushered the angelic guests in, with Rufus close enough to be his shadow. Rufus knelt down, and still his head grazed the ceiling.

"Sweetheart, this is Saul and Hank from California. They have come to encourage us and pray for you. God used Saul in a mighty way to support William Blake just before God healed him."

Jane Cooper was sitting up in her bed with Lucy still asleep next to her. She couldn't take her eyes off Rufus, who was kneeling next to Mr. Cooper.

Shiny explained why they were there. "Mrs. Cooper, we're messengers from heaven sent to let you know that God is more than able to heal you."

Hercules jumped right in. "Jane—may I call you Jane?"

Mrs. Cooper nodded as she kept her eyes fixed on Rufus.

Hercules continued. "Jane, we have been sent to you today to let you know God is going to heal you now!"

Hercules hesitated for a moment and then erupted. "And now means *now!*"

Hercules looked to Shiny for help, wondering, *Where in the world did all that come from?*

God whispered, "From yours truly. Take courage, for I am with you. Jane's faith has made her well. I have heard her prayers. She will live a long and fruitful life."

Mr. Cooper lovingly addressed his wife. "Jane, I think we should let these young men pray for you now."

The three angels weren't quite sure what Ben Cooper heard, from his response.

Rufus spoke up. "Mrs. Cooper, you see me, don't you?"

Jane Cooper affirmed Rufus with yet another silent nod.

Rufus declared, "God will do what He says He will do. Your faith has made you well. God has heard your prayers. You will have a long and fruitful life. You're going to have an early Christmas! Now rise up out of your sickbed." Rufus smiled and winked.

Suddenly Lucy woke up. (God never gets tired of doing suddenly.) Lucy kept rubbing her eyes, trying to focus on what she was seeing.

Looking at Rufus, Lucy gasped. "Mommy!"

Finally, Jane Cooper spoke. "I know, Lucy. I see him too."

Rufus leaned in from his kneeling position to make direct eye contact with Lucy. He smiled and winked at her. Excitedly, Lucy smiled and waved back at Rufus.

Rufus told her, "Lucy, you're even cuter than Shiny described to me. God is going to heal your mommy for Christmas."

Lucy asked, "Why do we have to wait for Christmas for God to heal Mommy?"

"No, Lucy, what I mean is God's going to give you an early Christmas present."

Mr. Cooper interrupted. "Lucy, who are you talking to?"

She pointed past her father. "The angel, Daddy! The one right there next to you. He's so beautiful and funny too!"

Mr. Cooper spun around to have a look. Rufus looked directly at Mr. Cooper and smiled, but Mr. Cooper couldn't see Rufus.

Exasperated, Ben Cooper spun back toward his wife and daughter. "I don't see any angel."

Rufus shrugged his shoulders, winked at Lucy and her mom, and then he was gone. Rufus found himself back at the E-Max theater, receiving high fives and fist bumps as the angel army gave God the glory. Rufus and the boys celebrated late into eternity.

Back at the Coopers', Shiny and Hercules prayed for Lucy's mom.

Suddenly Jane got up out of bed and asked the visiting angels if they would like some dinner. Yes, God performed another sudden miracle, just like in the Bible. After six months of being weak and gravely ill, Jane Cooper sat up, rose from bed, and made dinner for her family.

The Coopers celebrated Christmas early. That evening, they opened presents, sang Christmas carols, and thanked God for sending the two young men from California and the special messenger from heaven to encourage them to believe.

Lucy spent most of the evening sitting on Hercules's lap, laughing and singing silly songs with him. The early Christmas went late into the early-morning hours.

Shiny and Hercules said their good-byes and gave everyone big hugs. The Coopers made them promise to stop by and visit anytime they were in town. Hercules assured Lucy she would see him again. What Hercules didn't realize was that God had predestined Hercules to be Lucy's guardian angel. Hercules was chosen by God to watch over Lucy for her entire life.

Mr. Cooper insisted he take Shiny and Hercules back to where they were staying. Shiny wasn't quite sure what to say, but God was faithful to fill his mouth. Shiny explained to Mr. Cooper they needed to stop and say good-bye to Mr. Blake before they left for home. "If you would be so kind to take us over to say merry Christmas to Mr. Blake before we leave for home, that would be great."

"Let me grab my coat and gloves. I will be more than happy to drive you over to William's house."

As the visiting angels were walking out the door, Aspen the cat spoke up. "Thanks, boys. God said He's very proud of you. Hey, Hercules, I'll see you soon, and Shiny, be sure to say hello to Jesus for me."

Shiny reached down and gave Aspen an affectionate little scratch under his chin. The little lynx just purred. Shiny would swear that Aspen smiled at him as he purred his pleasure.

Mr. Cooper drove Shiny and Hercules to William Blake's house.

With tear-filled eyes, Ben Cooper said good-bye to his new friends. "Saul, Hank, I will never be able to repay you for what you did tonight. You gave me back my wife and Lucy her mother. I was so afraid we would have to live without her."

"Mr. Cooper, please give God the glory. All we did was obey our Father in heaven. We asked Him to bring healing to your wife."

Hercules paused for a moment and then continued. "There is never any need to be afraid of the future. After all, if God is for you, who dare be against you? God has plans for your family. Now it's time to thank Him and ask what it is He would want you to do."

Shiny agreed and added, "Mr. Cooper, I think life is going to get really exciting for you and your family. Our Father loves to take people who receive miracles and use their story to bring hope to people who have lost their way. Trust in God, and He will be faithful to guide you along life's path."

Ben Cooper gave Shiny and Hercules a great-big group hug and said his final good-bye. He made them promise to always stop by and visit when they were in town.

With snowflakes falling to the ground, Shiny and Hercules stood outside William Blake's home, waving to Ben as his car drove away.

Hercules looked at Shiny. "Want to make some snow angels?"

"Why not?" Shiny laughed as he fell to the ground.

Hercules followed him. They lay on the ground, swinging their arms and legs back and forth, creating perfect snow angels in Mr. Blake's front yard.

Suddenly Shiny was gone, and Hercules was left behind to put his final touches on his snow angel.

Hercules looked to his left. Shiny had been there moments before, but all that remained now was just a perfect silhouette of a beautiful, bald snow angel that Shiny had left behind.

"Shiny? Shiny? Uh-oh. Father, where's Shiny?"

God spoke. "Don't worry about Shiny, My little chubby cherub. I am with you. Be strong and courageous; I have more for you to do. Get up and go knock on William's door. Exquisite snow angels, I might add."

Hercules leaped to his feet and started walking to the door, thinking out loud. "Being here alone is quite different. I hope I can handle this. I haven't ever been alone on earth. Well, I will trust and obey."

God spoke again. "You're never alone, little friend. I am always with you."

Suddenly the sun broke through the gray, snowy sky, and it was a new day. *A new day for sure,* the angel thought. Hercules was on his own. Jane Cooper was healed, and her family was looking forward to their future together. William Blake and Miriam were falling in love.

And the little bald angel was on his way to eternity past for a meeting with destiny—and Shiny is his name.

The King Is Here

S hiny found himself standing in the garden facing the east gate. Jesus stood behind him, tenderly instructing Shiny that there would be no turning back. The Father was preparing all eternity to receive the miracle of the Savior, the Son of God.

God the Father declared to the heavens, "For unto us, a Child is born, Unto us, a Son is given, and the government will be upon His shoulders. His name will be called Wonderful, Counselor, Mighty God, Everlasting Father, Prince of Peace."

Jesus and Shiny stood together in the garden, taking in the power of the words spoken by the God the Father.

Rufus and the angel army stood at the entrance of the garden, watching and listening.

When the Father stopped speaking, the Spirit of God came and filled all of heaven with songs of praise. The entire host of angels erupted in songs about how God is an awesome God and that He reigns from heaven above with wisdom, power, and love.

Shiny turned around and faced Jesus. "I love you, Jesus."

Jesus smiled and said, "Little friend, just be sure to let the glory of the Father shine, and everything will be okay. Follow My lead, and see how . beautiful it all turns out. I love you too."

Shiny got down on his knees and kissed the feet of Jesus. This so pleased God the Father that He released His glory down on Shiny's bent head. God's glory bounced off Shiny and caused Jesus to glow.

Rufus and the angel army erupted again with praise. All of heaven began chanting. "Jesus! Jesus! Jesus!"

In the distance, you could hear the chants coming from the reception stadium. It was being sung by people coming from the earth tunnel.

The stars in the galaxy sang out, "Jesus, Jesus, Jesus!"

All of creation was cheering the coming of the Son of God. The chants grew louder and louder until all of heaven was one, resounding in unison: "Jesus, Jesus, Jesus!"

Suddenly the Spirit of God descended on the east gate, causing it to open.

Then God spoke. "Go, My Son. I love you, and I am so pleased with you."

Jesus reached down and touched Shiny on the shoulder. "Shiny, get up. It's time to go. Step through the gate, and I will be right behind you. Our Father wants you to lead the way with His glory shining on your head."

"Really?"

"Yes, Shiny, really. Let's go, My little bald friend."

Jesus finished talking. Shiny turned and waved to his host of friends. Rufus, Louie, Herald, and the angel army were beaming with smiles as they cheered on their most precious friend. Shiny stepped through the east gate into eternity past with Jesus right behind.

William Blake opened his front door, and there stood Hercules in all his glory. William smiled and said, "Welcome, come in. I've been waiting for you."

Hercules, surprised by the response, uncharacteristically had few words to say. "You've been expecting me?"

"Yes, God spoke to me in a dream last night and said that you would be coming by to share some good news with me."

Hercules stepped into Mr. Blake's house. "My, your house is light and bright. I like it."

God whispered, "Get used to it. This is going to be your home away from home."

Hercules giggled. When God whispers in Hercules's ears, it tickles and makes him laugh.

William Blake explained to Hercules that his house wasn't always bright and cheerful. "When I was blind, my house was dark and gloomy, but when God opened my eyes, I wanted to see everything God had given me to enjoy. So I decided to have a makeover of my house done. I wanted it to reflect how good God has been to me."

William paused and then asked, "So what's your real name?"

"Hercules."

Smiling, William remarked, "Hercules, that's a strong name. Very fitting for such a courageous one like you."

Hercules blushed and then said, "Thank you. God made me that way."

"So what good news do you have to share?"

Hercules looked confused. "I'm not sure. I really don't think I have anything to share just yet. God hasn't told me what to say to you. He will, though. God is faithful. Oh, do you happen to have some root beer? I'm very thirsty."

William Blake laughed and said, "Sure, I think I might have a bottle or two in the refrigerator. Why don't we go into the kitchen, and you can have an ice-cold root beer for breakfast."

Hercules followed Mr. Blake to the kitchen. "That would be wonderful."

As they were walking to the kitchen, Hercules remembered something Shiny had taught him: When you don't know what to share with someone, flap your wings, and God will be faithful to back your act.

Hercules stood up in the kitchen and started flapping his wings.

William Blake was astonished at the beauty of Hercules's wings as he poured Hercules a glass of root beer. "Hercules, why are you doing that?"

"This is how I get God's attention. I learned this from Shiny. I'm trying to find out what He wants me to share with you."

William just said, "Wow!"

Hercules flapped and flapped. Finally, he stopped and took a swig of root beer. "Boy, that's good."

William Blake asked, "Did God show you anything?"

"No, but He will be faithful to speak when it's time." Hercules paused and chuckled. "I think God wants me to enjoy this root beer first."

William laughed out loud. The two new friends shared stories of God's faithfulness. The doorbell rang. William Blake excitedly jumped up, excusing himself as he rushed to see who was there. Hercules gulped down more root beer while thinking, *I know who that is.* Hercules was sure it was Miriam by the excitement that William displayed as he went to answer the door.

Meanwhile, in eternity past, Shiny appeared to Joseph. "Joseph, how's it going?"

Joseph was very happy to see Shiny again. "It's been very difficult. I think Mary is about to deliver baby Jesus, and there is no room in the inn. We have been staying in this dirty, old manger where all the animals feed and sleep. It's quite smelly, Shiny, but I feel like this is where God would have us stay. I prayed to our Father, and I have peace. Even though Mary is very uncomfortable, she says she feels peace also."

Mary interrupted Joseph and asked, "Joseph, who are you talking to?"

"The angel, darling. He has returned, and I was speaking to him."

Mary seemed very relieved. "Oh, how wonderful that the angel is back. Maybe that means it's time for me to deliver our baby."

Shiny shrugged as he addressed Joseph. "I haven't a clue as to the time of Jesus's birth, but I do know God spoke and said it's time to go. Jesus is right behind me. He's coming soon. The Father knows the time. Joesph, why don't we worship God and wait and see what happens?"

Joseph nodded in agreement as he began to sing. He put his hand on Mary's stomach as he sang. Shiny and Mary joined in singing beautiful songs to God and the baby Jesus inside of Mary. As they sang, God's glory reflected off Shiny's head and lit up the entire manger. Joseph and Mary were both aware of the change in the atmosphere as a result of God's glory.

In heaven, Rufus, Louie, Herald, and the angel army looked down over the historic event from the E-Max theater.

Rufus called out the play-by-play. "Hey, look over there to the left in that field—I bet those are the shepherds who are going to come visit the baby Jesus when He's born. They're headed in the direction of the manger." He also noted to the angel onlookers of how the wise men were being prepared to visit as well.

Louie blew his horn like never before. "I can't contain myself! I am about to come unglued by the joy I feel in my soul."

Rufus encouraged him to play some soulful jazz in the background while he continued to give his commentary on the earthly events happening in eternity past.

Joseph asked Shiny, "Are you going to be around after Jesus is born?

"I'm not sure. Why do you ask?"

Joseph answered, "I don't know if I'm up to this task. God has asked much of me. I love the Lord God with all my heart, and I want to serve Him as the earthly father to His Son. I want to be sure I raise Jesus the way God desires. Shiny, I'm a poor man. I don't even have a lamb to offer at His dedication. At best, I'll have two small pigeons."

"Joseph, God will supply everything you need. Now, take courage, my friend, and trust God. He will see you through. I know life is hard for you right now, but trust and obey; there's no other way."

"You're right, Shiny, I must trust God. He has been faithful to me my entire life. He has provided, and He will provide, you're right."

Mary screamed, "Joseph, I think it's started! The pain is worse. What do I do? Help!"

"Mary, stay calm. God will see us through."

Joseph stayed right by her side through the night, helping her with the delivery of the baby named Jesus.

Then God spoke. "Shiny, let Joseph know I have a quick assignment for you. Tell him you won't be gone long."

Shiny obeyed. "Okay, Father, I will let Joseph know."

"I have to step out for just a moment; our Father has a short assignment for me, but I'll be right back."

Joseph desperately looked at Shiny as he knelt next to Mary on the dirt floor. "You'll be right back?"

"Right back. I won't be long; I promise."

Shiny stepped outside of the manger under a sky blanketed with stars. He heard from heaven,

"Flap those wings; it's time."

Shiny flapped with all his might. He propelled straight up into the sky like a helicopter. Looking down on the historic evening as he hovered over the earth, he could see the wise men pointing in his direction. God opened Shiny's ears to hear what they were saying.

"Look! There's the star. The baby is over there. All glory to God, who reigns forever."

Shiny watched as the wise men knelt and bowed to worship God. They rose up, tied their robes between their legs, and starting running in Shiny's direction. As Shiny began to descend, he turned to his left. In a distant field, he could see shepherds also running toward him.

Shiny touched down and slipped back into the manger. "Joseph, I'm back. How's it going?"

Joseph turned toward Shiny, and there in his arms was the newborn baby Jesus in swaddling clothes, tightly wrapped like a tiny burrito. Tears were streamed down Joseph's face. All Joseph could say was, "Praise God, praise God in heaven."

Joseph kept repeating his praise over and over, no matter what Shiny tried to ask him. Shiny leaned over and looked into the little baby's face peeking out from the swaddling clothes. As he pulled back the cloth, he would have sworn that the little baby Jesus winked at him.

(He didn't actually swear, though, because angels don't swear.)

The E-Max was out of control with shouting, cymbals crashing, and other sounds of ecstasy. Seraphim were flying all around, and cherubs were playing harps and other stringed instruments. Louie was leading a little jazz ensemble. Rufus was screaming at the top of his lungs through his megaphone.

"The King is here, The King is here! He's alive! The King is here!"

Back in the manger, the animals were out of control. The cows, sheep, and camels all joined the heavenly host praising God. Emmanuel had arrived!

Shiny knelt next to the baby in the manger and sang a lullaby over him. When Shiny opened his mouth, the most beautifully inspired song came out.

> *Oh, baby Jesus, what a miracle you are.*
> *You are God! You stepped out of heaven just to be with us.*
> *Oh, baby Jesus, what a miracle you are.*
> *You gave up Your throne just to take the cross.*
> *This baby in the manger is the Savior of the world.*
> *The baby in the manger is Jesus.*

Shiny was mesmerized by the way God had inspired him to sing out. Shiny looked to the heavens and rejoiced. "Thank You, Father, for giving me such a beautiful song."

Then God spoke. "Yes, Shiny, I have been holding that song in My heart for quite some time. Sing it again and see what happens."

Shiny sang the Christmas lullaby again. As he sang with all his heart, the shepherds came and joined in singing with him. The wise men knelt down and presented the Son of God with the most beautiful gifts. The animals joined in and sang also.

All of heaven sang the Christmas lullaby.

Heaven and earth had never been as united as it was at that moment, singing the pronouncement that God Himself had come to earth as a baby to take away the sin of the world.

He would grow up to be a faithful Son, following through to the cross so all the world would have the opportunity to be restored with God the Father through His salvation. Shiny stepped outside to be alone with God for a quiet moment. He stood under the blanket of stars, looked to heaven, and declared, "Father, I love You. Thank You for letting me be a part of this miraculous story. I want to serve You forever." Jumping up and down, he yelled, "I love, love, love, love, love, *love* You!"

From heaven, Shiny heard, "I love, love, *love* you too, My shiny-headed friend—and don't worry. I have plenty for you to do. Now do you understand why I made you bald?"

Suddenly Shiny sensed he wasn't alone. He spun around and saw Joseph standing there.

"Shiny, what can I say? Thank you, my dear friend and loyal servant of the Most High God."

Shiny hugged Joseph and kissed him on the forehead. "Joseph, it is you who are now the loyal servant of the Most High God. Trust Him, and He will be faithful to give the provision you need to raise His Son."

Shiny smiled, waved, and gave Joseph a knowing wink. Joseph was left standing in the starlit evening as he watched Shiny fly up into heaven.

Back on earth, Hercules and William Blake were having a discussion.

"God is faithful once again!" Hercules announced to William and Miriam that they were to wed on Christmas Eve. God was going to raise them up to be missionaries and take William's testimony on the road. They would travel all over the world together, telling of God's faithfulness to heal blind eyes and do so much more.

(Oh, and there is more about Shiny—much more Shiny to come.)

A CHRISTMAS MIRACLE

CHAPTER 1

The Lion and the Lamb

There was something different about this day. Shiny looked out his bedroom window and observed the peace of God as far as the eye could see. All was quiet on this calm day, and all creation seemed at rest. Then Shiny thought, *This is what the Sabbath was meant to be. Nothing to do today, and it's okay. How wonderful not having to strive for God's approval.* Shiny had always had it in his heart to please God, but he finally realized that there was nothing he could do to earn God's approval.

God had always loved him, even when he didn't have wings and couldn't sing. God's love can't be earned, and Shiny was enjoying the reality of resting in God's presence without having to strive for approval. Shiny thought, *That's the beauty of the Sabbath. It was our chance to enter into the rest God designed for us, just as when God Himself rested on the seventh day after He spent six days creating everything.* Shiny was learning that he could enter into God's rest anytime he wanted to cease striving.

Wow, I love this, thought Shiny. *This is the way God intended it to be.*

Shiny drove himself deeper into the stillness of the moment. He pulled the covers up tight around his neck and let his little angelic body sink deep into the comfort of his featherbed.

Yes, Shiny had a featherbed—and it was not just *any* featherbed.

He had an angel-feather bed. You see, from time to time, angels shed their feathers and grow a whole new set. In heaven, God is always making everything new. He does things we could never dream or imagine. Lying still in his bed, Shiny had no thoughts or tasks for the day.

He was experiencing the peace of God which goes beyond understanding. In the quietness, his heart began flooding with thanks for God transforming him into a messenger of hope. He was humbled.

Then it happened: God began sharing with Shiny about future opportunities that would arise. He shared how He would call Shiny to visit people in need to speak of God's ability to deliver them from challenging circumstances. God displayed in a vision how He would use Shiny and other angels to bring the good news of Jesus. God would snatch people out of the dark side and bring them into the light that only Jesus can offer.

Shiny was ever so still as he saw future opportunities unfold right before his eyes. He saw Billy Smith as an adult. He was a father and a husband. God would use Shiny to come alongside Billy the rest of his life.

In the vision, Shiny was present at little Lucy's wedding. He saw the birth of William and Miriam Blake's child. God flooded Shiny with visions of future opportunities. Shiny was enjoying being with God. Resting and waiting for new assignments was just what he was supposed to do on the Sabbath.

Someone knocked on his door. Abruptly Shiny sat up and said, "Oh, I know what that means. Someone is here to visit me."

God spoke. "You've been paying attention, haven't you?"

Shiny flew out of bed, grabbing his robe of confidence. He opened the door, and there was little Hercules, looking up at Shiny with a discouraged, downcast, and most desperate look on his face.

"Herc, are you okay? Please come in." Shiny motioned for Hercules to follow him into his home.

"Shiny, I think I blew it."

"What do you mean?"

"Shiny, I think I lost out on a future opportunity."

Shiny repeated, "A *future* opportunity?"

"Yes, God spoke to me and said to go and spend time with Lucy. He gave me some instructions to encourage her and protect her from harm."

Shiny was puzzled. "So what happened? I don't understand. How did you miss out on a future opportunity?"

"Well, I was thinking about how wonderful it would be to go to earth and have some root beer. While I was daydreaming, I drifted off into a deep sleep. It was quiet and peaceful. It was how I imagined the Sabbath

130

to be. I dreamt I was back at Mr. Blake's, hanging out with William and Miriam. We decided to go to Murph's for a float. I was so distracted by how good the float would taste that I forgot *why* I was there. I looked out the window, and there was Lucy walking across the street. Just then I woke up and had a sick feeling that Lucy had been hit by a car. I was so troubled I didn't know what else to do but to come and talk with you."

Shiny silently studied Hercules's eyes.

Then God interrupted. "It was a warning dream of what could happen if I don't send Hercules to protect Lucy. I'm teaching you the responsibilities of being a guardian for My children. Remember I see the past, present, and future and know all things."

God was silent.

Shiny and Hercules didn't say a word. The peace of God filled Shiny's home. The two angels soaked in the peace that surrounded them. Shiny broke the silence. "See, Herc? You didn't blow a future opportunity. God was preparing you for what will happen."

Hercules rejoiced. "God is so good. I'm going to be the best guardian angel."

Shiny smiled and said, "I'm sure you will be. You have the heart to serve, and you care about others. You'll be just fine, my little cherub."

Shiny walked Hercules to the door and blessed him to be on his way. "Herc, always remember that God is always with you; He will never leave you. He is the one who makes miracles happen. You don't have to worry or strive; all you have to do is rest."

"Thanks, Shiny. I can't wait to get to earth and do my part to guard little Lucy."

Shiny waved good-bye as he encouraged Hercules. "Get some rest, Herc. God is with you. Shine on!"

Hercules pumped his fist in the air and declared, "Shine on!"

The chubby little cherub went on his way down the Street of Gold. He whistled all the way to the earth tunnel. When he arrived at the tunnel, Hercules was greeted by Louie and his band of angels. They were setting up to give a jazz concert for the new arrivals coming home to heaven from earth.

Louie tooted his horn in the direction of Hercules. "Hey, Herc, where's Shiny?"

"He's home taking a Sabbath rest. I think God is getting ready to send Shiny back to eternity past. I have the feeling that something big is brewing. You know that peace which comes when God is getting you ready to do His will? I sensed the same peace in Shiny's house."

Louie listened to Hercules as the band of angels warmed up for the concert. "I think Shiny is going to be gone for a while. He seemed like he was preparing himself for a long journey."

Louie tooted his horn and said, "I just love it when God uses Shiny that way. It brings so much hope. I look forward to seeing what God will do."

"Me too. Well, I better get going. I have my own assignment down on earth. Say hi to Rufus and the angel army. See you later."

Hercules took a running start and jumped right into the earth tunnel. Louie waved good-bye and then directed his band to start playing. Heaven was filled with jazz music as people flooded in from the earth tunnel and made their way onto the gold landing pad on their way to the throne of Jesus. The reception stadium seemed louder than ever, as friends and family members cheered for their loved ones coming home.

Shiny stepped out of his high-rise apartment and made his way down the garden path. He stopped at the still waters and rested as he waited for God to give him his assignment. He laid down in the green pastures next to the still waters and listened for God to speak to him.

As he was lying down listening to the birds singing and the trees blowing in the gentle breeze, a lamb came and laid down by his side. "Good afternoon," he said. "My name is Lamb of God. Have you seen my friend, Lion of Judah?"

Shiny marveled at the lamb. "Why, no, I haven't."

The Lamb of God asked, "Shiny, may I lie down and rest with you?"

"How do you know my name?"

"I know you. You're the angel who went with Jesus to eternity past to help Joseph understand what God was doing."

"That's right."

The Lamb of God continued, "God is incredible, and He's always looking to work through us. What are you doing here at the still waters?"

"I'm waiting for God to give me my next assignment. Until then, I'm resting and waiting. I'm enjoying the Sabbath."

"Isn't the Sabbath beautiful? It's so full of God's peace. It's important that we rest and wait so God can do all He has planned for us. It really was worth the sacrifice."

Shiny agreed with the precious Lamb of God. Shiny was honored that the Lamb of God would want to share the Sabbath with him. As Shiny lay with the Lamb by the still waters, they heard a tremendous roar come from the direction of the forest that lined the green pastures.

The Lamb of God rose excitedly and called out, "Judah, over here!"

Shiny and the lamb directed their attention to the forest. Shiny was shocked by the appearance of the most majestic creature in the kingdom of God.

The Lion of Judah made his regal entrance as he stepped out from between the trees onto the green pasture.

Shiny was frozen as heaven shook with each powerful step from the approaching lion.

His mane blew freely in the gentle breeze coming from the still waters. With each step Judah took, Shiny could feel his heart filling with excitement. Hope flooded Shiny's heart as the Lion of Judah stopped short of the bald angel and the Lamb of God.

"Where did you go? I've been looking for you," said the lamb.

Judah roared, "I was resting in the forest. It's the Sabbath. I was listening to the Father."

The Lamb of God invited the Lion of Judah to lie down.

Shiny was silent as he listened to the lion and the lamb. Judah flopped down and took his place next to the lamb. Shiny couldn't believe he was lying down with the lion and the lamb. It was still and quiet once again. The fullness of the Sabbath was soaked in. Shiny knew he was exactly where God wanted him to be. He was learning the importance of being still and knowing who God is, and was, and is to come.

Hercules touched down on earth and found himself in a familiar location. He now stood in the front yard of William Blake and his new bride, Miriam. He took a good look around and discovered earth didn't smell quite as hopeless as it had on his last visit. Immediately, he began flapping his wings to get God's attention.

As Hercules flapped his wings, he thought, *Why am I at the Blakes' house when I need to be guarding Lucy?*

God spoke. "I will get you to where you need to be, but for now, enjoy the moment and know I am with you. Don't be concerned about anything; I am in control. By the way, don't go overboard with the root beer floats this visit."

Hercules heard God chuckling in the distance. He waited for God to say more, but it was quiet.

Suddenly (and yes, *suddenly* happens even on the Sabbath), Hercules heard a familiar voice coming from the Blakes' front porch. "Is that you, Hank?"

Hercules looked in the direction of the front porch and saw that Miriam Blake waving to him.

Hercules acknowledged her. "Miriam, how are you doing?" He boldly walked toward Miriam.

She ran down the steps of her front porch and met Hercules with a big hug. "It's so good to see you. Where's Saul?"

"Oh, our Father has some business for Saul to attend to back at home."

Miriam had a puzzled look on her face as she responded. "When you get back to California, please be sure to give Saul our love. William will be disappointed that Saul isn't here, but he will be so happy to see you. Please come in. I have some cold root beer in the refrigerator."

"Root beer?" Hercules had a spring in his step as he followed Miriam up the front porch and into the house.

Miriam poured a cold root beer for Hercules and let him know that William would be home from work soon. She also let him know that William would want Hercules to be their guest and stay in the extra bedroom for as long as he was visiting.

Then God affirmed, "Say yes, and let Miriam know you would be honored to stay with them."

Hercules obeyed. "Miriam, I would be honored to be your guest and stay here with you and William."

"I was hoping you would. Please feel free to make yourself comfortable. I'm going to finish making dinner before William gets home. I hope you like pot roast. For dessert, I've made angel food cake with fresh strawberries."

"Angel food cake?" Hercules was speechless.

"I hope you like angel food cake. I picked the strawberries fresh from our garden this morning."

"It's sounds heavenly; I can't wait to taste it." Hercules could hear more chuckles come from heaven.

Rufus and the angel army were at the E-Max, enjoying a good laugh with God as they watched Hercules's every move play out as he visited with Miriam. Rufus explained to the host of angels how God loves to have fun, even on the Sabbath. He went on the explain how people on earth had tried to turn the Sabbath into a religious activity to attempt to please God with their own efforts. "All God really wants for us is to rest in His presence and enjoy being with Him."

Rufus continued, "God wants all His children to enjoy the benefits of being part of the family of God. One of the most significant benefits is enjoying a good laugh with the Father. A cheerful heart is good medicine."

The E-Max theater was filled with laughter as they watched Hercules drink root beer, eat pot roast, and enjoy not one, not two, but three pieces of angel food cake topped with strawberries and whipped cream.

William Blake was excited to see Hercules. He shared how hope had been restored in his town since Hercules and Shiny had been visiting. Mr. Blake showed Hercules to his room and asked him if he needed anything before they went to bed. Hercules asked Mr. Blake if he had anything for a bellyache.

More laughter erupted throughout the E-Max.

Mr. Blake asked Hercules to pray with him before they went to bed. "Sure, I would love to pray for you. Anything in particular?"

Mr. Blake sheepishly shared his heart's desire. "Well, Miriam and I would like to have a baby. Could you pray that God would allow us to have a baby?"

"Great! Let's do it. Let's ask God to give you and Miriam a baby."

But before Hercules could say anything, God interrupted from heaven. "Tell William I have unique plans for them. Tell them to rest, and I will bring them a special child to raise. Let him know it's a done deal."

Hercules looked at William Blake and proclaimed, "God said it's done. He has heard your prayers, and He's bringing a special child for you and Miriam to raise."

William gave Hercules a big hug and said good night. With tears running down his face, he turned off the light. Hercules laid down on his bed and thanked God for hearing Mr. Blake's prayers and for taking away his bellyache.

Then God answered, "You're welcome. It's what I do. Now get some rest. Don't forget it's the Sabbath."

Shiny was so full of peace as he lay quietly with the lion and the lamb. The gentle breeze blowing off the still waters made the grass sway ever so gently as it ushered in the peace of God and refreshed the little bald angel.

Suddenly the lion roared. "God is sending you to help Joseph through a difficult season of life. God will use you to bring hope to Joseph. Shiny, let Joseph know that Mary and Jesus will be okay and that God the Father will be sure to see His plan to completion."

Shiny asked the lion if he knew what Joseph was going to have to endure.

The lion lay back down, and then the lamb spoke up. "Shiny, Joseph will raise Jesus to be a young man, and then God is going to call Joseph home. Our heavenly Father will use you to come alongside Joseph every step of the way. Be strong and courageous."

Shiny watched the lion and the lamb lying together as he stood up and said good-bye. Shiny walked away, knowing deep in his heart that he had been changed forever by spending the Sabbath with the Lion of Judah and the Lamb of God.

CHAPTER 2

Murph's Conversion

The little bald angel strolled through the garden and approached the east gate to eternity past.

Each step ushered Shiny closer to the ever-increasing presence of God. Standing in front of the gate, Shiny took a breath and reached for the gate's handle.

"Wait!"

Shiny looked over his shoulder as he turned toward the voice. Standing just a few steps behind him was a serenading seraph, crying out, "Wait! Hold on!"

Shiny stood frozen, unable to respond to the angelic presence. The seraph flew around the little bald angel with two of his wings while using two more wings to cover its face and two more wings to cover its feet. The six-winged seraph seemed to be entertaining Shiny in an attempt to stall. Shiny stared up at the seraph while it continued to fly around him in circles. Finally, the seraph went back to its post at the entrance and sang out, "Holy, holy, holy," joining the other seraphim.

Shiny turned back toward the east gate and saw Jesus standing in front of him. "Are you ready to go and encourage Joseph?"

"Yes."

The little bald angel was without words as he beheld the beauty of the Lord. He thought, *I will never get tired of being in God's presence and seeing the beauty of His holiness.*

Jesus opened the gate and invited Shiny to go ahead of him. "You first, My little bald friend."

Jesus smiled and rubbed the top of Shiny's head and motioned for Shiny to step through the gate first. Shiny obeyed and stepped into eternity past.

"Where have you been? I could've really used your help."

Joseph didn't wait for Shiny to respond. "Shiny, last week we lost Jesus for three days, and Mary was in a panic."

"What do you mean you 'lost' Jesus? How could you lose the Son of God?"

Joseph answered with his head bent and shoulders slumped. "It's not easy, believe me. We went to Jerusalem for the festival, and there was a large crowd. I thought Jesus was with Mary, and she thought He was with His friend Lazarus. We had been a day into our journey back home before we realized He was lost. We looked everywhere but couldn't find Him."

Shiny interrupted. "Believe me, Joseph—I know what you mean. I have been with Jesus, and then suddenly He's gone. But with all due respect, how did you not notice He was gone—for a whole day?"

Joseph seemed a little defensive. "Shiny, you have to understand something. He is the perfect child. He's always so obedient. Most of the time we don't even notice He's around. I thought He was with some of the other travelers, sharing the love of God. He never stops telling people how much God loves them."

Shiny motioned for Joseph to continue.

"When we realized He was gone, I told Mary not to panic and that we would find Him. We looked everywhere, but He was nowhere to be found. Like I said, an entire day had passed, and I didn't know what to do."

Joseph had Shiny's full attention now. "So what did you do?"

"What did I do? I prayed! I prayed with all my might! Shiny, I lost the Son of God. I thought how could God ever trust me again?"

Shiny smiled as he responded, "You know, Joseph, I felt that way once."

"What do you mean? What happened?"

Joseph listened intently to Shiny. "I thought I had completely blown an assignment God had given me. When I got back to heaven, I thought our Father was going to be furious."

Joseph interrupted. "Was He angry?"

"No! Joseph, all He did was love me and tell me how well I did."

"He what?"

"Yes, Joseph. He told me to sit on His lap, and He loved me and told me how well I did. It changed me forever."

The two friends sat silently basking in the magnitude of God's love. Then Shiny broke the silence. "So what happened next?" Joseph seemed to be lost in the thought of how much God really loves. Shiny prodded Joseph. "Joseph, what happened next?"

"We went back to Jerusalem and asked around to see if anyone had seen a young boy twelve years of age."

"Then what happened?" Shiny was captivated now and wanted to hear the rest of the story.

"We looked for another day and a half and still couldn't find him."

"Oh my!" Shiny said. "Were you worried?"

Joseph looked straight into Shiny's eyes. "Sure, I was worried, but we kept praying and trusting God would help us. Finally on the third day, we checked the temple and went to ask the rabbi if he had seen our Son, and you wouldn't believe what we saw."

"What? What did you see?" Shiny was all ears as he hung on Joseph's every word.

"Mary and I walked into the temple courts, and there was Jesus, talking with all the elders. It was like *He* was teaching *them*. They would ask Him questions, and He had all the answers."

"Wow! That's so amazing."

"Yes, Shiny, it was incredible. The authority with which He spoke was truly astonishing."

Joseph paused for a moment, smiled, and then continued. "But then Mary stepped in—"

"What do you mean *Mary stepped in*?"

"Well, it wasn't pretty. I'll tell you that."

Joseph chuckled and then shared with Shiny what happened next. "Mary walked up to Jesus, and right in the middle of what appeared to be a very special moment, she interrupted Him and said, 'Young man, what in the world were You thinking? Do You realize what You have done to Your father and me? We have been worried sick for three days, thinking something terrible had happened to You!'"

Again, all Shiny could say was "Oh my."

"Then the most amazing thing happened. Jesus said, 'Why were you looking for Me? Didn't you know that I had to be in My Father's house?'"

Shiny and Joseph sat there for what seemed like eternity, pondering the words of young Jesus. Then the little bald angel spoke up. "Joseph, do you understand what is going on here?"

Joseph paused before he responded to Shiny's question. "I think I do. I believe my Son has to be about what His heavenly Father is calling Him to, and Mary and I need to stay out of the way and support and raise Him the best we know how. Shiny, it is not easy raising the Son of God."

Shiny put his arm around Joseph and encouraged him. Before Shiny could say anything, Joseph spoke up. "Boy, Mary was mad! She didn't say one word all the way home. Then when we got home, Jesus told her how much He loved her, and she just melted."

Shiny gave Joseph another squeeze, and the two friends just laughed.

Joseph tried to speak through his laughter. "I attempted to console her that night when we went to bed, and all she kept saying was, 'I don't know what I'm going to do with that boy. I can't stay mad at Him when all He ever says is how much He loves me.'"

Joseph and Shiny laughed louder. Mary walked in and asked Joseph what was so funny. Joseph tried to respond, but before he could get a word out, Mary asked him if he had seen Jesus. Joseph looked at Shiny, and the two broke out laughing again. Mary glared at Joseph. "Joseph, son of David, what in the world is so funny about that?"

He tried to explain that his angel had returned, and he was sharing what had happened and they were having a good laugh over it. As he was attempting to share, Jesus walked in the room.

"There you are, Mom. I was looking for you."

"What do you need, Son?" Mary waited for an answer.

"I just wanted to say how much I love you and what a great mom you are."

Joseph looked at Shiny, and the two laughed out loud.

Jesus looked at Shiny and said, "I know you; you're one of My Father's messengers, aren't you?"

Shiny nodded through his laughter. Jesus smiled, and as He was walking out of the room, He said to Mary, "Mom, I'm going to go pray for a while. Is there anything you would like Me to pray for?"

Mary quickly answered, "Yes, pray Your father quits acting so crazy."
Jesus smiled. "Okay, Mom. I love you."

Mary gave Joseph another glaring look. "Don't you dare say a word."

"I was just going to tell you how much I love you too."

"Joseph, son of David, stop it."

Just as Mary was getting ready to leave the room, God spoke. "Shiny, are you prepared to help Me lighten up the mood and have some real laughs?"

"Absolutely."

God caused His glory to shine down on the little bald angel's head and open Mary's eyes. The room lit up, and she was able to see Shiny in all of God's glory, smiling at her. Mary stood still, not knowing how to respond.

God directed Shiny, "Open your mouth, and I will fill it."

The brightly glowing angel obeyed. "Mary, I'm Joseph's angel messenger. I come to bring good tidings of great joy. I was with you when you traveled to Bethlehem, and I come to bring you good news."

Shiny paused and waited for God to give him more. Mary just stared. Joseph laughed, and Jesus was in the other room praying. Shiny opened his mouth again. "Could I have a cup of water?"

Mary nodded and went to go get the angel a cup of water. She handed it to Shiny ever so carefully. Shiny took the water and drank it. "Why, that tastes heavenly. Thank you."

Again Mary just nodded. Joseph laughed some more, and Jesus was still praying in the other room. Shiny opened his mouth again. "Do you like to dance?"

Mary nodded. Joseph was now on the ground, rolling around laughing. Shiny took Mary by the hand and danced with her. Suddenly Mary started laughing. The three were filled with the joy of the Lord, refreshing Joseph and Mary's faith.

And Jesus was still praying in the other room.

Jesus loved to pray, even as a young boy. Yes, Jesus loved spending time with God the Father when He was on earth. Shiny opened his mouth one more time and asked Mary and Joseph if he could spend the night. Through their laughter, they said yes.

The morning seemed to come early.

Hercules awoke to pots and pans clanging in the kitchen. He put on his robe and made his way to the kitchen. He stopped at the bathroom on the way to fluff his curly red locks. He walked into the kitchen and saw Miriam cooking away at the stove; William was sitting at the table, reading his Bible.

"Good morning, Hercules. Did you sleep well?"

Hercules answered William with a word: "Heavenly."

Miriam joined the conversation. "That's wonderful, Henry."

God had still not opened Miriam's eyes for her to see the chubby little cherub for who he really was.

"I hope you're hungry, because Miriam makes the best french toast in the world."

Hercules asked William, "What's french toast?"

Miriam couldn't believe the young man from California had never eaten french toast. William helped explain the confusion. "Oh, Henry, you're quite the clown. Have a seat. You are in for a real treat, my friend. Miriam, why don't you put some fresh strawberries and some homemade whipped cream on the french toast for our guest?"

Miriam served Hercules a heaping plate of french toast topped off with fresh strawberries, whipped cream and dripping with maple syrup to boot. Hercules's eyes were as big as saucers as he surveyed the beautiful presentation.

"This looks delightful! Can I pray over the meal?"

William acknowledged the little heavenly guest. "We would be honored."

The three bowed their heads as Hercules prayed the most precious prayer. He ended it by thanking God for keeping him from getting yet another bellyache. Hercules didn't say a word after taking a bite. His eyes rolled back behind his eyelids from the sheer delight of his first bite of french toast. As he shoveled in one bite after the other, William and Miriam watched with glee as the little heavenly guest hummed with every bite. Hercules cleaned his plate as he took his final bite. William and Miriam sat in amazement.

William finally spoke up. "Henry, what did you think of Miriam's french toast?"

Hercules responded as he wiped the maple syrup off his chubby little chin. "I never thought there could be anything that tasted better than a root beer float."

William and Miriam chuckled as Miriam went to the kitchen to prepare more french toast. She didn't bother to even ask Hercules; she just filled his plate with a second helping. Hercules was elated to be staying with William and Miriam.

"So, Henry, do you have plans today?" asked William.

"I only have to do what my Father wants me to do today."

Again, Miriam had a puzzled look on her face. William jumped in. "Why don't you come with me to the store this morning? We'll surprise Murph. I'm sure he'll be overjoyed to see you."

Through another maple syrup–soaked bite of french toast, Hercules answered. "I think that would be just what my Father would want me to do."

William gave Miriam a kiss good-bye as Hercules waited at the front door. Miriam gave Hercules a big hug and let him know how excited she was to have him staying as a guest.

William and Hercules made the short walk to Murph's Corner Market. Hercules shared with William how God had called him to be the guardian of little Lucy. William asked many questions as they strolled down Main Street.

"So there really are guardian angels?"

Hercules chuckled as he responded, "You're looking at one."

They turned onto Center Avenue before arriving at Murph's Corner Market. Murph greeted them at the door and was excited to see Hercules with William Blake.

"Come in, come in. Hank, it's great to see you. Where's Saul?"

Hercules informed Murph that Shiny was busy doing his Father's business. He let William and Murph know that Shiny's work involved some important historical ramifications.

"Shiny has gone back to eternity past to be with Jesus and his earthly father, Joseph. Our heavenly Father has assigned him to be the friend of Joseph."

Murph was utterly confused. "Really?"

William was awestruck. "Really?"

Hercules continued. "Yes, our heavenly Father is changing the course of history with the love of his Son. He wants the world to know that hope only comes through His Son Jesus. Our Father in heaven is holy, and He wants all His children to be holy like Him. The only way the children of God can be holy is through the transforming work of Jesus and the cross."

Hercules stopped and was amazed how God was filling his mouth. Suddenly God opened Murph's ears and allowed him to hear the truth and beauty of the good news of Jesus.

Then Murph spoke up. "You know, Hank, I thought if I went to California for a while, I would find happiness. I listened to you and Saul tell stories of how great it was in California. So I thought I would go and experience it for myself. It was beautiful. The beaches, the mountains, even the people, but I came home and still felt empty. For my entire life, I have gone to church and have tried to be good. I've attempted to make right choices, but something was missing. I've always called myself a religious man, but today, when you were speaking about the good news of Jesus, I realized something."

Murph stopped to collect his thoughts. The pause was long and uncomfortable. Hercules decided to help Murph. "Mr. Murphy, religion is like filthy rags to God. He knows we can't please Him by being good. Only God is good. Matter of fact, He is so good He gave His Son Jesus to die on the cross for your sins so you can have a relationship with God, so you can enter into the family of God and be one of His children. You see, Murph, it's not about 'religion' or 'being good.' God just wants to have a relationship with you."

Tears began to fill Murph's eyes. William's eyes were also tearing up as he silently prayed.

Murph addressed Hercules. "I have been so lonely most of my life. I thought if I went to California for a while, I would find something or someone to fill the loneliness. You know, most days I love coming to the store and serving people. I try to help out in any way I can, but at the end of the day, I go home, and the loneliness overwhelms me."

"Only the love of God can fill that lonely place in you, Mr. Murphy." Hercules paused briefly and then continued. "I think God had me come visit you today to offer the free gift of His Son Jesus to you. You have to understand just one thing: *everyone has sinned.* Everyone has fallen short of the goal to please God and find peace. All you have to do is believe that Jesus came to die for your sins, and then confess to God that you need the forgiveness that He offers you through Jesus. Believe that Jesus is the Son of God—and you will be saved."

Murph dropped to his knees right there in the little corner market where he had been coming for over fifty years to serve others. Murph cried out as his knees smacked the floor. "God, I am a sinner. Forgive me. I believe Jesus is Your Son, and He died for me."

Hercules thought, *I didn't even have to lead him in a prayer. How cool is that? God, You're so good to me.*

Murph raised his head and looked up at William and Hercules. "What do I have to do?"

William responded. "My dear friend, you just did it. You just asked Jesus into your life. The Bible says you are a new creation in Christ Jesus. All the old stuff of your life is gone, passed away like a dead person. God has now made everything in your life new and alive."

Tom Murphy stood up, and William gave him a big hug. "Welcome to the family of God, my dear friend."

The two friends continued to embrace each other. As Hercules looked on, his heart was flooded with praise to his heavenly Father, and he witnessed yet another miracle. The words of Murph's good friend Mr. Thomas filled his heart. "The Lord is your Shepherd."

As Murph held William ever so tightly, he glanced over at Hercules. Suddenly God opened his eyes, and Murph saw the chubby little cherub in all of God's glory.

Smiling back, Hercules declared, "What do you think of God now, Mr. Murphy?"

CHAPTER 3

Hercules to the Rescue

Shiny was stirred in his sleep. From another room, he could hear a voice crying out. As he tossed and turned, trying to get back to sleep, he could hear the voice from the other room becoming more impassioned. Shiny decided to get up and find out for himself if everything was okay.

In the darkness of the night, he found his way to a small alcove off the main room of Joseph and Mary's one-room home. Shiny went through the opening and found himself in a space that was dimly lit by one candle. There were a few small animals asleep in a corner of some stacked hay. Shiny recognized it as Joseph's workshop and barn. The humble surroundings moved the bald angel's heart. In the shadows of the candlelight, Shiny could see a silhouette in the corner.

Shiny called out into the darkness, "Hello? Is anyone there?"

From the shadows, a young boy's voice called back. "Over here, Shiny."

Shiny walked toward the light, and he saw young Jesus on his knees, looking up at him.

"Shiny, what are you doing up at this hour?"

"I heard a voice coming from this direction."

"I'm so sorry. I like to get up in the middle of the night and come out here to pray to our Father."

Shiny was impressed by the maturity of the boy Jesus. "Why do you come out here in the barn?"

"My family works hard; they need their sleep. Mom and Dad work very hard all day. My brothers and sisters need their rest too." Jesus paused. "Would you like to join Me in prayer?"

146

Shiny didn't hesitate. "I would love to."

"Father, thank You for sending Shiny to encourage My father, Joseph. Would You let Shiny know how pleased You are with him?"

Jesus was quiet for the longest time. Shiny waited for Jesus to pray some more. He waited and waited. Jesus was still and silent. Shiny waited longer. He waited for over an hour.

Shiny grew impatient, "Uh, Jesus? Do you want me to pray something?"

"Would you like to pray?"

Shiny wasn't sure what to say. "I thought You were waiting for me to pray."

"Oh no, I was just listening to our Father."

Shiny was again impressed by the young boy's maturity. "Wow, our Father must have had a lot to say."

The young Jesus smiled. "Yes, He does. I think most people don't take the time to listen to all He has to say."

Shiny was very impressed by the wisdom from the young lad. "How did you learn this?"

Jesus answered, "I read the scrolls in the book of Samuel, where God spoke to the boy Samuel. Remember, Shiny—he thought it was Eli. Eli told Samuel to go back and say, 'speak, for your servant listens.'"

Shiny listened. "When I read that, I thought I could do the same thing. So a few years ago, I started asking our Father to speak to me. Every night, He wakes Me up, and I come out here and listen. It is so wonderful to hear the voice of God the Father. It prepares Me for the day. You know, Shiny, I'm learning to say only what our Father says and to only do what I see our Father doing. It really is an excellent way to live life."

Shiny didn't know what to say. He realized that Jesus was growing up to be an extraordinary young man. He felt privileged for being taught by the young rabbi in training. Shiny bowed his head and prayed. "Our Father, thank You for allowing me to spend time with Your Son Jesus. Thank you for letting me play a small part in His story."

God spoke. "I have plans to use you much more in the life of My Son while He's on earth."

Shiny was shocked.

Then Jesus replied, "Thank You, Papa!"

Jesus smiled at Shiny and gave him a big hug. "Shiny, we are going to serve our Father together. Watch what He will do as we trust and obey Him."

Jesus finished as the first light of day broke through the cracks in the wall. The animals began to stir. Jesus jumped up and informed Shiny that He had to feed the animals and get His chores done. Shiny offered to help Jesus feed the animals and help with His other chores.

"Good morning, Son," Joseph said as he entered the barn. "Good morning, Shiny. Did you both get a good night's rest?"

Jesus answered Joseph. "Yes, Father, we rested in the presence of our heavenly Father."

"Did you both spend most of the night out here praying?"

"Yes, Father, and it was great. Shiny's bald head helped make the candlelight brighter."

The three laughed and spent the morning sharing God's Word as they did their morning chores.

Shiny learned the fine art of milking goats and cleaning up after the animals and the mess they make. He enjoyed serving in any way he could. Shiny found Mary warming up to him as well. After breakfast, she taught Shiny how to sew and mend the children's clothes.

Once the morning chores were taken care of, Jesus came to Shiny and asked if he wanted to go to the temple to meet with the rabbi and study the scrolls.

"Yes, I would love to go with You to the temple."

Jesus explained to Shiny on the way how he was preparing for his bar mitzvah. He shared with the little bald angel how it was important to come under the authority of God's law and become part of the Jewish community. He wanted to be obedient in every way possible.

"I love to go to the temple and study the scrolls. Our Father's Word is so life giving. It helps prepare Me for what My Father in heaven has for Me."

Shiny questioned Jesus as they approached the temple courts. "What does our Father have waiting for You?"

Jesus stopped walking. "I must give up My life for those our Father loves. You see, Shiny, I have come not to do away with the law of God but to fulfill it. I have come to serve and not be served."

Shiny and Jesus walked into the temple courts together.

In heaven the E-Max theater was completely silent. Rufus quietly studied the events that were taking place in eternity past. Then he turned his attention to what was happening on earth with Murph and Hercules. Rufus's eyes were filled with tears as he watched the miracles taking place. He watched in utter amazement how God was using both of them, in the past and present at the same time.

Louie, the trumpeting angel, stood up and blew his horn. "We must be ready to defend what Jesus will go through. He is about to step into manhood, and we must get prepared to be there for Him."

Rufus broke his silent retreat. "Louie, we must stand and watch, but we can only do what our Father commands. God will stand with his Son Jesus, and the two alone are more than capable of defeating anything that may come against Jesus."

The entire angel army stood as Rufus spoke. In one voice, the angel army responded and filled the E-Max theater with songs of praise. The theater shook with the presence of God as He inhabited their praise.

Rufus cried out, "All glory, honor, and praise to You, oh God!" as they watched Murph, William Blake, and Hercules.

Then God responded, "I am going to bring victory through My Son, and all creation will be restored."

The E-Max was silent. The angels were frozen with their heads bowed toward earth. The presence of God brought peace on earth, and another Christmas season was ushered in. The angels in heaven had ushered in Thanksgiving by praising God, and now it was time to get ready for Christmas.

"Mom, can I get a bike for Christmas?" Lucy was very excited for Thanksgiving to be over, knowing Christmas was right around the corner.

Mrs. Cooper smiled at her daughter. "Well, let's wait and see what Christmas brings this year."

Lucy sighed, as she displayed the impatience of a six-year-old waiting to receive the treasures that only Christmas brings. Mrs. Cooper could see the impatience of her daughter manifesting before her. "Lucy, why don't we get ready to go shopping. We'll stop off at Murph's Corner Market and get some lunch."

"Okay, Mommy, I love going to Murph's."

"I know you do. Now go get ready so we can get going."

Jane Cooper was sure to give God praise for healing her as she sat down in front of the mirror to put her makeup on. As she brushed her hair, she prayed. "Heavenly Father, thank You for healing me and allowing me to spend another Christmas with my family. Thank You for Your goodness."

Lucy walked into her mom's bedroom and announced she was ready to go. "Mommy, I know what we can do today."

"And what would that be?"

"Mommy, after we get our lunch and have an ice-cream cone at Murph's, maybe we can stop at the bicycle shop and look at what bike would be just right for me."

Jane Cooper smiled at her little salesman daughter. "I don't recall saying anything about an ice-cream cone." She smiled at Lucy. "Let's go."

They walked out the door and got in the car. Lucy took her place in the backseat. As she strapped herself into her car seat, she made one last sales pitch. "Mommy, I was just thinking about how much you love a double ice-cream cone with a scoop of chocolate chip and a scoop of strawberry."

Mrs. Cooper smiled back at Lucy through the rearview mirror and started the car.

Murph kept staring at the little cherub, asking, "So you're an angel from heaven? God sent you to help us here on earth?"

Hercules kept nodding, affirming Mr. Murphy as he sipped on a freshly poured, ice-cold root beer.

"So does that mean that Saul is an angel too?"

Hercules smiled at Murph, never letting go of the straw with his mouth. Murph was awestruck by the thought that Saul was also an angel.

William added, "And Shiny is his name."

Murph was mute. God was revealing to him that Saul was not only Shiny, but he was also Sam the bald biker who had saved him from getting robbed.

Murph gasped.

William was concerned. "Are you okay, Tom?"

"William, remember a few years ago, just before God healed your eyes, when I shared with you about a bald biker named Sam?"

William told Murph that he indeed remembered. Hercules just sipped root beer as he listened. Murph continued, "God just spoke to me, Murph. Sam the bald biker was Shiny."

Hercules stopped sipping just long enough to chime in, "That would be correct, and that same bald biker named Sam was the one that very day who was with you, William, when Lefty and his boys tried to break into your house."

Murph, William, and Hercules had a good laugh over the thought that Shiny's bald head had saved the day.

Hercules finally took another break from sipping his root beer and explained what was happening to the two mortals. "You should see when God's glory comes down on Shiny's head in heaven. All eternity lights up."

There was more laughter from the little corner market.

Murph shared how excited he was to be able to go to church, knowing that his salvation was secure in what Christ had done for him on the cross. He asked Hercules if he could share with people about his newfound friends from heaven.

"Only God can reveal the angelic hosts to people. You can share that you have seen angels, but people will see us how God wants us to be seen until He decides to reveal who we are."

Hercules stopped to sip on his root beer and then added, "Like seeing us as bikers, doctors, or upstanding young men from California."

"So have you ever been to California?" Murph asked.

Hercules looked up from his root beer as he continued to sip. "Nope. Why would I want to go there? The root beer isn't as good."

William and Murph laughed as they pondered what Hercules had shared.

Murph asked, "So is your name really Hank?"

Still sipping root beer, the little cherub just said, "Nope."

"So what's your name?"

"Hercules."

William asked Murph. "What do you think of that, Murph?"

Mr. Murphy just shook his head and thought about the events of the day. He had received Jesus Christ as his Lord and Savior, he had met a real live angel from heaven, and on top of all that, the angel's name was Hercules. Murph stared out the window of his store, trying to comprehend

151

everything that was happening to him. As he was staring out the window, he noticed Lucy and her mom walking into the bicycle store across the street.

"Hey, there's Jane and Lucy Cooper going into the bike shop. I bet they're doing some Christmas shopping."

Hercules stopped sipping and immediately was reminded of his dream about little Lucy. "Are you sure that was Lucy and Mrs. Cooper?"

"I'm sure it was, Hank. Why?"

Murph was puzzled by Hercules's suspicious question. "Do you know the Coopers?"

"You can call me Herc, and yes, I know the Coopers. Shiny and I prayed for Mrs. Cooper."

"That's right, William, you told me about how God used Saul and Henry to heal Mrs. Cooper! I had forgotten. Herc, why are you so concerned about the Coopers?

Murph paused to hear Hercules's answer. "God sent me here to be Lucy's guardian. I have a feeling I'm going to protect her today from some harm."

Murph were puzzled by what Hercules had shared. "So there really are guardian angels?" he asked. "You've come to protect Lucy from harm?"

"Yes, that's my assignment. There have always been guardian angels."

"So you think something is going to happen to Lucy?" William asked.

"No. God will show me what to do so no harm comes her way. God has plans for Lucy."

Murph asked, "Should we pray?"

Hercules was very proud to hear Murph's desire to seek the Father. "Prayer always helps. God loves when His children ask Him for help. He likes to answer the prayers of His children. Would you like to pray, Mr. Murphy?"

"Hank—I mean, Herc—I would love to pray for little Lucy."

Hercules encouraged Murph. "Go for it!"

Murph bowed his head, and William and Hercules followed. "Dear heavenly Father, please hear our prayer as we lift little Lucy up to You. We ask, Father, that You would protect her from all harm. We bless the plans that You have for her life and ask that You would cause those plans to come to pass. Amen."

The three lifted their heads and looked out the window. There was the bicycle-store owner, Mrs. Cooper, and little Lucy. The store owner was wheeling out a pretty new pink bicycle. He steadied the bike so Lucy could get on it. It appeared that Lucy was being prepped to take the pink beauty out for a test ride.

Hercules heard from heaven, "Go! Serve and protect! I will be with you."

"Got to go!" Hercules jumped off his bar stool, leaving a half-filled glass of root beer at the counter.

William and Murph watched as Hercules bolted out the front door. Just as he stepped out of the corner market, he saw a large dump truck barreling down the street. Lucy took off on the bicycle. As she tried to maneuver the bike, her mother called out, "Lucy, be sure you look both ways."

Lucy turned toward her mother and lost control of the bicycle. The front wheel jumped the curb, and Lucy's bike began rolling down the middle of the street. Hercules took one quick leap of faith and yelled out, "God is with me!"

He positioned himself between Lucy and the oncoming dump truck. Facing the vehicle, Hercules held up both hands and proclaimed. "Stop in the name of the Lord!"

With sheer bravery, Hercules held his ground as the driver slammed on his brakes, locking up the wheels of the truck. The truck came to a screeching halt, and Hercules's nose now touched the front grille of the truck. Everyone stood in silent shock as Lucy gained control of the bike. After she turned it around, she waved at the driver as she made her way back to the curb.

Jane Cooper grabbed Lucy off the bike and held her tightly. The bicycle-store owner took control of the bike and brought it back up to the sidewalk. Hercules smiled at the stunned driver and walked back across to the corner market.

God had made Hercules invisible to everyone except the driver of the dump truck. Lucy, Jane, and the bicycle store owner never had a clue that God had used the heavenly hero to secure Lucy's safety.

The dump truck driver slowly rolled down the street, and his eyes never left Hercules as the angel walked back to the market.

Hercules turned one last time and waved to the driver as he walked back into the store. The chubby little cherub looked up to heaven and said, "Thank You, Father! That was so very cool!"

God had allowed Murph and William to watch Hercules's heroics. "Hercules, that was incredible!"

Hercules responded to William, "To God be the glory; great things He has done."

Murph jumped in. "God answered our prayer."

"Yes, He did answer our prayer. God is faithful." Hercules paused to take a sip of his temporarily abandoned root beer and then continued, "You know, people always question God's ways. They say why is it that God allows bad things to happen to good people? They ask, if God is so good, why do people suffer?" Again Hercules paused and took another sip. "God is in control, and it is our job to trust Him. He knows what's best for us."

Murph interrupted, "Herc, so the bad things that happen, aren't they a result of the sin in this world? It's not God's fault that bad things happen to people, right?"

"That's right, Mr. Murphy. God has provided an eternal answer through His Son Jesus. That doesn't mean that life will always be easy, but God will take care of His children for all eternity. Matter of fact, Shiny is helping to usher in God's answer to sin as we speak." Hercules stopped talking and slurped the last drops of root beer through his straw.

William and Murph looked confused. William asked, "What's Shiny doing?"

"God's will." Hercules sipped on.

Back at the E-Max theater, Rufus and the angel army were going absolutely nuts over Hercules's heroics. All the angels were rocking out to some of Louie's jazz band tunes. There was shouting, dancing, and singing throughout heaven. The angels were giving God the glory for how He used the chubby little cherub to protect Lucy.

To God be the glory; great things He has done.

Chapter 4

Rufus the Prophet

William Blake wasn't sure if he would ever see again. After being blind for almost half his life, God had healed his eyes. God had given him a beautiful wife in Miriam, and now he had angel friends in Shiny and Hercules. He was witnessing miracles almost on a daily basis. As he walked home from the corner market with Hercules, William was lost in his thoughts of how good God had been to him. He mindlessly began humming one of his favorite praise songs.

"I love that song," Hercules said as hummed along with Mr. Blake.

"What would you like to do this evening, Hercules?"

"Oh William, I never make plans."

William Blake and Hercules turned the corner and walked down Third Street. William opened the gate to his yard and gestured Hercules to go ahead.

"What is that smell? It smells heavenly."

William laughed and said, "Smells like Miriam has been busy in the kitchen. Smells like some of her fresh lasagna."

"Lasagna? I hope it's as good as pot roast."

William opened the front door for Hercules. "You've never had lasagna?"

Miriam greeted William with a big kiss and a hug and then gave Hercules a welcoming hug. "How did your day go, dear?"

"Oh, it was quite the day. I don't know where to begin."

Hercules jumped right into the conversation. "Why don't you start with Mr. Murphy accepting Jesus as his Savior?"

"What?" Miriam looked at William. "Is that right?"

Again Hercules jumped in. "It's true! I always tell the truth." Hercules smiled at William and Miriam with his big dimpled grin.

At dinner, William shared the events of the day. Miriam was very excited to hear that Murph gave his life to Christ. She was amazed when William shared how God had used Hercules to protect Lucy from the dump truck. Hercules was also amazed at how delicious Miriam's homemade lasagna was.

"What's for dessert?" he asked.

William and Miriam were getting quite used to Hercules's boldness when it came to food (and especially sweets). Miriam answered Hercules. "I made a special treat for you tonight."

"Really?" Hercules sat up in his chair and readied himself for the surprise. Miriam brought out a freshly baked chocolate cake covered with white frosting. Hercules's eyes were as big as silver dollars.

"Oh my, what is that called? It smells delicious."

"This is a devil's food cake with cream frosting."

Hercules's face grew sullen. William asked Hercules what was wrong. "I don't think I can eat that." Hercules dropped his head.

Suddenly Hercules thought, *It's been a while since there was a suddenly.* Suddenly the doorbell rang. William looked at Miriam and said, "Were we expecting a guest tonight?"

"I didn't invite anyone over."

William got up from the table and went to answer the front door. To his surprise, there was Shiny standing at the front door with a big smile on his face. William lunged at Shiny and gave him a big bear hug.

"Shhhh, I've come to surprise Hercules and bring him a message from our heavenly Father."

William and Shiny entered the dining room as Miriam gasped at the appearance of the angelic presence. God opened Miriam's eyes to see Shiny in all of God's glory. His head seemed brighter than ever.

Miriam asked, "Are you an angel?"

"Yes, and Shiny is my name. By the way, check out my friend Hercules."

Hercules raised his head from the disappointment of thinking he couldn't partake of the decadent dessert. Miriam saw Hercules with opened eyes. With tears running down her face, she proclaimed, "You too?"

"Yep, my name is Hercules!"

Hercules flew out of his seat and latched on to Shiny for dear life. "Shiny! I thought you were with Jesus. What are you doing here?"

"Well, first of all, our Father says it's okay to eat the cake. I was with Jesus, but our Father called me here."

Everyone laughed at Shiny's heavenly announcement. Shiny continued. "Our Father has another assignment for you, and He wants me here with you. He said we will be going back and forth from heaven to earth until Christmas."

Hercules couldn't decide what was more exciting, the thought of being around for Christmas or being able to eat the chocolate cake. Miriam wasn't quite sure how to react at the thought of two angels visiting her home. Then it hit her: "Wait! William, didn't you say the angel who visited you with the news that God was going to heal your eyes was named Shiny?"

William nodded, and before he could say a word, Shiny looked at Miriam and announced, "Fear not, the Lord is with you, and you will bring forth a child, but first our Father wants to know if you will obey Him."

Miriam squealed, "Yes!"

William sat stunned by the announcement of a child.

Then Shiny said, "On behalf of our Father in heaven, will you adopt an orphan who is troubled by the circumstances of life?"

Now William spoke up. "Yes! How do we do this?"

Hercules joined the conversation. "God will give you the answer on Christmas."

Shiny looked at Hercules and thought, *Where did that come from?*

Hercules smiled at Shiny and pointed up to the sky.

Shiny smiled and continued, "William and Miriam, God is about to bless you. He is calling you to follow Him to do the work of His kingdom. He will provide."

It was silent in the Blakes' dining room as Shiny completed his announcement. Then Miriam spoke up. "What does this mean?"

There was more silence. No one in the room seemed to have an answer to Miriam's question.

Hercules broke the silence like only Hercules could. "I don't know what it means, but I know our Father is faithful to fulfill the plans He has for you. Now I think it's time to have some of that cake."

There was more silence as Miriam cut the cake into triangular slices and presented her heavenly guests with devil's food cake smothered in vanilla-cream frosting. Everyone enjoyed the cake as they listened to Hercules hum his way through three pieces. Every so often, he would stop humming and declare, "God is so good."

The doorbell rang again. William looked at Miriam, who shrugged and got up to answer the door. When he opened the door, she saw Ben Cooper, his wife Jane, and little Lucy.

"Why, Ben, Jane, Lucy—what a pleasant surprise. What brings you here at this hour?"

Ben Cooper answered William's inquiry. "We were out for a walk, and Lucy said we were supposed to go over to your house."

William responded, "Really?"

Then Ben continued, "Yes, we tried to explain to her it would be rude, but she kept insisting that you had something very important to share with us. Please forgive us for just dropping in like this, but Lucy insisted. She even said God told her."

Miriam called from the dining room, "William, who is it?"

Before William could answer, Shiny whispered to Miriam, "It's the Coopers."

Miriam looked at Shiny. For a moment, she wondered how he did that—and then she realized Shiny had help from above.

"It's the Coopers!" William led the Coopers into the living room.

Lucy screeched when she saw Hercules and Shiny. "Hank, Saul! I knew we were supposed to come over."

Jane Cooper teared up when she saw the two young men who had been used by God to usher in her healing. Ben greeted Shiny and Hercules with a big hug. Lucy jumped up on Hercules's lap without an invitation. Hercules gave Lucy a big squeeze. "Please have a seat. Would you like to have some cake? We were just having dessert with our guests."

Ben Cooper resisted Miriam's offer. "Oh, no, we've already had dinner. We're just out for an evening walk."

At the same time, Lucy blurted out, "I would love some cake. Do you have ice cream to go with it?"

Hercules followed. "Ice cream?"

Embarrassed, Jane Cooper tried to reprimand Lucy, but she was too late.

Miriam answered Lucy. "Sure, you could have a piece of cake with some ice cream—if it's okay with your mom."

Miriam winked at Jane, who nodded.

"Ice cream and cake it is," Miriam confirmed as she made her way into the kitchen.

Hercules offered to help, but Miriam resisted. "No, Hank, you stay right there with Lucy."

Miriam was still processing the reality of two angels being in her home, proclaiming such outlandish things from God. While Miriam was in the kitchen getting the ice cream, Lucy asked William, "When are you and Mrs. Blake going to have a baby?"

Jane came to William's rescue. "Lucy, those aren't the kind of questions we ask."

Hercules jumped in. "Why not? We were just talking about babies."

William saved both Lucy and Hercules. "It's okay, Jane. We were just discussing our plans with Saul and Hank. We think we will have a child sooner than we had planned, Lucy. We may even adopt."

The room went silent again as Miriam entered the room with two big bowls of ice cream and freshly cut slices of chocolate cake for the Coopers.

God spoke, and the E-Max theater went silent. The only sound you could hear was the wind blowing through the wings of the angels who were flying from one end of the theater to the other. The angel army sat with their heads bowed low. Most covered their heads with their wings.

"Rufus, My faithful servant, rise."

Rufus stood to attention. He stood up from his seat in the E-Max theater, and the presence of God caused Rufus to continue to rise. Before he knew it, he was hovering at the highest point of the theater.

Looking down over all creation, the angel answered, "Yes, Father?"

"I'm sending you to visit Jane Cooper again. I will fill your mouth when you get there. Trust me—this is going to be big. I have excellent news for the Coopers."

Rufus slowly descended back to his theater seat. The heavens erupted with praise and adoration for God. Herald led the angel army in a rendition of, "Go, Rufus, go! If God is with you, who dare be against you?" The angels sang it over and over. Rufus got up, hiked his robe around his legs, and began running for the earth tunnel. Rufus approached the cavernous entrance and took a leap. He found himself racing through the tunnel like his friends before him. To his left, he saw faces speeding by on their way home to heaven.

Rufus came to an abrupt landing in the Blakes' front yard. "Wow, that was even more amazing than what Shiny and Hercules had described." He took a look around and then gave his wings a quick flap up and down.

Then God spoke. "Rufus, let's have some fun. I want you to walk through the dining room wall and make a surprise entrance."

Rufus stood still and thought about that for a moment. *Walk through the dining room wall? Really?*

God spoke. "Yes, just walk right through. I will be with you, and I can make it happen. I have plans to share with the Blakes and the Coopers."

Rufus thought, *How did God know what I was thinking?* Then he remembered, *Oh, yeah! He is God. He knows our every thought.* The visiting messenger walked around to the side of the house and could see light coming through the dining room window. Rufus took a deep breath, closed his eyes, and took a step through the wall. When he opened his eyes, he was staring at the Coopers, the Blakes, and Shiny and Hercules. Jane Cooper saw him first and gasped at the visitation of the angel who had appeared to her in her sickbed.

Lucy looked up and yelled, "Mommy, he's back!"

Shiny and Hercules both laughed out loud and greeted Rufus. Miriam and William Blake gasped at the size of Rufus. Again the angel messenger was forced to bend over to keep from banging his head against the ceiling. As he finished his last few bites of devil's food cake, Ben Cooper thought, *Not again!* Mr. Cooper turned to see what his daughter was pointing at, but again he could not see Rufus.

Then God spoke. "Rufus, tell Jane she is pregnant with Lucy's brother. Tell her that this boy is to be set apart for My purposes."

Rufus immediately responded, "Okay, Father. Jane, God wants you to know you're pregnant with Lucy's little brother. Set him apart for God."

The room was silent. As usual, Hercules broke the silence with a timely response. "Lucy, how cool is that? You're going to have a brother!"

Lucy looked up at Hercules and proclaimed, "This is going to be the best Christmas ever. A new pink bicycle and a new baby brother? God really does answer prayers."

With tears streaming down her face, Jane laughed out loud at Lucy's remarks.

Shiny spoke up. "God has spoken His blessings over your family."

"What in the world is going on?" Ben Cooper asked. "Jane, are you okay?"

Jane nodded.

Lucy continued to eat her cake and ice cream.

Then God spoke again. "Rufus, tell William and Miriam I am going to send them to Africa to adopt a special boy. Let them know they will fall in love with the people and make many trips back as missionaries. Be sure to tell them I will provide."

Rufus responded. "Really?"

"Yes, Rufus, really." God smiled down on Rufus.

"Okay, Father."

Rufus cleared his throat and said, "William, Miriam, God, is going to send you to Africa to adopt a special boy. You will fall in love with the people. Through the years, you will make many trips as missionaries. God is going to use your testimony of how He opened your eyes to help save an entire nation. Oh, and God will provide." Rufus stopped and thought, *Where in the world did that "save an entire nation" part come from?*

God just smiled.

William and Miriam were both flooded with faith as Rufus's words penetrated their hearts. Both started weeping at the news from heaven. Shiny and Hercules were also moved to tears. The love of God filled the dining room.

Finally, Ben Cooper spoke up. "What in the world is going on here? It's Christmas; we're supposed to be happy—and everyone is crying!"

Suddenly Rufus tapped Ben on the shoulder. As Ben turned, God opened his eyes. Rufus leaned down and gave Ben a big smile and a wink.

"God is going to bless your socks off, young man. You are going to get the baby boy you've always wanted. Merry Christmas."

Rufus stopped speaking, and the next thing he knew, he was back at the E-Max theater. The angel army bombarded him with cheers and back-slapping like heaven had never seen.

Ben Cooper sat staring at his half-empty bowl of ice cream. The dining room erupted with laughter. Shiny looked at Ben Cooper and asked, "Mr. Cooper, are you okay?"

Ben looked around the room, tears streaming down his face. He tried to talk but couldn't.

Jane asked, "Ben, are you all right?"

Ben could hardly get the words out. "Did … did … did you see … what I … I saw?"

Hercules looked at Ben and said, "Merry Christmas, Mr. Cooper."

Everyone laughed. There was much rejoicing in heaven and at the Blakes' home. God called Shiny and Hercules back to heaven. The Coopers strolled in the crisp night air back to their home. William and Miriam cleaned up and went to bed, praising God for the hope of a future family. God smiled down on everyone, excited about the thought of another Christmas filled with miracles.

CHAPTER 5

No More Limping for Lefty

Shiny and Hercules found themselves racing through the earth tunnel.
"I never get tired of doing this, Shiny. I love seeing the faces of people coming home to heaven. Look over there! See that elderly woman? Look how she's regaining her youthfulness. She looks like she just won the lottery."

Shiny had one response, and he yelled with all his might: "Praise God! You are more than marvelous—You are God!"

Shiny and Hercules rejoiced all the way back to heaven. Upon their arrival, they were welcomed home by Rufus and the angel army. They spent most of the afternoon hanging out at the reception stadium, watching people coming home to heaven to meet with the King of kings at His throne in the center of the stadium. The next morning, Shiny, Hercules, and Rufus got together with the angel army and waited for God to reveal His holiday plans.

There was tremendous excitement in the heavens. "Shiny, do you think God is going to send us back to earth for Christmas? Do you think He'll send you to eternity past to be with Joseph?"

Shiny wasn't sure. "Well, all I know, Herc, is whatever God has for us will be the very best. God always has us do His will."

Hercules quietly soaked in Shiny's wisdom.

Rufus added, "You know, Herc, God delights in our desire to do His will and please Him. That's why we are here—to please Him."

Hercules smiled his big cherub grin at the thought of pleasing God. "I just had a thought."

William Michael Cuccia

Shiny responded, "What's that, Herc?"

"I just thought, when we please God, I wonder if it's like what I feel when I drink an ice-cold root beer?"

Shiny and Rufus laughed, and then they picked up Hercules and threw him onto a big cloud. Hercules rolled around in the cloud, laughing and rejoicing at the thought of bringing God pleasure. Suddenly trumpets began to blow, and angelic voices broke out with beautiful songs. The heavens opened, and the voice of God rang throughout the heavens.

Then it was silent. The entire angel army stood still with their heads bowed.

Shiny, Hercules, and Rufus bowed low. Then the glory of God came down on Shiny's head. The heavens were brilliant from the reflection coming off his head. All of heaven was filled with the glory of God reflecting off the little bald angel. Then the King of kings rose from the throne in the center of the reception stadium.

Jesus stood up from His throne and proclaimed, "I have come to bring good news. I am the Lord. I will take care of the brokenhearted. I will set captives free. This is the year of My favor. The whole world will see My splendor. The beauty of My holiness will be displayed throughout the world."

King Jesus sat back down on His throne. All of heaven erupted at the announcement of the good news. Shiny lifted his head and was bewildered by what he saw. Heaven was lit up like never before. It was lit with expectation, and joy filled the heavens. The angel army was filled with hope. Hercules raised his head and saw the same. Rufus raised his head and also saw the light of expectation filling heaven.

"What's going on?" Hercules asked.

"God is getting ready to usher in another Christmas that will bring peace and hope. People need to know that God is alive and is victorious. People need to know Jesus is alive."

When Rufus was done making his proclamation, Hercules shouted with all his might, "Victory!"

Shiny and Rufus shook their heads and called out to Hercules to follow them. They made their way over to the E-Max to see what was happening back at Murph's Corner Market. To their surprise, half the town was at

164

the store. Murph, William and Miriam, Benny, Lenny, Lefty and his boys. They were planning an evening of Christmas caroling.

Well, maybe not half the town, Rufus noted, *but a small group of carolers showed up.*

Hercules made his request known from his seat at the E-Max. "I wish we could be there to go Christmas caroling with all our friends."

"That would be fun," replied Shiny.

Rufus encouraged Hercules, "Maybe God will give you the desires of your heart."

Suddenly God answered them. "My dear ones, I will send you to help sing in My presence. I have a special Christmas surprise for Lefty and his two friends."

Hercules spun around as he screamed, "Shiny, Rufus did you hear that? We get to go sing Christmas carols—and drink root beer!"

Rufus corrected Hercules. "I think you mean hot chocolate or cider."

"Hot chocolate? Are you kidding me?"

Hercules was filled with glee at the thought of drinking hot chocolate.

Rufus exhorted, "We'd better get some rest if we're going back to earth."

"Herc, I'll see you as soon as our Father calls."

"Okay, Shiny, I'm going to go get some rest. See you later."

Rufus, Shiny, and Hercules all went their separate ways to get rested up for the Christmas caroling event. As Rufus was walking back to his heavenly home, he heard a voice call out in the distance, "Would you like to help me?"

Rufus turned around and was awestruck. Jesus was standing there in the beauty of His holiness, and His eyes looked like flames of fire. His hair and beard were white and flowing. The train of His robe seemed to go on forever. Rufus bowed low before King Jesus.

Jesus reached down and tapped Rufus on his shoulder. "Get up, My friend. I have an assignment for you."

Rufus stood and tried to gaze into His eyes of fire. His heart melted with the love of God that overwhelmed him. His heart burned with desire to please King Jesus. Rufus realized he was looking into the eyes of perfection.

"Will you go and bring My love to the downcast?"

With tears streaming down his cheeks, Rufus answered the call. "Yes, I will go for You."

Jesus looked at Rufus with eyes of compassion. "Rufus, you have been faithful and patient. You have encouraged My servants, Shiny and Hercules. You have desired to see My plans fulfilled in them. You have patiently waited, and it's time for you to go and serve Me in love. I am going to overwhelm you with My love for the lost and hurting."

Rufus buckled under the weight of God's love. The angel collapsed under the holy weight, and he wept. Jesus reached down and pulled the bundle of love up close to Him and stared straight into Rufus's eyes. "Are you ready?"

Rufus, still sobbing, nodded in affirmation. Jesus commanded Rufus with a word: "Go!"

Suddenly Rufus was standing at the corner of Center Avenue and Main Street. Rufus kept rubbing his eyes, trying to focus and figure out how in the world he had arrived on earth. Attempting to regain his bearings, he spun around and found himself standing in front of Murph's Corner Market. He peeked into the front window, and saw the Christmas carolers making their plans for the evening.

"Excuse me, sir, are you lost?"

Rufus felt a finger tapping him on the back of his leg. He looked back down over his shoulder and saw little Lucy looking up at him. Before Rufus could respond, Lucy announced, "My parents are across the street at the bike shop, looking at the bicycle I want for Christmas. Do you have a bike?"

Rufus knelt down and addressed Lucy. "Young lady, I do not have a bicycle, but they look like they would be loads of fun."

"You're very tall. What's your name?"

"My name is Rufus, servant of the Most High God."

"Are you from Spain, Ree-car-do?"

Confused, Rufus once again patiently answered Lucy's question. "No, why do you ask?"

"Your accent sounds like you're from Spain, and your name is Ree-car-do."

"Good afternoon, Lucy," Tom Murphy said. "Where are your parents?"

Rufus immediately stood up, and it appeared as if he was unfolding himself in sections. Lucy and Murph looked on; it seemed like it took Rufus forever to finally erect himself to his final stature. Murph looked up at Rufus and introduced himself.

"Good afternoon, sir. My name is Tom Murphy, and I am the owner of this corner market."

"Hello. My name is Rufus, servant of the Most High God, and I've come to bring the love of God to the lost and hurting."

Murph looked down at Lucy, who just shrugged. Rufus patiently waited for Murph to respond. "Ricardo, would you and Lucy like to come in and have an ice-cold root beer on me while we wait for the Coopers to get done with their Christmas shopping?"

Lucy yelled, "Yes! Yes! Yes!"

Rufus shrugged and followed Murph and Lucy into the crowded corner market.

"Hey everyone," Murph said, "I want you to meet someone."

The small crowd of carolers turned and looked at Rufus as Murph introduced him. "This here is Ricardo, and he just arrived for the holidays."

Everyone greeted Rufus. Lucy greeted everyone as well and announced that the root beers were on Murph.

Lenny confirmed, "Yep."

Lefty extended his hand to Rufus. "My name is Larry, but everyone calls me Lefty because I broke my left leg years ago when I was a kid. I jumped out of a window at a house I was robbing, and since then, I have this pretty bad limp, so everyone calls me Limp Leg Lefty. Since I have given my life to Christ, I don't steal anymore. I sing in the choir and do what I can to make an honest living. It's hard, though, 'cause I can't do much with this limp."

The store was silent. Rufus just stared at Lefty.

Suddenly the heavens opened. "Rufus, ask Lefty if he believes I can heal his leg."

"Lefty, do you believe God can heal your leg?"

"Why, sure! He healed William's blind eyes and Billy's legs a few years ago on Christmas Eve. That's was the night I gave my life to Christ."

William Blake acknowledged Rufus. "It's true, Ricardo. I was completely blind, and God healed my eyes. Now I have a wonderful life. This is my beautiful wife, Miriam."

Miriam turned and gave Rufus a welcoming smile.

William continued, "On top of that, God has blessed us with the opportunity to go to Africa and adopt a child."

Rufus addressed William and Miriam. "Not only that, but God is going to allow you to become pregnant while you're in Africa. Your boys will grow up together and be lifelong friends who will serve God all the days of their lives."

The visitor's words silenced the crowd. Rufus thought, *Oh my, I wonder where that all came from. I just opened my mouth, and it poured right out.* Miriam and William sat in silence, pondering the words.

Officer Benny asked Rufus, "Are you a prophet from God?"

Rufus quickly replied, "No, sir, I'm a servant of the Most High God. I was called to share His love with the lost and hurting."

Again the heavens opened. "Rufus, you're doing fine. Let Lefty know I heard his prayer last night when he asked Me for a Christmas miracle."

Rufus didn't hesitate. His heart felt like it was pounding out of his chest from the love he was feeling. "Lefty, God heard your prayer last night when you asked Him for a Christmas miracle."

Lefty's jaw dropped as he listened to the words of love coming from the visitor's mouth.

"Would you like for us to pray for you right now? I believe God wants to heal your leg and send you on your way."

Lefty responded to Rufus's invitation. "Are you kidding me? Yes! I would love for you to pray for me."

Rufus could clearly hear the voice of God in his heart directing him. "I'm not going to pray for you, but I will believe for you. William and Miriam, would you pray for Lefty? God is announcing here today that He is going to use you both to heal the sick wherever He sends you. Your faith in God will heal the sick."

In heaven, Shiny and Hercules were enthralled by what they were seeing. Hercules elbowed Shiny from his seat at the E-Max. "Shiny, are you seeing what I'm seeing?"

"I know! God is really using Rufus in a powerful way. God is so awesome."

"I'll say. God is going to heal Lefty. I wonder if they will all drink root beer to celebrate after God heals his leg."

Shiny gave Hercules a smile and ruffled his curly red locks. William and Miriam made their way over to where Lefty was sitting. The people in the small corner store gathered around Lefty and surrounded him with love and faith. Rufus stood behind them all, rejoicing in his spirit as he watched the releasing of faith for God to perform yet another Christmas miracle. William and Miriam knelt down and placed their hands on Lefty's leg.

Everyone bowed their heads as William prayed a prayer of faith. William concluded his short prayer, and then he did something very peculiar. He stood up and looked right at Rufus. Rufus engaged him with a smile. William nodded and winked at Rufus, and Rufus returned the wink with one of his own.

Full of faith, William turned and addressed Lefty. "The Lord is telling me your faith has made you well, Lefty. Rise up and walk."

Lefty raised his head and looked at William. Lefty stood up from the bar stool he had been sitting on. He took a few cautious steps and then looked at everyone. "Oh my God! I'm healed! I'm healed! Thank you, Jesus!"

He took off running around the aisles of the corner market. Every few steps, he would leap up into the air and exclaim, "I'm healed!"

Everyone in the corner market erupted with shouts of joy. Ben and Jane Cooper entered the store. Ben addressed the joyous carolers. "What's going on?"

Lucy answered her father. "Daddy, Limp Leg Lefty just got healed like Mommy and Mr. Blake and Billy Smith. This nice man said God would heal Lefty, and God did it."

The Coopers turned and looked at Rufus. God opened Jane Cooper's eyes as she turned to look at Rufus. She recognized him as the messenger who had visited her when she was deathly ill. Rufus winked at Jane Cooper—and then he was gone.

Hercules elbowed Shiny and asked, "Hey, wait a minute—did everyone at Murph's see Rufus disappear?"

"I don't know, Herc. You know that God reveals what is necessary to accomplish His will."

Jane Cooper stared into the vacant space left by Rufus.

"Jane, are you okay?" asked Ben.

"Yes, I believe I'm quite fine." She smiled at Ben and then asked Lucy, "What did you say the nice gentlemen's name was who said Lefty would be healed?"

"His name is Ree-car-do, and he's right there."

Lucy pointed to where Rufus had been standing, but he was gone. "Hey, where did he go?"

Everyone turned in the direction of where Rufus had been standing.

Murph parroted Lucy as he began to pour root beers for everyone. "Where did Ricardo go?"

Lefty was still spinning around, rejoicing over his miracle. The corner store was buzzing with faith. William and Miriam shared with the Coopers what the visitor had told them about having a baby of their own and the proclamation that God would use them to heal the sick. Benny and Lenny were still shocked at the fact they had watched their old nemesis, Limp Leg Lefty, get healed right before their eyes. Everyone in the little corner market was inspired from the healing of Lefty's leg. Jane Cooper stared out the window, pondering the goodness of God, lost in the knowledge that she was pregnant as well.

Lefty spoke into the silence of the corner market. "Do you think Ricardo was really an angel in disguise?"

Lenny just said, "Yep."

At the E-Max, Rufus was received with high fives, fist bumps, and head slaps from the angel army. Hercules shouted out to Rufus, "You should have hung around long enough to drink some root beer."

Shiny shook his head and announced, "Rufus, you were great! You obeyed God and ushered in an incredible miracle."

Rufus smiled at Shiny and said, "Hope on, my friend, hope on."

Hercules jumped up on his seat and yelled, "Hope on, Ree-car-do, hope on!"

Shiny and Rufus grabbed Hercules and flung him onto a big cloud.

CHAPTER 6

The Bake Sale

"**M**ommy, did you and Daddy buy my new pink bike for Christmas?"

"Lucy, you will just have to wait and see what Christmas brings."

The Coopers were still stunned by yet another Christmas miracle as they made the walk home from the little corner market. Snowflakes fell and kissed the pavement as the Coopers made their way up the walk to their front door.

"I hope I get the bike. It's such a beautiful bike."

The Coopers entered the front door of their home and spent the evening recapping the exciting events of the day. Lucy said her prayers before she went to bed. Jane tucked Lucy in and prayed with her. Ben came in to join his family in prayer, and the three thanked God for healing Lefty and for allowing Jane to be pregnant.

In heaven, Shiny woke up to the singing of birds. His heart was filled with thanksgiving, knowing that God was filling the earth with hope. "Thank You, God, for the beauty of Your presence. I love the way the birds sing Your praise."

Still reeling from the way God had used him, Rufus had woken up a few hours earlier.

Hercules was still asleep, dreaming of root beer floats and angel food cake smothered with whipped cream and strawberries.

On earth, Billy Smith woke up to a ringing doorbell. He jumped out of bed and found a half dozen of his friends at the front door, calling for him to come out and play some ball in the schoolyard. "Mom, is it okay if I go down to the school to play ball?"

"Yes, Billy, but be home by noon so we can go to the church for the bake sale."

Running out the door, Billy grabbed his glove and hat. "Thanks, Mom. I'll be home by eleven thirty. Love you!"

Billy's mom barely got out, "Love you too, son," before the front door slammed.

Alone in the house, Billy's mom sang God's praises for healing her son's crippled legs. "Heavenly Father, thank You again for healing Billy's legs and allowing him the gift to play and run and experience life. I will forever give You thanks. I praise You for being a miracle-working God. I dedicate my son to You."

In heaven, God commanded Shiny, "Go!"

The next thing Shiny knew, he was being blown by the east wind in the direction of earth tunnel. It was as if God's simple command to go was like a slingshot catapulting Shiny to an unknown assignment. Shiny found himself standing in front of Billy's mom. Billy's mom was on her hands and knees, washing the kitchen floor, totally unaware of the bald angel's presence. Shiny watched her scrubbing the floor while singing God's praise. Suddenly God's glory filled Billy's house and lit up Shiny's head.

Billy's mom became aware of the visitor from heaven. "Are you the bald angel?"

Shiny looked down at Billy's mom as she looked up at him from her knees on the kitchen floor.

"Yes, ma'am, I am the bald angel."

"So Billy does have a bald angel who visits him."

"Yes, ma'am, that would be me."

Billy's mom was struck by the beauty of God's glory reflecting off Shiny's head. Finally, she asked, "What's your name?"

"Shiny."

Billy's mom broke out crying and laughing at the same time. Right there on the kitchen floor, God released joy on Billy's mom as she took in the reality that her son did have an angel who had visited him with the good news that he would be healed.

Shiny asked Billy's mom, "Are you okay?"

Mrs. Smith explained that she was full of God's joy because she knew that Billy's angel had come to visit her too. Shiny quietly waited for direction from God. He wasn't quite sure how he should respond to her. He decided to flap his wings to get God's attention. The flapping of his wings caused more of God's joy to fall on Billy's mom. She found herself lying on the kitchen floor, laughing uncontrollably. Shiny flapped harder, and God released more joy. This seemed to go on until Billy's mom was totally exhausted.

When Shiny opened his mouth, God filled it. "God says that He has completely healed you from the grief of Billy's crippled years. He has set plans in place for Billy to serve Him all the days of his life. Billy will experience great success playing ball. God will call him to leave baseball and serve as a pastor and teacher of His Word."

Shiny stopped flapping his wings after he gave Billy's mom the message. Mrs. Smith received the words with tears streaming down her cheeks as she lay in a crumpled ball on the kitchen floor. She was so moved by the message and the outpouring of God's joy that she appeared to be utterly exhausted.

Then she spoke up. "Shiny, this is the answer to all my prayers. God has heard the cry of my heart and has answered me today."

Shiny gave Billy's mom a big smile as he reached down and helped her up. Shiny looked into her eyes and encouraged her to continue to be strong and courageous. Shiny encouraged her to pray for Billy and the plans that God had laid out for him.

Suddenly Billy came bolting through the back kitchen door. "Shiny!"

"Billy, it's so good to see you."

Billy was excited and confused at the presence of Shiny. "What are you doing here?"

"I don't know, Billy. Our Father just told me to go. The next thing I knew, I was here with your mom." Shiny stood silently waiting for God to speak. Shiny had learned the importance of waiting and obeying.

"See, Mom? I told you Shiny was real."

Billy's mom stood quietly in the middle of the kitchen. "Do you eat?"

Shiny was surprised by her question. "Why, yes, I do eat. That is one of the blessings God has given us in heaven. He prepares quite the table for us to eat from in heaven. He's a good Father."

"I just prepared some sugar cookies cut in the shape of angels for the Christmas bake sale. Would you like to try one?"

Billy's mom felt awkward talking to the bald angel, but Shiny was delighted with the invitation. "I would love to have one of your cookies. I would prefer to eat one with hair."

Shiny smiled at Billy's mom, trying to make her feel at ease. "Oh, I would never make a bald angel cookie. I mean I wouldn't want to offend you by having anyone bite off your head. I mean, your head is so beautiful. You are beautiful. I just wouldn't want to offend you."

The more Billy's mom tried to explain herself, the more embarrassed she felt. She found herself still struggling with the fact that there was a real live angel standing in her kitchen, and a bald one at that. She was trying to grasp the reality that she was having a conversation about whether she would make a bald angel cookie with a live bald angel. Shiny made it easy on her and surveyed the plate filled with cookies.

He reached for one, saying, "This one here actually looks good. It reminds me of my friend Hercules."

In unison, Billy and his mom both said, "Hercules?"

"Yes, Hercules is my most precious friend in heaven. He is a cute, chubby little cherub."

Again in unison they both said, "Cherub?"

Shiny took a big bite of the cookie and declared, "This is quite heavenly. Very delightful. I'm sure Hercules would love these cookies. I wish he was here with us."

The three stood quietly in the kitchen as Shiny devoured the cookie. Billy's mom offered Shiny another one. He declined and declared, "Oh no, these cookies are for the bake sale. You better save them."

Then God invoked, "Shiny, ask her why the church is raising funds."

Shiny obeyed and inquired. Billy beat his mom to the punch. "The church is raising money to help send the Blakes to Zimbabwe. They're going to adopt a baby. Isn't that cool, Shiny?"

"Why, yes, it is, Billy. That is quite exciting. I look forward to seeing William and Miriam fulfill the plans God has for their lives."

Billy and his mom both responded to Shiny in unison. "You know the Blakes?"

"Oh yes. I met William when he was still blind."

Billy's mom was stunned by Shiny's words. "Wait, are you the angel who visited William and told him that God would heal his blind eyes?"

"That would be me. God is so good."

Billy boldly jumped in as well. "I remember Mr. Blake sharing about an angel who visited him. He never said he was bald."

Shiny chuckled and said, "Well, Billy, Mr. Blake was still blind, so he couldn't see me; he could only hear me."

The three had a good laugh, and Billy's mom said, "Billy, we better get going to the bake sale, or we'll be late." She turned to Shiny. "Would you like to go with us, or will you be staying here?"

"Oh, I would love to go to church with you."

Billy's mom sighed and said, "Okay then; let's all go to the church for the bake sale."

The three got into the car. Billy opened the door for Shiny and let him sit in the front seat. Shiny was very excited to be going for a ride in a car. Billy's mom was a bit nervous driving her car with a real live angel in it. Billy was ecstatic to be riding with Shiny in his car. On the way to the church, Billy leaned forward from the backseat to ask Shiny, "Would you like to go Christmas caroling with us tonight?"

Shiny asked back, "Are you going with the Blakes and Murph?"

With amazement, Billy's mom said, "Why, yes we are. How did you know that?"

"My friend Rufus was at Murph's yesterday when they were practicing. Our Father in heaven did another big miracle while Rufus was there."

Billy's mom asked, "You have a friend named Rufus? Is he an angel?"

"Yes, ma'am."

Shiny tried to continue, but Billy interrupted. "What miracle did God do?"

Shiny shared the good news about Lefty's leg. "While everyone was getting ready to practice singing carols at Murph's Corner Market, our Father sent Rufus to earth to share the good news that God would heal Lefty's leg. William and Miriam led everyone in a healing prayer for Lefty. God heard their prayer and answered. Lefty doesn't limp anymore. He's healed!"

The three drove down the street to the church in silence. The weight of Shiny's testimony of what God had done for Lefty seemed to fill the car.

Finally, young Billy spoke up and said, "God healed Lefty's leg, just like he healed my legs, Mom."

Billy's mom drove down the street, trying to grasp the reality of what was happening. Her thoughts were running wild. *I'm driving down the road with an angel in my car who is telling me he has two angel friends named Hercules and Rufus. On top of that, this angel just shared how God healed Lefty's leg like He had healed my son's legs a few years before.*

Suddenly Billy's mom was overcome with the emotion of the truth she was processing. She began singing God's praises right there in the car as she drove down the street to the church.

Billy and Shiny joined in with her, and the three sang praises to God all the way to the church.

When they arrived, Mrs. Smith looked at Shiny and asked, "So are you going to go Christmas caroling with us?"

Shiny looked at Billy and his mom and announced, "We will see what our Father has planned."

Billy, Mrs. Smith, and the bald angel carried the trays of cookies from the car to the church. As the three walked up to the front of the church, they were met by Pastor Andrews.

"Good afternoon, Mrs. Smith. Good afternoon, Billy. I see you've brought a visitor to the bake sale today."

Pastor Andrews extended his hand to welcome Shiny. The bald angel smiled and shook the pastor's hand. Billy proudly introduced Shiny to the pastor. "Pastor, this is Shiny the angel I told you about, the one who shared the good news that I would be healed."

Pastor Andrews seemed confused at Billy's introduction as he greeted the bald angel. "It is a delight to have you visiting us today, Saul. I've always wanted to visit California."

Now Billy and his mom were confused. Shiny smiled and said, "I look forward to seeing all the goodies at the bake sale today. I only wish my friend Hercules had come with me. He loves sweets, especially root beer floats."

Pastor Andrews responded, "We have quite the display of goodies here today; your friend Henry is really missing out. Not to mention we have the best root beer this side of the Mississippi at Murph's Corner Market."

Shiny smiled and followed Pastor Andrews into the church. Billy and his mom followed behind, trying to figure out what was going on. Shiny reached back and put his arms around Billy and his mom's shoulders and helped usher them into the church hall. Shiny whispered, "Our Father will reveal His plans to your pastor all in good time."

Hercules couldn't contain himself. He was bouncing up and down on his seat at the E-Max. Rufus was still reeling from the excitement of being used by God to share the messages of hope to Lefty, William, and Miriam. With every bounce, Hercules blurted out, "I hope I get to go to the bake sale with Shiny. Oh, Father, let me go and share some good news and eat some cookies."

Rufus and the angel army laughed as they watched the chubby little cherub trying to tug on the heartstrings of God to get his way.

Suddenly the heavens began to shake, and God spoke. "I'm sending a host of angels to earth to usher in My glory for Christmas. I'm releasing more miracles this season. Many will give their lives to My Son and receive eternal life when they witness the miracles I'm stringing together. This will be a Christmas to remember."

The heavens calmed as the angel army absorbed the shock of God's goodness. His proclamation reverberated throughout heaven, and every angel was flooded with faith. Simultaneously the angel army erupted with shouts of joy.

Hercules asked Rufus, "Does that mean I get to go to the bake sale?"

Rufus ruffed Hercules's curly top. "Yes, my chubby little friend, you get to go to the bake sale."

"Are you sure?"

"Hercules, is our Father good or is He good?"

"He is so good!"

"Does our Father delight in giving us the desires of our hearts?"

Now Hercules was bouncing way off his seat. "Yes! Yes! Yes!"

Rufus boldly proclaimed, "Hercules, go in the strength of the Lord, and I'll see you there."

God was pleased with Rufus's faith-filled proclamation. God smiled, and the heavens lit up.

Hercules found himself flying toward the earth tunnel.

Rufus shouted out, "Go, little buddy, you go!"

Billy escorted Shiny over to his best friend, Eric Swan, and introduced him. "Eric, this is Shiny, the bald angel I told you about."

Eric Swan's eyes were as big as saucers. "It's really true? You're real?"

"Why, yes I am, and I'm delighted to meet you, Eric. I think you play some great second base."

"Thank you," was all Eric Swan could muster up as a response to the angelic presence.

Shiny reached out to shake Eric's hand, and as he did, the bald angel looked across the hall and saw a familiar face on the other side of the room. Much to Shiny's surprise, there was Hercules, waving to him with his dimpled grin, simultaneously taking a bite from one of Miriam Blake's homemade brownies.

"Shiny, I made it to the bake sale. Our Father is so good. As we delight in Him, He does give us the desires of our hearts."

Shiny shook his head and walked over to hug his big surprise from heaven. As Shiny greeted Hercules, he thought, *I wonder why God opened Eric Swan's eyes to see me—but not Pastor Andrews's?*

God answered, "Childlike faith, My friend, childlike faith. Remember—unless they become like little children, no one will see My kingdom."

Shiny thought, *that makes sense.*

CHAPTER 7

The Christmas Carolers

"**M**iriam, how did the bake sale go today?" William Blake was anxious to hear how much money was raised.

"Pastor Andrews said they would make the announcement tomorrow at the Sunday service. He asked if we would be willing to go up on the platform and let everyone know who the money was being raised for."

Miriam paused and could tell her husband was disappointed that he had to wait another day to find out how much money was raised for their trip to Africa. "I do have a surprise for you, sweetheart."

William perked up as he tried to anticipate what kind of surprise would raise his spirits. Just then Hercules came out of the guest bedroom and made his entrance into the living room where William and Miriam were sitting.

"Hercules! When did you get here?"

"Just in the nick of time to participate in the bake sale. William, our Father let me come and enjoy the bake sale, and on top of that, I get to go Christmas caroling with everyone tonight."

William's spirits were visibly lifted as he listened to his heavenly friend share how wonderful the goodies were at the bake sale. "I hope you didn't eat all our profits for the trip." William smiled as he gave Hercules a big hug, and then he continued to razz the chubby little cherub. "I hope you left some room in that tummy of yours for dinner."

Hercules smiled and rubbed his tummy. "I think there's plenty of room in here for some of Miriam's home cooking."

Suddenly there was a knock on the door. William went to the door, and to his surprise, there was Shiny standing on the front porch. Shiny greeted William with a big hug.

"Shiny, come in, come in." William was getting quite used to these surprise visitations. "I assume you know that Hercules is here."

"Oh yes, I saw him at the bake sale earlier today."

"Why am I not surprised to hear that you were at the bake sale too?"

William put his arm around Shiny's shoulders and ushered him into the house.

"Hey, Shiny," Herc said, "you're here just in time for dinner."

Shiny blushed at the boldness of Hercules's announcement. Miriam saved Hercules. "Shiny, you know you are always welcome here anytime, and that means for meals too."

"Thank you, Miriam, that's very kind." Shiny paused, looked at Hercules, and then continued. "We're happy to be here and excited to be able to go Christmas caroling with all our earthly friends."

William invited everyone to follow him to the dining room as Miriam made her way into the kitchen. They all sat down at the dining room table, and Miriam served them heaping servings of homemade macaroni and cheese with baked chicken. Hercules asked if he could pray. William affirmed him, and everyone bowed their heads as they held hands.

"Dear Father, we are so grateful for Your goodness. Thank You for blessing William and Miriam. We thank You for the good news coming their way tomorrow morning. Please bless this food now. In Jesus's name, amen. Let's eat!"

Hercules dug into the mac and cheese, humming his way through every bite. Shiny thanked William and Miriam for being so gracious. They spent most of the evening talking about the wonderful miracle of Lefty's leg.

In heaven, Rufus waited patiently for his next assignment. He was filled with faith as he anticipated the miracles God had announced were coming. Rufus sat at the entrance of the reception stadium, enjoying the music of Louie and his band, who were playing for the new arrivals coming home to heaven. Rufus began singing praises and thanking God for allowing him to be used in such a powerful way in the lives of those God loves.

Rufus paused and soaked in the presence of God—which is always present, everywhere, all the time in heaven. He realized how wonderful it was to always be in the presence of God, whether in heaven or on earth.

Is it true that God is always everywhere all the time in heaven? Rufus wondered. He realized something profound. *It's the same here as it is on earth: all one has to do is just acknowledge His presence. Everything in all of creation is contained in God, and God is in everything.* Rufus was now deeply lost in his thoughts.

Then God spoke. "Let Me explain it this way, Rufus. If you put a bucket in the depth of the ocean, the entire bucket would be contained by the ocean, and the ocean would also completely fill the bucket."

Rufus replied, "So You're like the ocean, and all of creation is the bucket?"

"Yes, except I'm bigger than the ocean. I have no beginning and no end. I am always present, everywhere, all the time!"

Rufus thought, *Wow! God, You're immeasurably big!*

God smiled and said, "Yep."

Rufus was entirely consumed by the presence and love of God. He laid his head back and let the music penetrate him. The heavens opened while he was being saturated with God's love. God gave Rufus the most beautiful vision. God the Father showed Rufus everything that would result from the Christmas caroling. He explained that the heart of His people would move God to perform more miracles. Rufus couldn't contain himself. He jumped up and began praising God with all his might. He sang and danced his way into a frenzy. The entire angel army followed his lead. God was so moved by the extravagant display of worship that it caused Him to throw his head back and laugh hilariously. Heaven was filled with so much joy that it spread throughout the world.

Earth would never be the same.

Then God said, "Rufus, My servant, I want you to go and join Shiny and Hercules. The three of you will sing with My children. Lead them to worship Me and spread My love. I will deliver My people from pain and hopelessness. I will bring victory to those who only have known defeat. I will bring joy to the world."

Rufus bowed low and worshipped God. All the angels bowed low and worshipped. All the saints in heaven bowed low and worshipped. All creation glorified God.

Miriam served plum pudding for dessert. Hercules hummed his way through not one, not two, but three bowls of plum pudding. Watching Hercules eat brought Miriam great joy. William announced that they must get ready to go to Murph's to meet up with the gang so they could go Christmas caroling. Shiny helped Miriam and William clear the table while Hercules finished his fourth bowl of plum pudding.

At the Coopers' house, Jane was getting Lucy dressed for her first Christmas caroling experience.

Lefty and the boys were already at Murph's, helping put the final touches on the Christmas tree in the front window. Lefty was full of God's praise. He kept saying, "Hey, guys, check it out." He would dance around the store, and every so often, he would jump up in the air. "God is good! God is great."

Billy and his mom were still trying to convince his dad that the bald angel was real. "Come now, we must get going to Murph's."

"Okay, Dad, but I'm telling you, Shiny did come and visit us today. Ask Mom."

Billy's mom tried to share with her husband how Shiny just appeared in the kitchen, but the more she shared, the crazier it sounded.

"Okay, okay! The bald angel visited you today. Now let's get going, or we will be late for the caroling."

Billy's dad reminded them they had to stop by to pick up Eric Swan on the way. Eric's parents were not churchgoers, but they allowed him to participate in church activities with the Smith family. When Billy and his parents arrived at the Swans', they were confronted by Eric's dad.

"Eric tells me that he met a real live angel today at the bake sale."

Billy looked at his mom and then decided he would address the difficult question. "Mr. Swan, with all due respect, you do know that I was crippled and in a wheelchair and that the doctors said I would never walk again, right?"

"Yes, Billy."

"You are also well aware that God healed me. You can't deny that, right? Here I am standing before you, Mr. Swan."

Mr. Swan dropped his head and nodded.

Then Billy continued, "Mr. Swan, I would never lie to you. God did send an angel to me to share the good news that I would be healed. This same angel came to my house today. He is the bald angel—and Shiny is his name."

Mr. Swan stood stunned and had no response. Eric Swan stepped off his front porch and asked, "Shouldn't we get going?"

Mr. Swan nodded one more time. After Eric Swan jumped in the backseat with Billy, they were on their way down the road to Murph's. Back at the little corner market, it seemed as though everyone was arriving at once. The Coopers were already there when the Blakes came with Shiny and Hercules. Those whose eyes had been opened recognized Shiny and Hercules; the rest saw them as Saul and Henry. It was quite the crowd. Benny and Lenny were there in their best Christmas caroling attire.

Just as the Smith family was walking up, Rufus appeared at the corner of Center and Main. Mr. Smith opened the door and motioned Rufus to enter ahead of him and his family.

Rufus walked in the little corner market, and Lucy squealed, "Ree-car-do, you're back!"

Jane Cooper immediately recognized Rufus as her bedside angel. Shiny and Hercules were more than delighted to see their heavenly buddy. Everyone gathered together around the Christmas tree in front of the store. William Blake prayed over the evening's events.

When William finished his prayer, Shiny was overwhelmed by the presence of God. He began singing the most beautiful rendition of the Christmas lullaby, the song he had sung over baby Jesus the night of His miraculous birth.

Shiny sang out, "O baby Jesus, what a miracle You are. You are God. You stepped out of heaven just to be with us. O baby Jesus, what a miracle You are. You are the Lord. You gave up Your throne just to take the cross. That baby in the manger is the Savior of the world. That baby in the manger is Jesus."

When Shiny stopped singing, it was a silent night at the little corner market. Even Hercules and Rufus had tears running down their faces. The presence of God was so thick no one could move.

Finally, little Lucy had the courage to whisper, "That was so beautiful."

Miriam agreed. "Yes, that was beautiful."

Hercules said, "Heavenly."

Lenny also agreed. "That was beautiful."

Suddenly everyone turned to Lenny, amazed at his response. It was the first time anyone heard him say anything more than "yep." God was obviously present in the little corner market.

Murph just wept. So did Billy's father. Suddenly God opened Billy's dad's eyes to see Shiny in all of God's glory.

Billy's dad gasped, "Oh my, it's true!"

Shiny just winked and announced to everyone, "To God be the glory!"

Everyone joined Shiny in singing another round of the Christmas lullaby. The carolers sang out with their hands lifted high, and their hearts surrendered. Murph served a round of hot cider to everyone except Hercules (who was given a root beer float with a candy cane for a stir stick). The little corner market was filled with joy and laughter as the carolers prepared to go out and usher in a night of miracles.

Hercules discovered the delicious taste of a candy cane. All was well at the little corner market.

Hercules hummed above the crowd.

CHAPTER 8

God Is Real—See!

Super-sized snowflakes fell from heaven outside the little corner market. Inside, God's presence ushered in an extra measure of joy to the small gathering of carolers. Everyone put on their coats, scarves, mittens, and knit caps. There was a supernatural expectation in the air.

Eric Swan pointed to the front window. "Look! It's snowing!"

Lenny confirmed, "Yep."

Officer Benny handed out a lawful exhortation. "Everyone be careful out there; it will be wet and slippery. Be sure to proceed with caution."

The three children were encouraged to lead the way. Billy, Lucy, and Eric walked out into the crisp, snow-covered night, and the adults followed. Rufus took the position as the rear guard.

The carolers did not yet know that they were on their way to a miracle-filled evening. Murph walked out with Rufus, a large thermos of hot chocolate in hand as he locked the door behind.

The carolers started north toward First and Main Street. Turning down First Avenue, the singing began. The songs seemed to warm the frigid evening air. As they walked down First Avenue, the carolers approached a dimly lit corner, where a streetlamp had been broken. Officer Benny led the way with his policeman's flashlight. He pointed the flashlight in the direction of a dark corner. To his surprise, the light was met by a presence of what appeared to be an old woman hunched over, sitting on the curb.

Hercules ran ahead of the carolers and acknowledged the woman wrapped tightly in a ragged blanket. "Excuse me," he said. "Are you okay?"

Hercules waited for a response. The woman never lifted her head. The unresponsive women sat with her head covered. Hercules flapped his wings to ask God to help this poor lost soul. The group of carolers was now standing huddled just behind Hercules.

God filled Hercules with boldness. Without hesitation, the chubby little cherub opened his mouth. "I command all shame to be gone. Emily, look at me."

Hercules waited for a response. The woman raised her head and looked into Hercules's eyes. "No one has called me Emily in twenty years. How did you know my name?"

"God knows your name. He wants you to know that tonight all your shame is gone. He's going to do a miracle in your life, and everything that has been stolen from you is going to be restored."

Emily unfolded herself and stood. She stared at Hercules for a moment and then looked around at all the carolers' faces, one by one, in a calculated, deliberate attempt to try to make a connection. Turning her attention back to Hercules, she asked, "Are you an angel?"

"I'm a messenger of God, sent to you tonight to bring you a message of hope that will cause you to believe that God will provide for you."

The carolers huddled even closer, surrounding Hercules and Emily, providing warmth. Murph handed Emily a freshly poured cup of hot chocolate. Emily grabbed the cup with both hands, exposing worn-out mittens with missing fingers and numerous holes.

Emily made quick eye contact with Murph, and then she turned away while muttering, "Thank you."

Jane Cooper and Miriam put their arms around Emily and displayed a warmth of love that had been absent from the woman's tattered life for a very long time. Emily crumbled in their embrace and wept. They held her close and let God's love permeate her. The rest of the carolers softly sang over her.

Then Emily announced, "It's been years since I've felt the touch of another human being."

The carolers and Emily had made a connection. William prayed a beautiful prayer over Emily.

Shiny invited Emily to come along with them. From that moment, Emily Wilson's life was changed forever. She joined the carolers as they strolled down First Avenue. With snowflakes falling all around her, Emily experienced the warmth and acceptance of God's unconditional love.

Lucy pointed to a house on First Avenue. "Look, that's the only house on the street that's not decorated for Christmas, and it's the largest house on the block. Let's go sing there."

Billy Smith announced, "I'm not sure we should go there."

Shiny stepped in. "Why not?"

Eric Swan answered. "That's Mr. Howling's estate. He doesn't like children."

Hercules reacted. "How sad it that? God loves children."

Rufus held his position at the rear. He quietly prayed, "Father, what should we do? Should we go or should we stay?"

God responded, "Rufus, go and share the love that only I can give. I'm about to unravel Mr. Howling's world and release him to be the giver I have always intended him to be. No longer will his life be dreary and desolate."

Ben Cooper grabbed his daughter's hand and asked, "Isn't Mr. Howling the wealthiest man in town?"

Billy Smith's father responded, "Yes, he's a very wealthy and very private man. I'm not sure it's a good idea to disturb him."

Rufus spoke from his position in the rear. "God says we are to go. We are to share His love and watch what happens. God is going to do something special tonight for Mr. Howling."

Everyone turned their attention to Rufus. The Christmas-sized snowflakes continued to fall as the small collection of carolers absorbed Rufus's words. Emily asked Murph if she could have another cup of hot chocolate. As Murph filled her cup, Rufus walked to the front of the group and grabbed Lucy's other hand.

Lucy looked up at Rufus, way up at Rufus, and smiled. "Ree-car-do, I think we should do it."

Rufus turned back to the carolers and asked, "What do you think? Lucy's in; are you?"

Lenny joined in. "Yep."

The carolers said in unison, "Let's do it."

As the faithful carolers approached Mr. Howling's house, they began singing. With each step, faith grew in their hearts. Standing at the front gate of the Howling estate, Eric Swan declared, "I didn't realize how much bigger the Howling house was than all the rest of the houses on the street."

Rufus grabbed hold of the latch on the front gate and turned it. He opened the gate and stepped through. With Lucy's hand in his own, he motioned for everyone to follow. The carolers continued to sing out. It seemed like their singing caused the darkened grounds of the Howling Estate to brighten up. It took forever to make the walk down the stone pathway to the front doors. Standing at the base of a series of stone steps leading up to a pair of massive wooden doors, Rufus encouraged everyone to be bold in their faith. "God is going to pour out His love. Let's go share some good news."

Rufus, Lucy, and Ben Cooper led the carolers up the series of steps. Standing in front of the large wooden doors, Hercules whispered, "What now?"

Suddenly God spoke. "Sing like you've never sung before! Sing My praises! Watch and see what I will do."

Shiny was the first to sing. He sang with all his might, and God's glory came down. Shiny's head lit the darkened courtyard. All the carolers followed Shiny's lead. Those whose eyes had been opened were amazed at how brightly God's glory was reflecting off Shiny's head. The voices grew louder as they responded to God's presence, and the courtyard filled with joy.

There was no response.

The large wooden doors seemed welded shut by a dreary, desolate seal. It felt like it had been years since anyone had crossed the threshold of those doors that now loomed over the small collection of carolers. Shiny continued to lead the singing, and everyone's faith increased—as did the presence of God's glory.

Suddenly—and yes, this is a *big* suddenly—there was a loud creaking sound.

It seemed like the house itself was shifting. The two massive wooden doors began to separate, and the crowd of carolers went silent. The doors opened, and there stood a little man in the shadows. The house was dark inside. It was impossible to see the little man's face as he stood back, hidden in the darkness. "Did you not read my sign at the front gate?"

Rufus answered the voice from the darkness. "Sir, I didn't see the sign, but God has called us tonight to come and share His love with you."

Suddenly it was silent. It was so quiet you could hear the snowflakes kissing the stone pavement. The little man from behind the large doors resisted. "God? There is no God—now leave before I call the police!"

Officer Benny stepped forward. "Mr. Howling, this is Officer Benny. God does exist, and He loves you very much."

Officer Lenny confirmed, "Yep."

"If I have to call the mayor tonight, I will. Get off my property now! There is no God, I tell you!"

Mr. Howling began to slam the front door. Suddenly God filled Shiny's mouth. Shiny spoke, and God opened Mr. Howling's eyes. "God is real: see!"

Shiny stood before Mr. Howling in the all of God's glory. The glory of God reflected off the bald angel's head and blinded the dreary little man. Shiny continued as Mr. Howling attempted to shield himself from the brightness of God's glory. "God loves you with an everlasting love. His Son Jesus died for you. God will never leave you. Oh, and you will never be able to outgive God. Don't be afraid, Mr. Howling, God is going to increase your wealth as you give to His kingdom. And one more thing, my name is Shiny—and I will be back."

Shiny stood stunned as he processed his bold declaration. Mr. Howling stood stunned by the light of God's truth.

The little man slammed the door shut.

CHAPTER 9

Temporary Disappointment

In the silence of the evening, the small collection of carolers was at a loss.

Suddenly God spoke. "Get a move on," He said. "I have more for you to do tonight. Don't be discouraged; I have accomplished all that I have desired. Now move along, dear ones. More miracles are waiting."

Shiny, Rufus, and Hercules looked at each other and then turned to the discouraged carolers. Shiny spoke first. "Don't be discouraged! God has accomplished what He desired."

"Yes," Rufus said, "and God has more for us tonight."

Hercules jumped off the first step and yelled, "Merry Christmas, Mr. Howling! Come on, friends; let's get going and see what God has up His sleeves." He then skipped down the rest of the steps. Rufus and Shiny followed behind, along with the rest of the carolers.

Behind the two dreary, desolate wooden doors, Mr. Howling began to weep, wondering what had just happened. He had spent his entire life building an empire based on hard work and a belief that man was in control of his own destiny. For years, he held the belief that God did not exist. This self-made man was now facing the fact that his entire belief system was crumbling before his very eyes. He could not deny what he had just witnessed.

Collapsed in the darkness on his mansion floor, he struggled to get the image of the bald angel out of his mind. The harder he tried to erase the image, the more it burned in his mind. He feared it would be permanently etched in his brain. He feared every time he closed his eyes, he would see the bald angel proclaiming the reality that God did exist. He thought, *Could it be true that there is a God who loves me?*

He broke right there on the cold stone floor. "God, if You are real, please forgive me. Show me tonight that You exist and do in fact love me."

Exhausted, the little wealthy man lay in a heap behind the doors that had protected him for many years.

The carolers turned back up Main Street and made their way down Second Avenue. As they made the turn, God spoke to Shiny. He said, "Flap your wings, Shiny. I need you to trust Me."

Shiny trusted and obeyed. In an instant, he found himself standing over Mr. Howling. Full of God's glory, Shiny's head lit up the foyer. The shattered little man was stunned again by the light of God's presence reflecting off Shiny's bald head.

God filled Shiny's mouth. "God is for real, and He does, in fact, love you, Mr. Howling. He loves you with an everlasting love. There is nothing you can do to separate yourself from God's love."

Still in a heap, Mr. Howling just lay there sobbing.

"Merry Christmas, Mr. Howling!"

No sooner had those words rolled off Shiny's lips than he found himself with the carolers who were singing outside a little house on Second Avenue. Two young children ran to the front window and were peering out at the carolers. The door opened, and there was a young mother with a plate of cookies. The carolers graciously received the cookies.

Murph offered the young boy and girl a cup of hot chocolate. They were thrilled to have the hot chocolate to go with their Christmas cookies. Rufus asked the young family if there was anything the carolers could pray for them.

"Yes, please pray my daddy gets to come home for Christmas this year." It seemed like the words just erupted from the little boy.

His younger sister said, "We haven't seen our daddy in a very long time."

Rufus turned his attention to the young mother. With one lonely tear running down her cheek, she filled in the details for the carolers. "My husband is away at war. He is an army captain. Last year, he was supposed to come home for Christmas, but because of the conflict, he was forced to stay. So yes, we haven't seen him for almost two years."

The carolers quietly listened as the young mother continued, "It's not easy raising two young children on my own. They miss their daddy very much. They need their father."

Then Rufus asked, "May we pray for you? We know the heavenly Father, and I know He will hear our prayers for you."

"That would be wonderful."

The young mother brought her children to her side as a mother hen gathers her chicks. For the next few minutes, it seemed like just about every caroler and angel lifted up a prayer to heaven for this young family in need of a Christmas miracle. Every angel at the E-Max theater joined hands and hearts, agreeing with the prayers being offered on behalf of this desperate family.

The prayers came to an end, and there was a pause.

Everyone's heads were still bowed when Billy Smith began to pray. "Our Father in heaven, hear my prayer. Just like when You healed my crippled legs and sent my angel to encourage me so I would know that I would be healed, please do the same now for this dear family. You are the God of miracles, Lord. Please bring their daddy home. Give them a Christmas miracle, now in Jesus's name. Amen."

At that very moment, the heavens opened, and God's glory came down on Shiny. The young family's eyes were opened, and they experienced the joy of seeing the bald angel in all of God's glory. Shiny stood proud smiling at them with his head reflecting the glory of God. "I think this means you will see your dad for Christmas."

After Shiny had made his proclamation, he smiled and gave them an affirming wink. The young family stood together at their front door with mouths wide open. Hercules and Rufus both stepped up, and God allowed the young family to see them as angels also.

Hercules bent down and said to the two young siblings, "Isn't God good? You're going to see your daddy for Christmas."

Rufus added, "Merry Christmas!"

The carolers all gave the family a big hug and walked down the street, singing and rejoicing all the while. The young family just stood there at the front door, stunned by what they had just witnessed.

The rest of the evening, the carolers were able to sing and bless many families in their small town. It was truly a night of miracles. They prayed for a woman who had been in back pain for twenty-five years, and she was healed.

At another home, they were able to share the good news of Jesus Christ. They prayed with a gentleman to receive Jesus as his savior, and the man was saved right there on his front porch. He was so excited that he joined the carolers and went singing with them the rest of the evening.

It was truly a night of miracles. If all the things that God did that evening were shared, it would take another book, and there's only one more chapter. The carolers made it back to Murph's, where they rejoiced in the miracles God had performed. They ate together and sang some more. Everyone went home with hearts full of joy.

Sunday morning seemed to come quickly for everyone—except William Blake.

William had tossed and turned all evening. He was so excited to see the miracles God had done throughout the evening, but he still wondered if the bake sale had raised enough money to send them to Africa. This was a test of faith for the future missionary. William decided to get up before the rising of the sun. He knelt down in the living room and began to pray. "Heavenly Father, God of all miracles, You are the God who opened my blind eyes. I trust You with all my heart, and I lean not on my own understanding. In all my ways, I acknowledge You, knowing You will direct our path. I guess what I'm trying to say Lord is, it's all up to You, and I trust You. Amen."

In heaven, Shiny, Rufus, and Hercules watched intently from their seats at the E-Max. The angel army was still wildly buzzing in heaven over the previous evening's events. All of heaven was anticipating the final tally of the bake sale.

Hercules called out to Rufus and Shiny, "How much money do you think they raised?"

Shiny pondered the question and then gave his response. "Herc, just like William prayed, we must trust God. He will decide the outcome. God will provide."

Rufus agreed with Shiny and added, "Our Father owns the cattle on a thousand hills; this is no big deal. God said the Blakes would go to Africa to adopt a child, so I think He can back His act."

Hercules looked at Rufus and responded, "I love you, Roof."

Rufus ruffled Hercules's curls, and the three laughed as they watched with anticipation.

The little town church was filled with music as the singers on stage led the congregation in songs of worship. William Blake squirmed in his chair, and Miriam tried to comfort him with pats on his leg. Emily Wilson made her first public appearance in years. As she sat sandwiched between the Cooper and Smith families, Emily tried to remember the last time she had been around so many people.

The music seemed muffled; Emily was lost in her thoughts. She pondered her first night on the streets without food and money. That had been over twenty years ago, and she flashed back to the time when she was kicked out of her house as a teenager. She wondered how she would fare now that she was truly trusting God with her life. Each thought was accompanied by a peace that washed over her, and it gave her the confidence to rise up and accept that everything would be okay.

Emily had given her life to Christ as a young child. Many times during her homeless years, she had the effort to connect with her heavenly Father. She remembered how many times she had been in danger living on the streets, and how it seemed that God had always protected her from any evil that tried to come her way. Sandwiched between the two loving families, Emily was filled with a sense of comfort and confidence that she had not felt for a very long time. She stood with the rest of the congregation as they sang the final song. Emily Wilson sang with a grateful heart. The warmth of the church overwhelmed her as she sang praises to her God.

The singing ended, and little Lucy grabbed Emily's hand and whispered, "You sing so beautifully. You should be up on stage with the worship band."

Emily blushed and replied, "Thank you, Lucy."

To make it easier for them to go up on stage at the appropriate time, the Blakes sat toward the front with Murph. The morning announcements were given, and the offering was taken. It was now time for Miriam and William Blake to take their positions on the stage and receive the long-awaited news of the bake sale profits.

Filled with excitement, Shiny, Rufus, and Hercules leaned forward in their seats and looked down on the church service. Shiny turned to Rufus and declared, "This is it! Time for God our deliverer."

Rufus nodded. Hercules displayed his impatience. "Come on, come on! Why do pastors have to talk so much? Get on with the announcement! How much was raised at the bake sale?"

Pastor Andrews asked William and Miriam to come forward. It felt like a death march for William. He felt his legs go heavy as he stepped up on the stage. Pastor Andrews asked William and Miriam to share their desire to go to Africa and adopt an orphan. They shared how God had put it on their hearts not only go and adopt a child, but to share William's testimony that God had healed his blind eyes.

The moment arrived and Pastor Andrews announced that the bake sale had raised just shy of $1,400 and that the church had made a commitment to match what was raised. William tried to smile, but the reality of needing more than three times the amount overwhelmed him.

Miriam could feel her husband's faith draining out of him. She grabbed his hand and squeezed it to assure him all would be well.

As they stepped down off the stage, William heard deep down in his spirit the words: "Trust me."

"What's going to happen now? They don't have enough money." Hercules dropped his head in his hands as the last few words trailed off his lips.

Shiny exhorted Hercules. "We must trust our Father that He will provide. Remember, Herc, God is faithful, and if he has called William and Miriam, He will provide what they need. God has plans for their future."

Rufus followed up. "Herc, aren't you always saying how good God is? We have to trust that God will show His goodness to William and Miriam. Our Father knows best."

Hercules perked up. "You're right! God *is* good, He knows what's best, and He never lets his children down. He will provide! I'm so excited to see how He does it. I'm going to the concession stand to get some M&M's and popcorn; anyone want anything?"

Shiny and Rufus both shook their heads as Hercules made a quick flight to the concession stand to get some snacks.

William and Miriam drove home in silence. Miriam tried to encourage William that God would provide what they needed. William acknowledged the truth that his wife was sharing. When they arrived at their house,

William went straight to his study to kneel down and pray. Miriam went to the kitchen to cook up some lunch.

As soon as William's knees touched the carpet in his study, the doorbell rang. William said, "I'll get the door, dear."

To his surprise, everyone who had gone caroling the night before now stood on his front porch. The little group of carolers sang out the Christmas lullaby. When they finished, Ben Cooper spoke up. "William, we have come to pray with you for a miracle. We have come to pray to the God who healed your eyes."

William was moved by the love expressed by his friends. He invited them in as his eyes filled with tears.

The Blakes' home was filled with love, laughter, and stories about the miracles God had done for one small town in the heart of America.

CHAPTER 10

Christmas Miracles

Christmas morning was cold and crisp.

It had been three weeks since the bake sale results were announced. The Blakes had been spending most of their time trusting God for the trip to Africa. The trip seemed to be approaching faster than the money was, yet they clung to their faith that God would provide the rest of the money.

Most days, William spent his time thanking God for His faithfulness and trusting God's will for his life.

Shiny woke up early, excited for another Christmas. He reflected back on the Christmas when God had set Mr. Thomas free from his hopeless despair, healed Billy Smith's legs, and opened William Blake's eyes. He couldn't stop thinking about what God might do this Christmas. His heart was filled with hope. Walking down the Street of Gold, he met up with his two angel buddies. "Good morning, Rufus," he said. "Hey, Herc."

"Merry Christmas, Shiny."

Hercules was already flying around with anticipation of what God might do.

Rufus said, "Merry Christmas, Shiny."

God's voice rang out from the heavens, "Merry Christmas, My dear friends."

On earth, Lucy screeched, "I knew I would get my pink bike for Christmas!"

Moments earlier, she had come running down the hallway to see what Christmas had brought. The pink bike was definitely her prize possession.

"Come now, Lucy," her father said, "it's time to go to church." Ben Cooper was already out the door, getting his car ready for his growing family. Jane and Lucy followed him out the door.

Billy Smith and his parents were on their way to pick up Eric Swan and his parents, who had surprisingly accepted an invitation to the Christmas Day service.

The soldier's wife and her two children drove cautiously down the snow-covered streets as she made her way to another Christmas church service without her husband. She prayed, "Lord, bring us a miracle for Christmas. Keep my husband safe today, and bring him home soon."

Pastor Andrews positioned himself at his familiar post at the entrance of the church so he could greet all the arrivals. The little local church was buzzing with excitement, for another Christmas had arrived. The music started, and the people joined together in song. The church was united in one voice, lifting their praise to the God of all creation, the God who'd sent His Son in the form of a baby who was born in a manger. That same child who would grow to be fully God and fully man. The man who would give His life for all humankind so that they would have the opportunity to be reunited with their Creator for all eternity.

As the final song was sung, the doors at the back of the church flung open. Pastor Andrews took his position behind the pulpit, ready to give the Christmas announcements and then share the sermon he had worked hard at for over a month.

In heaven, the E-Max was rocking with songs, praise, laughter, and joy. It was so raucous that when God spoke, even the angel army was surprised. "Shiny, Rufus, Hercules, go usher in the gifts I have prepared for this day."

The three angel messengers didn't hesitate. Before they could take a step toward the earth tunnel, they found themselves flying around the church rafters.

Lucy looked up and gasped, "Mommy!" as she pointed upward toward the three angelic hosts.

Pastor Andrews announced, "Dear ones, today we have a particular family member who has not been with us for quite some time. Let me direct your attention to the back of the auditorium."

The entire congregation turned their attention to the back doors. U.S. Army Captain Samuel Morris walked into the church. His wife and two children got up, ran to the back of the church, and wrapped their arms around him. The Morris family was reunited for the first time in almost two years—and there wasn't a dry eye in the church.

Everyone watched Captain Morris escort his family to the front of the church. He stepped up on the stage to share the miraculous story of how God had suddenly made a way to bring him home for Christmas. Young Captain Morris was just finishing his story when another surprise visitor stepped through the doors and entered the sanctuary.

Pastor Andrews was stunned by this visitor. He was a man who had never stepped foot in the church. The entire church reacted to Pastor Andrews's response. Every eye in the church was fixed on the unfamiliar silhouette standing in front of the old wooden church doors.

There, to everyone's surprise, stood none other than Ulysses S. Howling. The church was silent.

The flapping of the three angels' wings was all that could be heard. Mr. Howling looked up and locked eyes on Shiny. Shiny winked and waved.

Mr. Howling took a deep breath and made his way to the front of the church. Without hesitation, he walked right up on stage and whispered in Pastor Andrews's ear. "Is it okay if I say something to your church?"

Pastor Andrews nodded and took a seat in the first row. Mr. Howling shared the story of his Christmas surprise. "Last night, I had a dream. In my dream, God asked me if I wanted to be part of the most beautiful Christmas miracle. I laid in bed, completely still as God shared with me how all my wealth had been given to me by Him and Him alone. He had planned and prepared me for this moment. He shared with me that there is a couple in the church whom He has called to go to Africa to adopt an orphan. He went on to say that not only are they going to adopt a child, but they are going to be used to establish orphanages in Africa. They will go as missionaries many times throughout their lives and bring the good news of Jesus Christ to the nations of Africa."

Mr. Howling paused to wipe his brow and clean his glasses. He also took the time to wipe a few tears running down his cheek.

"God then asked me if I would be obedient to answer the call to give my life to Jesus and serve Him only. Well, I said yes. God then asked if I would come today and share some more good news." Mr. Howling paused again. The entire church was silent as they hung on his every word. "I have come this morning to ask the couple called to Africa to come up on stage with me."

William and Miriam were stunned as they made the walk from their seats to the front stage.

Mr. Howling asked Pastor Andrews to come as well.

The little rich man presented William and Miriam with a check for $100,000.

When Pastor Andrews announced the amount, the church erupted. Mr. Howling shared that this was the seed money to start their missionary work in Africa. He encouraged the church to always be cheerful givers and to always trust God.

The Christmas service was full of a few more surprises. Mr. Howling asked if he could be baptized, and Pastor Andrews agreed. As a result of Mr. Howling's beautiful testimony of God's incredible faithfulness and provision, Eric Swan's mother and father, and a host of new converts also gave their lives to Christ that day.

Shiny, Rufus, and Hercules enjoyed the service while they sat perched on the church rafters.

Many in the congregation gave testimonies for months how they had seen the bald angel who had visited Billy Smith the crippled boy and William Blake the blind man. They testified that the bald angel was there on Christmas to the surprise of all.

Oh, and Shiny is his name.

Printed in the United States
By Bookmasters